Leonora

Arnold Bennett

LEONORA

A Novel

By

ARNOLD BENNETT

Author of *The Grand Babylon Hotel, The Gates of Wrath, Anna of the Five Towns,* etc.

1903

CONTENTS

CHAPTER I

THE HOUSEHOLD AT HILLPORT

She was walking, with her customary air of haughty and rapt leisure, across the market-place of Bursley, when she observed in front of her, at the top of Oldcastle Street, two men conversing and gesticulating vehemently, each seated alone in a dog-cart. These persons, who had met from opposite directions, were her husband, John Stanway, the earthenware manufacturer, and David Dain, the solicitor who practised at Hanbridge. Stanway's cob, always quicker to start than to stop, had been pulled up with difficulty, drawing his cart just clear of the other one, so that the two portly and middle-aged talkers were most uncomfortably obliged to twist their necks in order to see one another; the attitude did nothing to ease the obvious asperity of the discussion. She thought the spectacle undignified and silly; and she marvelled, as all women marvel, that men who conduct themselves so magisterially should sometimes appear so infantile. She felt glad that it was Thursday afternoon, and the shops closed and the streets empty.

Immediately John Stanway caught sight of her he said a few words to the lawyer in a somewhat different key, and descended from his vehicle. As she came up to them Mr. Dain saluted her with bashful abruptness, and her proud face broke as if by the loosing of a spell into a generous and captivating smile; Mr. Dain blushed, the vision was too much for his composure; he moved his horse forward a yard or two, and then jerked it back again, gruffly advising it to stand still. Stanway turned to her bluntly, unceremoniously, as to a creature to whom he owed nothing. She noticed once more how the whole character of his face was changed under annoyance.

'Here, Nora! ' he said, speaking with the raw anger of a man with a new-born grievance, 'run this home for me. I'm going over to Hanbridge with Mr. Dain. '

'Very well, ' she agreed with soothing calmness, and taking the reins she climbed up to the high driving-seat.

'And I say, Nora—Wo-*back*! ' he flamed out passionately to the impatient cob, 'where're your manners, you idiot? I say, Nora, I doubt I shall be late for tea—half-past six. Tell Milly she must be in.

1

The others too. ' He gave these instructions in a lower tone, and emphasised them by a stormy and ominous frown. Then with an injured 'Now, Dain! ' he got into the equipage of his legal adviser and departed towards Hanbridge, trailing clouds of vexation.

Leonora drove smartly but cautiously down the steep slope of Oldcastle Street; she could drive as well as a woman may. A group of clay-soiled girls lounging in the archway of a manufactory exchanged rude but admiring remarks about her as she passed. The paces of the cob, the dazzle of the silver-plated harness, the fine lines of the cart, the unbending mien of the driver, made a glittering cynosure for envy. All around was grime, squalor, servitude, ugliness; the inglorious travail of two hundred thousand people, above ground and below it, filled the day and the night. But here, as it were suddenly, out of that earthy and laborious bed, rose the blossom of luxury, grace, and leisure, the final elegance of the industrial district of the Five Towns. The contrast between Leonora and the rough creatures in the archway, between the flower and the phosphates which nourished it, was sharp and decisive: and Leonora, in the September sunshine, was well aware of the contrast. She felt that the loud-voiced girls were at one extremity of the scale and she at the other; and this arrangement seemed natural, necessary, inevitable.

She was a beautiful woman. She had a slim perfect figure; quite simply she carried her head so high and her shoulders so square that her back seemed to be hollowed out, and no tightness on the part of a bodice could hide this charming concavity. Her face was handsome with its large regular features; one noticed the abundant black hair under the hat, the thick eyebrows, the brown and opaque skin, the teeth impeccably white, and the firm, unyielding mouth and chin. Underneath the chin, half muffling it, came a white muslin bow, soft, frail, feminate, an enchanting disclaimer of that facial sternness and the masculinity of that tailor-made dress, a signal at once provocative and wistful of the woman. She had brains; they appeared in her keen dark eyes. Her judgment was experienced and mature. She knew her world and its men and women. She was not too soon shocked, not too severe in her verdicts, not the victim of too many illusions. And yet, though everything about her witnessed to a serene temperament and the continual appeasing of mild desires, she dreamed sadly, like the girls in the archway, of an existence more distinguished than her own; an existence brilliant and tender, where dalliance and high endeavour, virtue and the flavour of sin, eternal appetite and eternal satisfaction, were incredibly united. Even now, on her fortieth birthday, she still believed in the possibility of a conscious state of positive and continued happiness, and regretted that she should have missed it.

The imminence and the arrival of this dire birthday, this day of wrath on which the proudest woman will kneel to implacable destiny and beg a reprieve, had induced the reveries natural to it— the self-searching, the exchange of old fallacies for new, the dismayed glance forward, the lingering look behind. Absorbed though she was in the control of the sensitive steed, the field of her mind's eye seemed to be entirely filled by an image of the woman of forty as imagined by herself at the age of twenty. And she was that woman now! But she did not feel like forty; at thirty she had not felt thirty; she could only accept the almanac and the rules of arithmetic. The interminable years of her marriage rolled back, and she was eighteen again, ingenuous and trustful, convinced that her versatile husband was unique among his sex. The fading of a short-lived and factitious passion, the descent of the unique male to the ordinary level of males, the births of her three girls and their rearing and training: all these things seemed as trifles to her, mere excrescences and depressions in the vast tableland of her monotonous and placid career. She had had no career. Her strength of will, of courage, of love, had never been taxed; only her patience. 'And my life is over! ' she told herself, insisting that her life was over without being able to believe it.

As the dog-cart was crossing the railway bridge at Shawport, at the foot of the rise to Hillport, Leonora overtook her eldest daughter. She drew up. From the height of the dog-cart she looked at her child; and the girlishness of Ethel's form, the self-consciousness of newly-arrived womanhood in her innocent and timid eyes, the virgin richness of her vitality, made Leonora feel sad, superior, and protective.

'Oh, mother! Where's father? ' Ethel exclaimed, staring at her, struck with a foolish wonder to see her mother where her father had been an hour before.

'What a schoolgirl she is! And at her age I was a mother twice over! ' thought Leonora; but she said aloud: 'Jump up quickly, my dear. You know Prince won't stand. '

3

Ethel obeyed, awkwardly. As she did so the mother scrutinised the rather lanky figure, the long dark skirt, the pale blouse, and the straw hat, in a single glance that missed no detail. Leonora was not quite dissatisfied; Ethel carried herself tolerably, she resembled her mother; she had more distinction than her sisters, but her manner was often lackadaisical.

'Your father was very vexed about something, ' said Leonora, when she had recounted the meeting at the top of Oldcastle Street. 'Where's Milly? '

'I don't know, mother—I think she went out for a walk. ' The girl added apprehensively: 'Why? '

'Oh, nothing! ' said Leonora, pretending not to observe that Ethel had blushed. 'If I were you, Ethel, I should let that belt out one hole... not here, my dear child, not here. When you get home. How was Aunt Hannah? '

Every day one member or another of John Stanway's family had to pay a visit to John's venerable Aunt Hannah, who lived with her brother, the equally venerable Uncle Meshach, in a little house near the parish church of St. Luke's. This was a social rite the omission of which nothing could excuse. On that day it was Ethel who had called.

'Auntie was all right. She was making a lot of parkin, and of course I had to taste it, all new, you know. I'm simply stodged. '

'Don't say "stodged. "'

'Oh, mother! You won't let us say *anything*, ' Ethel dismally protested; and Leonora secretly sympathised with the grown woman in revolt.

'Oh! And Aunt Hannah wishes you many happy returns. Uncle Meshach came back from the Isle of Man last night. He gave me a note for you. Here it is. '

'I can't take it now, my dear. Give it me afterwards. '

'I think Uncle Meshach's a horrid old thing! ' said Ethel.

'My dear girl! Why? '

'Oh! I do. I'm glad he's only father's uncle and not ours. I do hate that name. Fancy being called Meshach! '

'That isn't uncle's fault, anyhow, ' said Leonora.

'You always stick up for him, mother. I believe it's because he flatters you, and says you look younger than any of us. ' Ethel's tone was half roguish, half resentful.

Leonora gave a short unsteady laugh. She knew well that her age was plainly written beneath her eyes, at the corners of her mouth, under her chin, at the roots of the hair above her ears, and in her cold, confident gaze. Youth! She would have forfeited all her experience, her knowledge, and the charm of her maturity, to recover the irrecoverable! She envied the woman by her side, and envied her because she was lightsome, thoughtless, kittenish, simple, unripe. For a brief moment, vainly coveting the ineffable charm of Ethel's immaturity, she had a sharp perception of the obscure mutual antipathy which separates one generation from the next. As the cob rattled into Hillport, that aristocratic and plutocratic suburb of the town, that haunt of exclusiveness, that retreat of high life and good tone, she thought how commonplace, vulgar, and petty was the opulent existence within those tree-shaded villas, and that she was doomed to droop and die there, while her girls, still unfledged, might, if they had the sense to use their wings, fly away.... Yet at the same time it gratified her to reflect that she and hers were in the picture, and conformed to the standards; she enjoyed the admiration which the sight of herself and Ethel and the expensive cob and cart and accoutrements must arouse in the punctilious and stupid breast of Hillport.

She was picking flowers for the table from the vivid borders of the lawn, when Ethel ran into the garden from the drawing-room. Bran, the St. Bernard, was loose and investigating the turf.

'Mother, the letter from Uncle Meshach. '

Leonora took the soiled envelope, and handing over the flowers to Ethel, crossed the lawn and sat down on the rustic seat, facing the house. The dog followed her, and with his great paw demanded her attention, but she abruptly dismissed him. She thought it curiously characteristic of Uncle Meshach that he should write her a letter on her fortieth birthday; she could imagine the uncouth mixture of wit, rude candour, and wisdom with which he would greet her; his was a strange and sinister personality, but she knew that he admired her. The note was written in Meshach's scraggy and irregular hand, in three lines starting close to the top of half a sheet of note paper. It ran: 'Dear Nora, I hear young Twemlow is come back from America. You had better see as your John looks out for himself. ' There was nothing else, no signature.

As she read it, she experienced precisely the physical discomfort which those feel who travel for the first time in a descending lift. Fifteen quiet years had elapsed since the death of her husband's partner William Twemlow, and a quarter of a century since William's wild son, Arthur, had run away to America. Yet Uncle Meshach's letter seemed to invest these far-off things with a mysterious and disconcerting actuality. The misgivings about her husband which long practice and continual effort had taught her how to keep at bay, suddenly overleapt their artificial barriers and swarmed upon her.

The long garden front of the dignified eighteenth-century house, nearly the last villa in Hillport on the road to Oldcastle, was extended before her. She had played in that house as a child, and as a woman had watched, from its windows, the years go by like a procession. That house was her domain. Hers was the supreme intelligence brooding creatively over it. Out of walls and floors and ceilings, out of stairs and passages, out of furniture and woven stuffs, out of metal and earthenware, she had made a home. From the lawn, in the beautiful sadness of the autumn evening, any one might have seen and enjoyed the sight of its high French windows, its glowing sun-blinds, its faintly-tinted and beribboned curtains, its creepers, its glimpses of occasional tables, tall vases, and dressing-mirrors. But Leonora, as she sat holding the letter in her long white hand, could call up and see the interior of every room to the most minute details. She, the housemistress, knew her home by heart. She had thought it into existence; and there was not a cabinet against a wall, not a rug on a floor, not a cushion on a chair, not a knicknack on a mantelpiece, not a plate in a rack, but had come there by the design of her brain. Without possessing much artistic taste, Leonora had an extraordinary talent for domestic equipment, organisation, and management. She was so interested in her home, so exacting in her ideals, that she could never reach finality; the place went through a constant succession of improvements; its comfort and its attractiveness were always on the increase. And the result was so striking that her supremacy in the woman's craft could not be challenged. All Hillport, including her husband, bowed to it. Mrs. Stanway's principles, schemes, methods, even her trifling dodges, were mentioned with deep respect by the ladies of Hillport, who often expressed their astonishment that, although the wheels of Mrs. Stanway's household revolved with perfect smoothness, Mrs. Stanway herself appeared never to be doing anything. That astonishment was Leonora's pride. As her brain marshalled with ease the thousand diverse details of the wonderful domestic machine, she could appreciate, better than any other woman in Hillport, without vanity and without humility, the singular excellence of her gifts and of the organism they had perfected. And now this creation of hers, this complex structure of mellow brick-and-mortar, and fine chattels, and nice and luxurious habit, seemed to Leonora to tremble at the whisper of an enigmatic message from Uncle Meshach. The foreboding caused by the letter mingled with the menace of approaching age and with the sadness of the early autumn, and confirmed her mood.

Millicent, her youngest, ran impulsively to her in the garden. Millicent was eighteen, and the days when she went to school and wore her hair in a long plait were still quite fresh in the girl's mind. For this reason she was often inordinately and aggressively adult.

'Mamma! I'm going to have my tea first thing. The Burgesses have asked me to play tennis. I needn't wait, need I? It gets dark so soon. ' As Millicent stood there, ardently persuasive, she forgot that adult persons do not stand on one leg or put their fingers in their mouths.

Leonora looked fondly at the sprightly girl, vain, self-conscious, and blonde and pretty as a doll in her white dress. She recognised all Millicent's faults and shortcomings, and yet was overcome by the charm of her presence.

'No, Milly, you must wait. ' Throned on the rustic seat, inscrutable and tyrannous Leonora, a wistful, wayward atom in the universe, laid her command upon the other wayward atom; and she thought how strange it was that this should be.

'But, Ma— —'

'Father specially said you must be in for tea. You know you have far too much freedom. What have you been doing all the afternoon? '

'I haven't been doing anything, Ma. '

Leonora feared for the strict veracity of her youngest, but she said nothing, and Milly retired full of annoyance against the inconceivable caprices of parents.

At twenty minutes to seven John Stanway entered his large and handsome dining-room, having been driven home by David Dain, whose residence was close by. Three languorous women and the erect and motionless parlourmaid behind the door were waiting for him. He went straight to his carver's chair, and instantly the women were alert, galvanised into vigilant life. Leonora, opposite to her husband, began to pour out the tea; the impassive parlourmaid stood consummately ready to hand the cups; Ethel and Millicent took their seats along one side of the table, with an air of nonchalance which was far from sincere; a chair on the other side remained empty.

'Turn the gas on, Bessie, ' said John. Daylight had scarcely begun to fail; but nevertheless the man's tone announced a grievance, that, with half-a-dozen women in the house, he the exhausted breadwinner should have been obliged to attend to such a trifle. Bessie sprang to pull the chain of the Welsbach tap, and the white and silver of the tea-table glittered under the yellow light. Every woman looked furtively at John's morose countenance.

Neither dark nor fair, he was a tall man, verging towards obesity, and the fulness of his figure did not suit his thin, rather handsome face. His age was forty-eight. There was a small bald spot on the crown of his head. The clipped brown beard seemed thick and plenteous, but this effect was given by the coarseness of the hairs, not by their number; the moustache was long and exiguous. His blue eyes were never still, and they always avoided any prolonged encounter with other eyes. He was a personable specimen of the clever and successful manufacturer. His clothes were well cut, the necktie of a discreet smartness. His grandfather had begun life as a working potter; nevertheless John Stanway spoke easily and correctly in a refined variety of the broad Five Towns accent; he could open a door for a lady, and was noted for his neatness in compliment.

8

It was his ambition always to be calm, oracular, weighty; always to be sure of himself; but his temperament was incurably nervous, restless, and impulsive. He could not be still, he could not wait. Instinct drove him to action for the sake of action, instinct made him seek continually for notice, prominence, comment. These fundamental appetites had urged him into public life—to the Borough Council and the Committee of the Wedgwood Institution. He often affected to be buried in cogitation upon municipal and private business affairs, when in fact his attention was disengaged and watchful. Leonora knew that this was so to-night. The idea of his duplicity took possession of her mind. Deeps yawned before her, deeps that swallowed up the solid and charming house and the comfortable family existence, as she glanced at that face at once strange and familiar to her. 'Is it all right? ' she kept thinking. 'Is John all that he seems? I wonder whether he has ever committed murder. ' Yes, even this absurd thought, which she knew to be absurd, crossed her mind.

'Where's Rose? ' he demanded suddenly in the depressing silence of the tea-table, as if he had just discovered the absence of his second daughter.

'She's been working in her room all day, ' said Leonora.

'That's no reason why she should be late for tea. '

At that moment Rose entered. She was very tall and pale, her dress was a little dowdy. Like her father and Millicent, she carried her head forward and had a tendency to look downwards, and her spine seemed flaccid. Ethel was beautiful, or about to be beautiful; Millicent was pretty; Rose plain. Rose was deficient in style. She despised style, and regarded her sisters as frivolous ninnies and gadabouts. She was the serious member of the family, and for two years had been studying for the Matriculation of London University.

'Late again! ' said her father. 'I shall stop all this exam work. '

Rose said nothing, but looked resentful.

When the hot dishes had been partaken of, Bessie was dismissed, and Leonora waited for the bursting of the storm. It was Millicent who drew it down.

9

'I think I shall go down to Burgesses, after all, mamma. It's quite light, ' she said with audacious pertness.

Her father looked at her.

'What were you doing this afternoon, Milly? '

'I went out for a walk, pa. '

'Who with? '

'No one. '

'Didn't I see you on the canal-side with young Ryley? '

'Yes, father. He was going back to the works after dinner, and he just happened to overtake me. '

Milly and Ethel exchanged a swift glance.

'Happened to overtake you! I saw you as I was driving past, over the canal bridge. You little thought that I saw you. '

'Well, father, I couldn't help him overtaking me. Besides——'

'Besides! ' he took her up. 'You had your hand on his shoulder. How do you explain that? '

Millicent was silent.

'I'm ashamed of you, regularly ashamed... You with your hand on his shoulder in full sight of the works! And on your mother's birthday too! '

Leonora involuntarily stirred. For more than twenty years it had been his custom to give her a kiss and a ten-pound note before breakfast on her birthday, but this year he had so far made no mention whatever of the anniversary.

'I'm going to put my foot down, ' he continued with grieved majesty. 'I don't want to, but you force me to it. I'll have no goings-on with Fred Ryley. Understand that. And I'll have no more idling about. You girls—at least you two—are bone-idle. Ethel shall begin to go to the works next Monday. I want a clerk. And you, Milly, must take up the housekeeping. Mother, you'll see to that. '

Leonora reflected that whereas Ethel showed a marked gift for housekeeping, Milly was instinctively averse to everything merely domestic. But with her acquired fatalism she accepted the ukase.

'You understand, ' said John to his pert youngest.

'Yes, papa. '

'No more carrying-on with Fred Ryley—or any one else. '

'No, papa. '

'I've got quite enough to worry me without being bothered by you girls. '

Rose left the table, consciously innocent both of sloth and of light behaviour.

'What are you going to do now, Rose? ' He could not let her off scot-free.

'Read my chemistry, father. '

'You'll do no such thing. '

'I must, if I'm to pass at Christmas, ' she said firmly. 'It's my weakest subject. '

'Christmas or no Christmas, ' he replied, 'I'm not going to let you kill yourself. Look at your face! I wonder your mother——'

'Run into the garden for a while, my dear, ' said Leonora softly, and the girl moved to obey.

'Rose, ' he called her back sharply as his exasperation became fidgetty. 'Don't be in such a hurry. Open the window—an inch. '

* * * * *

Ethel and Millicent disappeared after the manner of young fox-terriers; they did not visibly depart; they were there, one looked away, they were gone. In the bedroom which they shared, the door well locked, they threw oft all restraints, conventions, pretences, and discussed the world, and their own world, with terrible candour. This sacred and untidy apartment, where many of the habits of childhood still lingered, was a retreat, a sanctuary from the law, and the fastness had been ingeniously secured against surprise by the peculiar position of the bedstead in front of the doorway.

'Father is a donkey! ' said Ethel.

'And ma never says a word! ' said Milly.

'I could simply have smacked him when he brought in mother's birthday, ' Ethel continued, savagely.

'So could I. '

'Fancy him thinking it's you. What a lark! '

'Yes. I don't mind, ' said Milly.

'You are a brick, Milly. And I didn't think you were, I didn't really. '

'What a horrid pig you are, Eth! ' Milly protested, and Ethel laughed.

'Did you give Fred my note all right? ' Ethel demanded.

'Yes, ' answered Milly. 'I suppose he's coming up to-night? '

'I asked him to. '

'There'll be a frantic row one day. I'm sure there will, ' Milly said meditatively, after a pause.

'Oh! there's bound to be! ' Ethel assented, and she added: 'Mother does trust us. Have a choc? '

Milly said yes, and Ethel drew a box of bonbons from her pocket.

They seemed to contemplate with a fearful joy the probable exposure of that life of flirtations and chocolate which ran its secret course side by side with the other life of demure propriety acted out for the benefit of the older generation. If these innocent and inexperienced souls had been accused of leading a double life, they would have denied the charge with genuine indignation. Nevertheless, driven by the universal longing, and abetted by parental apathy and parental lack of imagination, they did lead a double life. They chafed bitterly under the code to which they were obliged ostensibly to submit. In their moods of revolt, they honestly believed their parents to be dull and obstinate creatures who had lost the appetite for romance and ecstasy and were determined to mortify this appetite in others. They desired heaps of money and the free, informal companionship of very young men. The latter—at the cost of some intrigue and subterfuge—they contrived to get. But money they could not get. Frequently they said to each other with intense earnestness that they would do anything for money; and they repeated passionately, 'anything. '

'Just look at that stuck-up thing! ' said Milly laughing. They stood together at the window, and Milly pointed her finger at Rose, who was walking conscientiously to and fro across the garden in the gathering dusk.

Ethel rapped on the pane, and the three sisters exchanged friendly smiles.

'Rosie will never pass her exam, not if she lives to be a hundred, ' said Ethel. 'And can you imagine father making me go to the works? Can you imagine the sense of it? '

'He won't let you walk up with Fred at nights, ' said Milly, 'so you needn't think. '

'And your housekeeping! ' Ethel exclaimed. 'What a treat father will have at meals! '

'Oh! I can easily get round mother, ' said Milly with confidence. 'I *can't* housekeep, and ma knows that perfectly well. '

'Well, father will forget all about it in a week or two, that's one comfort, ' Ethel concluded the matter. 'Are you going down to Burgesses to see Harry? ' she inquired, observing Milly put on her hat.

'Yes, ' said Milly. 'Cissie said she'd come for me if I was late. You'd better stay in and be dutiful. '

'I shall offer to play duets with mother. Don't you be long. Let's try that chorus for the Operatic before supper. '

* * * * *

That night, after the girls had kissed them and gone to bed, John and Leonora remained alone together in the drawing-room. The first fire of autumn was burning in the grate, and at the other end of the long room dark curtains were drawn across the French window. Shaded candles lighted the grand piano, at which Leonora was seated, and a single gas jet illuminated the region of the hearth, where John, lounging almost at full length in a vast chair, read the newspaper; otherwise the room was in shadow. John dropped the 'Signal, ' which slid to the hearthrug with a rustle, and turned his head so that he could just see the left side of his wife's face and her left hand as it moved over the keys of the piano. She played with gentle monotony, and her playing seemed perfunctory, yet agreeable. John watched the glinting of the four rings on her left hand, and the slow undulations of the drooping lace at her wrist. He moved twice, and she knew he was about to speak.

'I say, Leonora, ' he said in a confidential tone.

'Yes, my dear, ' she responded, complying generously with his appeal for sympathy. She continued to play for a moment, but even more softly; and then, as he kept silence, she revolved on the piano-stool and looked into his face.

'What is it? ' she asked in a caressing voice, intensifying her femininity, forgiving him, excusing him, thinking and making him think what a good fellow he was, despite certain superficial faults.

'You knew nothing of this Ryley business, did you? ' he murmured.

'Oh, no. Are you sure there's anything in it? I don't think there is for an instant. ' And she did not. Even the placing of Milly's hand on Fred Ryley's shoulder in full sight of the street, even this she regarded only as the pretty indiscretion of a child. 'Oh! there's nothing in it, ' she repeated.

'Well, there's *got* to be nothing in it. You must keep an eye on 'em. I won't have it. '

She leaned forward, and, resting her elbows on her knees, put her chin in her long hands. Her bangles disappeared amid lace.

'What's the matter with Fred? ' said she. 'He's a relation; and you've said before now that he's a good clerk, '

'He's a decent enough clerk. But he's not for our girls. '

'If it's only money——' she began.

'Money! ' John cried. 'He'll have money. Oh! he'll have money right enough. Look here, Nora, I've not told you before, but I'll tell you now. Uncle Meshach's altered his will in favour of young Ryley. '

'Oh! Jack! '

John Stanway stood up, gazing at his wife with an air of martyrised virtue which said: 'There! what do you think of that as a specimen of the worries which I keep to myself? '

She raised her eyebrows with a gesture of deep concern. And all the time she was asking herself: 'Why did Uncle Meshach alter his will? Why did he do that? He must have had some reason. ' This question troubled her far more than the blow to their expectations.

John's maternal grandfather had married twice. By his first wife he had had one son, Shadrach; and by his second wife two daughters and a son, Mary (John's mother), Hannah, and Meshach. The last two had never married. Shadrach had estranged all his family (except old Ebenezer) by marrying beneath him, and Mary had earned praise by marrying rather well. These two children, by a useful whim of the eccentric old man, had received their portions of the patrimony on their respective wedding-days. They were both dead. Shadrach, amiable but incompetent, had died poor, leaving a daughter, Susan, who had repeated, even more reprehensibly, her father's sin of marrying beneath her. She had married a working potter, and thus reduced her branch of the family to the status from which old Ebenezer had originally raised himself. Fred Ryley, now an orphan, was Susan's only child. As an act of charity John Stanway had given Fred Ryley a stool in the office of his manufactory; but, though Fred's mother was John's first cousin, John never acknowledged the fact. John argued that Fred's mother and Fred's grandfather had made fools of themselves, and that the consequences were irremediable save by Fred's unaided effort. Such vicissitudes of blood, and the social contrasts resulting therefrom, are common enough in the history of families in democratic communities.

Old Ebenezer's will left the residue of his estate, reckoned at some fifteen thousand pounds, to Meshach and Hannah as joint tenants with the remainder absolutely to the survivor of them. By this arrangement, which suited them excellently since they had always lived together, though neither could touch the principal of their joint property during their joint lives, the survivor had complete freedom to dispose of everything. Both Meshach and Hannah had made a will in sole favour of John.

'Yes, ' John said again, 'he's altered it in favour of young Ryley. David Dain told me the other day. Uncle told Dain he might tell me. '

'Why has he altered it? ' Leonora asked aloud at last.

John shook his head. 'Why does Uncle Meshach do anything? ' He spoke with sarcastic irritation. 'I suppose he's taken a sudden fancy for Susan's child, after ignoring him all these years. '

'And has Aunt Hannah altered her will, too? '

'No. I'm all right in that quarter. '

'Then if your Aunt Hannah lives longest, you'll still come in for everything, just as if your Uncle Meshach hadn't altered his will? '

'Yes. But Aunt Hannah won't live for ever. And Uncle Meshach will. And where shall I be if she dies first? ' He went on in a different tone. 'Of course one of 'em's bound to die soon. Uncle's sixty-four if he's a day, and the old lady's a year older. And I want money. '

'Do you, Jack, really? ' she said. Long ago she had suspected it, though John never stinted her. Once more the solid house and their comfortable existence seemed to shiver and be engulfed.

'By the way, Nora, ' he burst out with sudden bright animation, 'I've been so occupied to-day I forgot to wish you many happy returns. And here's the usual. I hadn't got it on me this morning. '

He kissed her and gave her a ten-pound note.

'Oh! thanks, Jack! ' she said, glancing at the note with a factitious curiosity to hide her embarrassment.

'You're good-looking enough yet! ' he exclaimed as he gazed at her.

'He wants something out of me. He wants something out of me, ' she thought as she gave him a smile for his compliment. And this idea that he wanted something, that circumstances should have forced him into the position of an applicant, distressed her. She grieved for him. She saw all his good qualities—his energy, vitality, cleverness, facile kindliness, his large masculinity. It seemed to her, as she gazed up at him from the music-stool in the shaded solitude or the drawing-room, that she was very intimate with him, and very dependent on him; and she wished him to be always flamboyant, imposing, and successful.

'If you are at all hard up, Jack——' She made as if to reject the note.

'Oh! get out! ' he laughed. 'It's not a tenner that I'm short of. I tell you what you *can* do, ' he went on quickly and lightly. 'I was thinking of raising a bit temporarily on this house. Five hundred, say. You wouldn't mind, would you? '

The house was her own property, inherited from an aunt. John's suggestion came as a shock to her. To mortgage her house: this was what he wanted!

'Oh yes, certainly, if you like, ' she acquiesced quietly. 'But I thought—I thought business was so good just now, and——'

'So it is, ' he stopped her with a hint of annoyance. 'I'm short of capital. Always have been. '

'I see, ' she said, not seeing. 'Well, do what you like. '

'Right, my girl. Now—roost! ' He extinguished the gas over the mantelpiece.

The familiar vulgarity of some of his phrases always vexed her, and 'roost' was one of these phrases. In a flash he fell from a creature engagingly masculine to the use-worn daily sharer of her monotonous existence.

'Have you heard about Arthur Twemlow coming over? ' she demanded, half vindictively, as he was preparing to blow out the last candle on the piano. He stopped.

'Who's Arthur Twemlow? '

'Mr. Twemlow's son, of course, ' she said. 'From America. '

'Oh! Him! Coming over, did you say? I wonder what he looks like. Who told you? '

'Uncle Meshach. And he said I was to say you were to look out for yourself when Arthur Twemlow came. I don't know what he meant. One of his jokes, I expect. ' She tried to laugh.

John looked at her, and then looked away, and immediately blew out the last candle. But she had seen him turn pale at what Uncle Meshach had said. Or was that pallor merely the effect on his face of raising the coloured candle-shade as he extinguished the candle? She could not be sure.

'Uncle Meshach ought to be in the lunatic asylum, I think, ' John's voice came majestically out of the gloom as they groped towards the door.

'We shall have to be polite to Arthur Twemlow, when he comes, if he is coming, ' said John after they had gone upstairs. 'I understand he's quite a reformed character. '

* * * * *

Because she fancied she had noticed that the window at the end of the corridor was open, she came out of the bedroom a few minutes later, and traversed the dark corridor to satisfy herself, and found the window wide open. The night was cloudy and warm, and a breeze moved among the foliage of the garden. In the mysterious diffused light she could distinguish the forms of the poplar trees.

Suddenly the bushes immediately beneath her were disturbed as though by some animal.

'Good night, Ethel. '

'Good night, Fred. '

She shook with violent agitation as the amazing adieu from the garden was answered from the direction of her daughter's window. But the secondary effect of those words, so simply and affectionately whispered in the darkness, was to bring a tear to her eye. As the mother comprehended the whole staggering situation, the woman envied Ethel for her youth, her naughty innocence, her romance, her incredibly foolish audacity in thus risking the disaster of parental wrath. Leonora heard cautious footsteps on the gravel, and the slow closing of a window. 'My life is over! ' she said to herself. 'And hers beginning. And to think that this afternoon I called her a schoolgirl! What romance have I had in my life? '

She put her head out of the window. There was no movement now, but above her a radiance streaming from Rose's dormer showed that the serious girl of the family, defying commands, plodded obstinately at her chemistry. As Leonora thought of Rose's ambition, and Ethel's clandestine romance, and little Millicent's complicity in that romance, and John's sinister secrets, and her own ineffectual repining—as she thought of these five antagonistic preoccupied souls and their different affairs, the pathos and the complexity of human things surged over her and overwhelmed her.

CHAPTER II

MESHACH AND HANNAH

The little old bachelor and spinster were resting after dinner in the back-parlour of their house near the top of Church Street. In that abode they had watched generations pass and manners change, as one list hearthrug succeeded another in the back-parlour. Meshach had been born in the front bedroom, and he meant to die there; Hannah had also been born in the front bedroom, but it was through the window of the back bedroom that the housewife's soul would rejoin the infinite. The house, which Meshach's grandfather, first of his line to emerge from the grey mass of the proletariat, had ruined himself to build, was a six-roomed dwelling of honest workmanship in red brick and tile, with a beautiful pillared doorway and fanlight in the antique taste. It had cost two hundred pounds, and was the monument of a life's ambition. Mortgaged by its hard-pressed creator, and then sold by order of the mortgagee, it had ultimately been bought again in triumph by Meshach's father, who made thirty thousand pounds out of pots without getting too big for it, and left it unspoilt to Meshach and Hannah. Only one alteration had ever been made in it, and that, completed on Meshach's fiftieth birthday, admirably exemplified his temperament. Because he liked to observe the traffic in Church Street, and liked equally to sit in the back-parlour near the hob, he had, with an oriental grandeur of self-indulgence, removed the dividing wall between the front and the back parlours and substituted a glass partition: so that he could simultaneously warm the fire and keep an eye on the street. The town said that no one but Meshach could have hit on such a scheme, or would have carried it out with such an object: it crowned his reputation.

John Stanway's maternal uncle was one of those individuals whose character, at once strong, egotistic, and peculiar, so forcibly impresses the community that by contrast ordinary persons seem to be without character; such men are therefore called, distinctively, 'characters'; and it is a matter of common experience that, whether through the unconscious prescience of parents or through that felicitous sense of propriety which often guides the hazards of destiny, they usually bear names to match their qualities. Meshach Myatt! Meshach Myatt! What piquant curious syllables to roll glibly off the tongue, and to repeat for the pleasure of repetition! And what a vision of Meshach their utterance conjured up! At sixty-four, stereotyped by age, fixed and confirmed in singularity, Meshach's figure answered better than ever to his name. He was slight of bone and spare in flesh, with a hardly perceptible stoop. He had a red, seamed face. Under the small, pale blue eyes, genial and yet frigid, there showed a thick, raw, red selvedge of skin, and below that the skin was loose and baggy; the wrinkled eyelids, instead of being shaped to the pupil, came down flat and perpendicular. His nose and chin were witch-like, the nostrils large and elastic; the lips, drawn tight together, curved downwards, indifferently captious; a short white beard grew sparsely on the chin; the skin of the narrow neck was fantastically drawn and creased. His limbs were thin, the knees and elbows sharpened to a fine point; the hands very long, with blue, corded veins. As a rule his clothes were a distressing combination of black and dark blue; either the coat, the waistcoat, or the trousers would be black, the rest blue; the trousers had the old-fashioned flap-pockets, like a sailor's, with a complex apparatus of buttons. He wore loose white cuffs that were continually slipping down the wrist, a starched dickey, a collar of too lenient flexure, and a black necktie with a 'made' bow that was fastened by means of a button and button-hole under the chin to the right; twenty times a day Meshach had to secure this precarious cravat. Lastly, the top and bottom buttons of his waistcoat were invariably loose.

He was of that small and lonely minority of men who never know ambition, ardour, zeal, yearning, tears; whose convenient desires are capable of immediate satisfaction; of whom it may be said that they purchase a second-rate happiness cheap at the price of an incapacity for deep feeling. In his seventh decade, Meshach Myatt could look back with calm satisfaction at a career of uninterrupted nonchalance and idleness. The favourite of a stern father and of fate, he had never done a hard day's work in his life. When he and Hannah came into their inheritance, he realised everything except the house and invested the proceeds in Consols. With a roof, four hundred a year from the British Empire, a tame capable sister, and notoriously good health, he took final leave of care at the age of thirty-two. He wanted no more than he had. Leisure was his chief luxury; he watched life between meals, and had time to think about what he saw. Being gifted with a vigorous and original mind that by instinct held formulas in defiance, he soon developed a philosophy of his own; and his reputation as a 'character' sprang from the first diffident, wayward expressions of this philosophy. Perceiving that the town not unadmiringly deemed him odd, he cultivated oddity. Perceiving also that it was sometimes astonished at the extent of his information about hidden affairs, he cultivated mystery, the knowledge of other people's business, and the trick of unexpected appearances. At forty his fame was assured; at fifty he was an institution; at sixty an oracle.

'Meshach's a mixture, ' ran the local phrase; but in this mixture there was a less tedious posturing and a more massive intellect than usually go to the achievement of a provincial renown such as Meshach's. The man's externals were deceptive, for he looked like a local curiosity who might never have been out of Bursley. Meshach, however, travelled sometimes in the British Isles, and thereby kept his ideas from congealing. And those who had met him in trains and hotels knew that porters, waiters, and drivers did not mistake his shrewdness for that of a simpleton determined not to be robbed; that he wanted the right things and had the art to get them; in short, that he was an expert in travel. Like many old provincial bachelors, while frugal at home he could be profuse abroad, exercising the luxurious freedom of the bachelor. In the course of years it grew slowly upon his fellow pew-holders at the big Sytch Chapel that he was worldly-minded and possibly contemptuous of their codes; some, who made a specialty of smelling rats, accused him of gaiety.

'You'd happen better get something extra for tea, sister, ' said Meshach, rousing himself.

'Why, brother? ' demanded Hannah.

'Some sausage, happen, ' Meshach proceeded.

'Is any one coming? ' she asked.

'Or a bit of fish, ' said Meshach, gazing meditatively at the fire.

Hannah rose and interrogated his face. 'You ought to have told me before, brother. It's past three now, and Saturday afternoon too! ' So saying, she hurried anxiously into the kitchen and told the servant to put her hat on.

'Who is it that's coming, brother? ' she inquired later, with timid, ravenous curiosity.

'I see you'll have it out of me, ' said Meshach, who gave up mysteries as a miser parts with gold. 'It's Arthur Twemlow from New York; and let that stop your mouth. '

Thus, with the utterance of this name in the prim, archaic, stuffy little back-parlour, Meshach raised the curtain on the last act of a drama which had slumbered for fifteen years, since the death of William Twemlow, and which the principal actors in it had long thought to be concluded or suppressed.

The whole matter could be traced back, through a series of situations which had developed one out of another, to the character of old Twemlow; but the final romantic solution was only rendered possible by the peculiarities of Meshach Myatt. William Twemlow had been one of those men in whom an unbridled appetite for virtue becomes a vice. He loved God with such virulence that he killed his wife, drove his daughter into a fatuous marriage, and quarrelled irrevocably with his son. The too sensitive wife died for lack of joy; Alice escaped to Australia with a parson who never accomplished anything but a large family; and Arthur, at the age of seventeen, precociously cursed his father and sought in America a land where there were fewer commandments. Then old Twemlow told his junior partner, John Stanway, that the ways of Providence were past finding out. Stanway sympathised with him, partly from motives of diplomacy, and partly from a genuine misunderstanding of the case; for Twemlow, mild, earnest, and a generous supporter of charities, was much respected in the town, and his lonely predicament excited compassion; most people looked upon young Arthur as a godless and heartless vagabond.

Alice's husband was a fool, impulsive and vain; and, despite introductions, no congregation in Australia could be persuaded to listen to his version of the gospel; Alice gave birth to more children than bad sermons could keep alive, and soon the old man at Bursley was regularly sending remittances to her. Twemlow desired fervently to do his duty, and moreover the estrangement from his son increased his satisfaction in dealing handsomely with his daughter; the son would doubtless learn from the daughter how much he had lost by his impiety. Seven years elapsed so, and then the parson gave up his holy calling and became a tea-blender in Brisbane. Twemlow was shocked at this defection, which seemed to him sacrilegious, and a chance phrase in a letter of Alice's requesting capital for the new venture—a too assured demand, an insufficient gratitude for past benefits, Alice never quite knew what—brought about a second breach in the Twemlow family. The paternal purse was closed, and perhaps not too early, for the improvidence of the tea-blender and Alice's fecundity were a gulf whose depth no munificence could have plumbed. Again John Stanway sympathised with the now enfeebled old man. John advised him to retire, and Twemlow decided to do so, receiving one-third of the net profits of the partnership business during life. In two years he was bedridden and the miserable victim of a housekeeper; but, though both Alice and Arthur attempted reconciliation, some fine point of conscience obliged him to ignore their overtures. John Stanway, his last remaining friend, called often and chatted about business, which he lamented was far from being what it ought to be. Twemlow's death was hastened by a fire at the works; it happened that he could see the flames from his bedroom window; he survived the spectacle five days. Before entering into his reward, the great pietist wrote letters of forgiveness to Alice and Arthur, and made a will, of which John Stanway was sole executor, in favour of Alice. The town expressed surprise when it learnt that the estate was sworn at less than a thousand pounds, for the dead man's share in the profits of Twemlow & Stanway was no secret, and Stanway had been living in splendour at Hillport for several years. John, when questioned by gossips, referred sadly to Alice's husband and to the depredations of housekeepers. In this manner the name and memory of the Twemlows were apparently extinguished in Bursley.

But Meshach Myatt had witnessed the fire at the works; he had even remained by the canal side all through that illuminated night; and an adventure had occurred to him such as occurs only to the Meshach Myatts of this world. The fire was threatening the office, and Meshach saw his nephew John running to a place of refuge with a drawer snatched out of an American desk; the drawer was loaded with papers and books, and as John ran a small book fell unheeded to the ground. Meshach cried out to John that he had dropped something, but in the excitement and confusion of the fire his rather high-pitched voice was not heard. He left the book lying where it fell; half-an-hour afterwards he saw it again, picked it up, and put it in his pocket. It contained some interesting informal private memoranda of the annual profits of the firm. Now Meshach did not return the book to its owner. He argued that John deserved to suffer for his carelessness in losing it, that John ought to have heard his call, and that anyhow John would surely inquire for it and might then be allowed to receive it with a few remarks upon the need of a calm demeanour at fires; but John never did inquire for it.

When William Twemlow's will was proved a few weeks later, Meshach Myatt made no comment whatever. From time to time he heard news of Arthur Twemlow: that he had set up in New York as an earthenware and glassware factor, that he was doing well, that he was doing extremely well, that his buyer had come over to visit the more aristocratic manufactories at Knype and Cauldon, that some one from Bursley had met Arthur at the Leipzig Easter Fair and reported him stout, taciturn, and Americanised. Then, one morning in Lord Street, Liverpool, fifteen years after the death of old Twemlow and the misappropriation of the little book, Meshach encountered Arthur Twemlow himself; Meshach was returning from his autumn holiday in the Isle of Man, and Arthur had just landed from the 'Servia. ' The two men were mutually impressed by each other's skill in nicely conducting an interview which ninety-nine people out of a hundred would have botched; for they had last met as boy of seventeen and man of forty. They lunched richly at the Adelphi, and gave news for news. Arthur's buyer, it seemed, was dead, and after a day or two in London Arthur was coming to the Five Towns to buy a little in person. Meshach inquired about Alice in Australia, and was told that things were in a specially bad way with the tea-blender. He said that you couldn't cure a fool, and remarked casually upon the smallness of the amount left by old Twemlow. Arthur, unaware that Meshach Myatt was raising up an idea which for fifteen years had been buried but never forgotten in his mind, answered with nonchalance that the amount certainly was rather small. Arthur added that in his dying letter of forgiveness to Alice the old man had stated that his income from the works during the last years of his life had been less than two hundred per annum. Meshach worked his shut thin lips up and down and then began to discuss other matters. But as they parted at Lime Street Station the observer of life said to Arthur with presaging calm: 'You'll be i' th' Five Towns at the end of the week. Come and have a cup o' tea with me and Hannah on Saturday afternoon. The old spot, you know it, top of Church Street. I've something to show you as 'll interest you. ' There was a pause and an interchange of glances. 'Right! ' said Arthur Twemlow. 'Thank you! I'll be there at a quarter after four or thereabouts. ' 'It's like as if what must be! ' Meshach murmured to himself with almost sad resignation, in the enigmatic idiom of the Five Towns. But he was highly pleased that he, the first of all the townsfolk, should have seen Arthur Twemlow after twenty-five years' absence.

When Hannah, in silk, met the most interesting and disconcerting American stranger in the lobby, the sound and the smell of Bursley sausage frizzling in the kitchen added a warm finish to her confused welcome. She remembered him perfectly, 'Eh! Mr. Arthur, ' she said, 'I remember you that *well*.... ' And that was all she could say, except: 'Now take off your overcoat and do make yourself at home, Mr. Arthur. '

'I guess I know *you*, ' said Twemlow, touched by the girlish shyness, the primeval innocence, and the passionate hospitality of the little grey-haired thing.

As he took off his glossy blue overcoat and hung it up he seemed to fill the narrow lobby with his large frame and his quiet but penetrating attractive American accent. He probably weighed fourteen stone, but the elegance of his suit and his boots, the clean-shaven chin, the fineness of the lines of the nose, and the alert eyes set back under the temples, redeemed him from grossness. He looked under rather than over forty; his brown hair was beginning to recede from the forehead, but the heavy moustache, which entirely hid his mouth and was austerely trimmed at the sides, might have aroused the envy of a colonel of hussars.

'Come in, wut, '[1] cried Meshach impatiently from the hob, 'come in and let's be pecking a bit, ' and as Arthur and Hannah entered the parlour, he added: 'She's gotten sausages for you. She would get 'em, though I told her you'd take us as you found us. I told her that. But women—well, you know what they are! '

[1] *Wut* = wilt.

'Eh, Meshach, Meshach! ' the old damsel protested sadly, and escaped into the kitchen.

And when Meshach insisted that the guest should serve out the sausages, and Hannah, passing his tea, said it was a shame to trouble him, Twemlow slipped suddenly back into the old life and ways and ideas. This existence, which he thought he had utterly forgotten, returned again and triumphed for a time over all the experiences of his manhood; it alone seemed real, honest, defensible. Sensations of his long and restless career in New York flashed through his mind as he impaled Hannah's sausages in the curious parlour—the hysteric industry of his girl-typist, the continuous hot-water service in the bedroom of his glittering apartment at the Concord House, youthful nights at Coster and Bial's music-hall, an insanely extravagant dinner at Sherry's on his thirtieth birthday, a difficulty once with an emissary of Pinkerton, the incredible plague of flies in summer. And during all those racing years of clangour and success in New York, the life of Bursley, self-sufficient and self-contained, had preserved its monotonous and slow stolidity. Bursley had become a museum to him; he entered it as he might have entered the Middle Ages, and was astonished to find that beautiful which once he had deemed sordid and commonplace. Some of the streets seemed like a monument of the past, a picturesque survival; the crate-floats, drawn by swift shaggy ponies and driven by men who balanced themselves erect on two thin boards while flying round corners, struck him as the quaintest thing in the world.

'And what's going on nowadays in old Bosley, Miss Myatt? ' he asked expansively, trying to drop his American accent and use the dialect.

'Eh, bless us! ' exclaimed Hannah, startled. 'Nothing ever happens here, Mr. Arthur. '

He felt that nothing did happen there.

'Same here as elsewhere, ' said Meshach. 'People living, and getting childer to worry 'em, and dying. Nothing'll cure 'em of it seemingly. Is there anything different to that in New York? Or can they do without cemeteries? '

Twemlow laughed, and again he had the illusion of having come back to reality after a long, hurried dream. 'Nothing seems to have changed here, ' he remarked idly.

'Nothing changed! ' said Meshach. 'Nay, nay! We're up in the world. We've got the steam-car. And we've got public baths. We wash oursen nowadays. And there's talk of a park, and a pond with a duck on it. We're moving with the times, my lad, and so's the rates. '

It gave him pleasure to be called 'my lad' by old Meshach. It was piquant to him that the first earthenware factor in New York, the

Jupiter of a Fourteenth Street office, should be addressed as a stripling. 'And where is the park to be? ' he suavely inquired.

'Up by the railway station, opposite your father's old works as was—it's a row of villas now. '

'Well, ' said Twemlow. 'That sounds pretty nice. I believe I'll get you to come around with me and show off the sights. Say! ' he added suddenly, 'do you remember being on that works one day when my poor father was on to me like half a hundred of bricks, and you said, "The boy's all right, Mr. Twemlow"? I've never forgotten that. I've thought of it scores of times. '

'Nay! ' Meshach answered carelessly, 'I remember nothing o' that. '

Twemlow was dashed by this oblivion. It was his memory of the minute incident which more than anything else had encouraged him to respond so cordially to Meshach's advances in Liverpool; for he was by no means facile in social intercourse. And Meshach had rudely forgotten the affecting scene! He felt diminished, and saw in the old bachelor a personification of the blunt independent spirit of the Five Towns.

* * * * *

'Milly's late to-day, ' said Hannah to her brother, timorously breaking the silence which ensued.

'Milly? ' questioned Twemlow.

'Millicent her proper name is, ' Hannah said quickly, 'but we call her Milly. My nephew's youngest. '

'Yes, of course, ' Twemlow commented, when the Myatt family-tree had been sketched for him by the united effort of brother and sister, 'I recollect now you told me in Liverpool that Mr. Stanway was married. Who did he marry? '

Meshach Myatt pushed back his chair and stood up. 'John catched on to Knight's daughter, the doctor at Turnhill, ' he said, reaching to a cigar-cabinet on the sideboard. 'Best thing he ever did in his life. John's among the better end of folk now. People said it were a come-down for her, but Leonora isn't the sort that comes down. She's got

28

blood in her. *That*! ' He snapped his fingers. 'She's a good bred 'un. Old Knight's father came from up York way. Ah! She's a cut above Twemlow & Stanway, is Leonora. '

Twemlow smiled at this persistence of respect for caste.

'Have a weed, ' said Meshach, offering him a cigar. 'You'll find it all right; it's a J. S. Murias. Yes, ' he resumed, 'maybe you don't remember old Knight's sister as had that far house up at Hillport? When she died she left it to Leonora, and they've lived there this dozen year and more. '

'Well, I guess she's got a handsome name to her, ' Twemlow remarked perfunctorily, rising and leaving Hannah alone at the table.

'And she's the handsomest woman in the Five Towns: that I do know, ' said Meshach as, in the grand manner of a connoisseur, he lighted his cigar. 'And her was forty, day afore yesterday, ' he added with caustic emphasis.

'Meshach! ' cried Hannah, 'for shame of yourself! ' Then she turned to Twemlow smiling and blushing a little. 'Oughtn't he? Eh, but Mrs. John's a great favourite of my brother's. And I'm sure her girls are very good and attentive. Not a day but one or another of them calls to see me, not a day. Eh, if they missed a day I should think the world was coming to an end. And I'm expecting Milly to-day. What's made the dear child so late — —'

'I will say this for John, ' asserted Meshach, as though the little housewife had not been speaking, 'I will say this for John, ' he repeated, settling himself by the hob. 'He knew how to pick up a d— —d fine woman. '

'Meshach! ' Hannah expostulated again.

Something in the excellence of Meshach's cigars, in his way of calling a woman fine, in the dry, aloof masculinity of his attitude towards Hannah, gave Twemlow to reflect that in the fundamental deeps of experience New York was perhaps not so far ahead of the old Five Towns after all.

There was a fluttering in the lobby, and Millicent ran into the parlour, hurriedly, negligently.

'I can't stay a minute, auntie, ' the vivacious girl burst out in the unmistakable accents of condescending pertness, and then she caught sight of the well-dressed, good-looking man in the corner, and her bearing changed as though by a conjuring trick. She flushed sensitively, stroked her blue serge frock, composed her immature features to the mask of the finished lady paying a call, and summoned every faculty to aid her in looking her best. 'So this chit is the daughter of our admired Leonora, ' thought Twemlow.

'I suppose you don't remember old Mr. Twemlow, my dear? ' said Hannah after she had proudly introduced her niece.

'Oh, auntie! how silly you are! Of course I remember him quite well. I really can't stay, auntie. '

'You'll stay and drink this cup of tea with me, ' Hannah insisted firmly, and Milly was obliged to submit. It was not often that the old lady exercised authority; but on that afternoon the famous New York visitor was just as much an audience for Hannah as for Hannah's greatniece.

Twemlow could think of nothing to say to this pretty pouting creature who had rushed in from a later world and dissipated the atmosphere of mediævalism, and so he addressed himself to Meshach upon the eternal subject of the staple trade. The women at the table talked quietly but self-consciously, and Twemlow saw Milly forced to taste parkin after three refusals. Even while still masticating the viscid unripe parkin, Milly rose to depart. She bent down and dutifully grazed with her lips the cheek of the parkin-maker. 'Good-bye, auntie; good-bye, uncle. ' And in an elegant, mincing tone, 'Good afternoon, Mr. Twemlow. '

'I suppose you've just got to be on time at the next place? ' he said quizzically, smiling at her vivid youth in spite of himself. 'Something very important? '

'Oh, very important! ' she laughed archly, reddening, and then was gone; and Aunt Hannah followed her to the door.

Leonora

'What th' old folks lose, ' murmured Meshach, apparently to the fire, as he put his half-consumed cigar into a meerschaum holder, 'goes to the profit of young Burgess, as is waiting outside the Bank at top o' th' Square. '

'I see, ' said Twemlow, and thought primly that in his day such laxities were not permitted.

Hannah and the servant cleared the tea-table, and the two men were left alone, each silently reducing an J. S. Murias to ashes. Meshach seemed to grow smaller in his padded chair by the hob, to become torpid, and to lose that keen sense of his own astuteness which alone gave zest to his life. Arthur stared out of the window at the confined backyard. The autumn dusk thickened.

Suddenly Meshach sprang up and lighted the gas, and as he adjusted the height of the flame, he remarked casually: 'So your sister Alice is as poorly off as ever? '

Twemlow assented with a nod. 'By the way, ' he said, 'you told me on Wednesday you had something interesting to show me. '

Meshach made no answer, but picked up the poker and struck several times a large pewter platter on the mantelpiece.

'Do you want anything, brother? ' said Hannah, hastening into the room.

'Go up into my bedroom, sister, and in the left-hand pigeon-hole in the bureau you'll see a little flat tissue-paper parcel. Bring it me. It's marked J. S.'

'Yes, brother, ' and she departed.

'You said as your father had told your sister as he never got no more than two hundred a year from th' partnership after he retired. '

'Yes, ' Twemlow replied. 'That's what she wrote me. In fact she sent me the old chap's letter to read. So I reckoned it cost him most all he got to live. '

'Well, ' the old man said, and Hannah returned with the parcel, which he carefully unwrapped. 'That'll do, sister. ' Hannah

31

disappeared. 'Sithee! ' He mysteriously drew Arthur's attention to a little green book whose cover still showed traces of mud and water.

'And what's this? ' Twemlow asked with assumed lightness.

Meshach gave him the history of his adventure at the fire, and then laboriously displayed and expounded the contents of the book, peering into the yellow pages through the steel-rimmed spectacles which he had put on for the purpose.

'And you've kept it all this time? ' said Twemlow.

'I've kept it, ' answered the old man grimly, and Twemlow felt that that was precisely what Meshach Myatt might have been expected to do.

'See, ' said Meshach, and their heads were close together, ' that's the year before your father's death—eight hundred and ninety-two pounds. And year afore that—one thousand two hundred and seven pounds. And year afore that—bless us! Have I turned o'er two pages at once? ' And so he continued.

Twemlow's heart began to beat heavily as Meshach's eyes met his. He seemed to see his father as a pathetic cheated simpleton, and to hear the innumerable children of his sister crying for food; he remembered that in the old Bursley days he had always distrusted John Stanway, that conceited fussy imposing young man of twenty-two whom his father had taken into partnership and utterly believed in. He forgot that he had hated his father, and his mind was obsessed by a sentimental and pure passion for justice.

'Say! Mr. Myatt, ' he exclaimed with sudden gruffness, 'do you suggest that John Stanway didn't do my father right? '

'My lad, I'm doing no suggesting.... You can keep the book if you've a mind to. I've said nothing to no one, and if I had not met you in Liverpool, and you hadn't told me that your sister was poorly off again, happen I should ha' been mum to my grave. But that's how things turn out. '

'He's your own nephew, you know, ' said Twemlow.

'Ay! ' said the old man, 'I know that. What by that? Fair's fair. '

Leonora

Meshach's tone, frigidly jocular, almost frightened the American.

'According to you, ' said he, determined to put the thing into words, 'your nephew robbed my father each year of sums varying from one to three hundred pounds—that's what it comes to. '

'Nay, not according to me—according to that book, and what your father told your sister Alice, ' Meshach corrected.

'But why should he do it? That's what I want to know. '

'Look here, ' said Meshach quietly, resuming his chair. 'John's as good a man of business as you'd meet in a day's march. But never sin' he handled money could he keep off stocks and shares. He speculates, always has, always will. And now you know it—and 'tisn't everybody as does, either. '

'Then you think——'

'Nay, my lad, I don't, ' said Meshach curtly.

'But what ought I to do? '

Meshach cackled in laughter. 'Ask your sister Alice, ' he replied, 'it's her as is interested, not you. You aren't in the will. '

'But I don't want to ruin John Stanway, ' Twemlow protested.

'Ruin John! ' Meshach exclaimed, cackling again. 'Not you! We mun have no scandals in th' family. But you can go and see him, quiet-like, I reckon. Dost think as John'll be stuck fast for six or seven hundred, or eight hundred? Not John! And happen a bit of money'll come in handy to th' old parson tea-blender, by all accounts. '

'Suppose my father—made some mistake—forgot? '

'Ay! ' said Meshach calmly. 'Suppose he did. And suppose he didna'.'

'I believe I'll go and talk to Stanway, ' said Twemlow, putting the book in his pocket. 'Let me see. The works is down at Shawport? '

'On th' cut, '[2] said Meshach.

[2] Cut = canal.

'I can say Alice had asked me to look at the accounts. Oh! Perhaps I can straighten it out neat——' He spoke cheerfully, then stopped. 'But it's fifteen years ago! '

'Fifteen! ' said Meshach with gravity.

'I'm d——d if I can make you out! ' thought Twemlow as he walked along King Street towards the steam-tram for Knype, where he was staying at the Five Towns Hotel. Hannah had sped him, with blushings, and rustlings of silk, from Meshach's door. 'I'm d——d if I can make you out, Meshach. ' He said it aloud. And yet, so complex and self-contradictory is the mind's action under certain circumstances, he could make out Meshach perfectly well; he could discern clearly that Meshach had been actuated partly by the love of chicane, partly by a quasi-infantile curiosity to see what he should see, and partly by an almost biblical sense of justice, a sense blind, callous, cruel.

CHAPTER III

THE CALL

It was the Trust Anniversary at the Sytch Chapel, and two sermons were to be delivered by the Reverend Dr. Simon Quain; during fifteen years none but he had preached the Trust sermons. Even in the morning, when pillars of the church were often disinclined to assume the attitude proper to pillars, the fane was almost crowded. For it was impossible to ignore the Doctor. He was an expert geologist, a renowned lecturer, the friend of men of science and sometimes their foe, a contributor to the 'Encyclopædia Britannica, ' and the author of a book of travel. He did not belong to the school of divines who annihilated Huxley by asking him, from the pulpit, to tell them, if protoplasm was the origin of all life, what was the origin of protoplasm. Dr. Quain was a man of genuine attainments, at which the highest criticism could not sneer; and when he visited Bursley the facile agnostics of the town, the young and experienced who knew more than their elders, were forced to take cover. Dr. Quain, whose learning exceeded even theirs—so the elders sarcastically ventured to surmise—was not ashamed to believe in the inspiration of the Old Testament; he could reconcile the chronology of the earth's crust with the first chapter of Genesis; he had a satisfactory explanation of the Johannine gospel; and his mere existence was an impregnable fortress from which the adherents of the banner of belief could not be dislodged. On this Sunday morning he offered a simple evangelical discourse, enhanced by those occasional references to palæozoic and post-tertiary periods which were expected from him, and which he had enough of the wisdom of the serpent to supply. His grave and assured utterances banished all doubts, fears, misgivings, apprehensions; and the timid waverers smiled their relief at being freed, by the confidence of this illustrious authority, from the distasteful exertion of thinking for themselves.

The collection was immense, and, in addition to being immense, it provided for the worshippers an agreeable and legitimate excitement of curiosity; for the plate usually entrusted to Meshach Myatt was passed from pew to pew, and afterwards carried to the communion rails, by a complete stranger, a man extremely self-possessed and well-attired, with a heavy moustache, a curious dimple in his chin, and melancholy eyes, a man obviously of considerable importance somewhere. 'Oh, mamma, ' whispered Milly to her mother, who was

alone with her in the Stanway pew, 'do look; that's Mr. Twemlow. '
Several men in the congregation knew his identity, and one, a
commercial traveller, had met him in New York. Before the final
hymn was given out, half the chapel had pronounced his name in
surprise. His overt act of assisting in the offertory was favourably
regarded; it was thought to show a nice social feeling on his part;
and he did it with such distinction! The older people remembered
that his father had always been a collector; they were constrained
now to readjust their ideas concerning the son, and these ideas,
rooted in the single phrase, *ran away from home*, and set fast by time,
were difficult of adjustment. The impressiveness of Dr. Quain's
sermon was impaired by this diversion of interest.

The members of the Stanway family, in order to avoid the crush in
the aisles and portico, always remained in their pew after service,
until the chapel had nearly emptied itself; and to-day Leonora chose
to sit longer than usual. John had been too fatigued to rise for
breakfast; Rose was struck down by a sick headache; and Ethel had
stayed at home to nurse Rose, so far as Rose would allow herself to
be nursed. Leonora felt no desire to hurry back to the somewhat
perilous atmosphere of Sunday dinner, and moreover she shrank
nervously from the possibility of having to make the acquaintance of
Mr. Twemlow. But when she and Milly at length reached the outer
vestibule, a concourse of people still lingered there, and among them
Arthur was just bidding good-bye to the Myatts. Hannah, rather
shortsighted, did not observe Leonora and Milly; Meshach gave
them his curt quizzical nod, and the aged twain departed. Then
Millicent, proud of her acquaintance with the important stranger,
and burning to be seen in converse with him, left her mother's side
and became an independent member of society.

'How do you do, Mr. Twemlow? ' she chirped.

'Ah! ' he replied, recognising her with a bow the sufficiency of which
intoxicated the young girl. 'Not in such a hurry this morning? '

'Oh! no! ' she agreed with smiling effusion, and they both glanced
with furtive embarrassed swiftness at Leonora. 'Mamma, this is Mr.
Twemlow. Mr. Twemlow my mother. ' The dashing modish air of
the child was adorable. Having concluded her scene she retired from
the centre of the stage in a glow.

Arthur Twemlow's manner altered at once as he took Leonora's hand and saw the sudden generous miracle which happened in her calm face when she smiled. He was impressed by her beautiful maturity, by the elegance born of a restrained but powerful instinct transmitted to her through generations of ancestors. His respect for Meshach rose higher. And she, as she faced the self-possessed admiration in Arthur's eyes, was conscious of her finished beauty, even of the piquancy of the angle of her hat, and the smooth immaculate whiteness of her gloves; and she was proud, too, of Millicent's gracile, restless charm. They walked down the steps side by side, Leonora in the middle, watched curiously from above and below by little knots of people who still lingered in front of the chapel.

'You soon got to work here, Mr. Twemlow, ' said Leonora lightly.

He laughed. 'I guess you mean that collecting box. That was Mr. Myatt's game. He didn't do me right, you know. He got me into his pew, and then put the plate on to me. '

Leonora liked his Americanism of accent and phrase; it seemed romantic to her; it seemed to signify the quick alertness, the vivacious and surprising turns, of existence in New York, where the unexpected and the extraordinary gave a zest to every day.

'Well, you collected perfectly, ' she remarked.

'Oh, yes you did, really, Mr. Twemlow, ' echoed Millicent.

'Did I? ' he said, accepting the tribute with frank satisfaction. 'I used to collect once at Talmage's Church in Brooklyn—you've heard Talmage over here of course. ' He faintly indicated contempt for Talmage. 'And after my first collection he sent for me into the church parlour, and he said to me: "Mr. Twemlow, next time you collect, put some snap into it; don't go shuffling along as if you were dead. " So you see this morning, although I haven't collected for years, I thought of that and tried to put some snap into it. '

Milly laughed obstreperously, Leonora smiled.

At the corner they could see Mrs. Burgess's carriage waiting at the vestry door in Mount Street. The geologist, escorted by Harry Burgess, got into the carriage, where Mrs. Burgess already sat; Harry followed him, and the stately equipage drove off. Dr. Quain had married a cousin of Mrs. Burgess's late husband, and he invariably stayed at her house. All this had to be explained to Arthur Twemlow, who made a point of being curious. By the time they had reached the top of Oldcastle Street, Leonora felt an impulse to ask him without ceremony to walk up to Hillport and have dinner with them. She knew that she and Milly were pleasing him, and this assurance flattered her. But she could not summon the enterprise necessary for such an unusual invitation; her lips would not utter the words, she could not force them to utter the words.

He hesitated, as if to leave them; and quite automatically, without being able to do otherwise, Leonora held her hand to bid good-bye; he took it with reluctance. The moment was passing, and she had not even asked him where he was staying: she had learnt nothing of the man of whom Meshach had warned her husband to beware.

'Good morning, ' he said, 'I'm very glad to have met you. Perhaps— —'

'Won't you come and see us this afternoon, if you aren't engaged? ' she suggested quickly. 'My husband will be anxious to meet you, I know. '

He appeared to vacillate.

'Oh, do, Mr. Twemlow! ' urged Milly, enchanted.

'It's very good of you, ' he said, 'I shall be delighted to call. It's quite a considerable time since I saw Mr. Stanway. ' He laughed. This was his first reference to John.

'I'm so glad you asked him, ma, ' said Milly, as they walked down Oldcastle Street.

'Your father said we must be polite to Mr. Twemlow, ' her mother replied coldly.

'He's frightfully rich, I'm sure, ' Milly observed.

At dinner Leonora told John that Arthur Twemlow was coming.

'Oh, good! ' he said: nothing more.

* * * * *

38

In the afternoon the mother and her eldest and youngest, supine and exanimate in the drawing-room, were surprised into expectancy by the sound of the front-door bell before three o'clock.

'He's here! ' exclaimed Milly, who was sitting near Leonora on the long Chesterfield. Ethel, her face flushed by the fire, lay like a curving wisp of straw in John's vast arm-chair. Leonora was reading; she put down the magazine and glanced briefly at Ethel, then at the aspect of the room. In silence she wished that Ethel's characteristic attitudes could be a little more demure and sophisticated. She wondered how often this apparently artless girl had surreptitiously seen Fred Ryley since the midnight meeting on Thursday, and she was amazed that a child of hers, so kindly disposed, could be so naughty and deceitful. The door opened and Ethel sat up with a bound.

'Mr. Burgess, ' the parlourmaid announced. The three women sank back, disappointed and yet relieved.

Harry Burgess, though barely of age, was one of the acknowledged dandies of Hillport. Slim and fair, with a frank, rather simple countenance, he supported his stylistic apparel with a natural grace that attracted sympathy. Just at present he was achieving a spirited effect by always wearing an austere black necktie fastened with a small gold safety-pin; he wore this necktie for weeks to a bewildering variety of suits, and then plunged into a wild polychromatic debauch of neckties. Upon all the niceties of masculine dress, the details of costume proper to a particular form of industry or recreation or ceremonial, he was a genuine authority. His cricketing flannels—he was a fine cricketer and lawn-tennis player of the sinuous oriental sort—were the despair of other dandies and the scorn of the sloven; he caused the material, before it was made up, to be boiled for many hours by the Burgess charwoman under his own superintendence. He had extraordinary aptitudes for drawing corks, lacing boots, putting ferrules on walking-sticks, opening latched windows from the outside, and rolling cigarettes; he could make a cigarette with one hand, and not another man in the Five Towns, it was said, could do that. His slender convex silver cigarette-case invariably contained the only cigarettes worthy of the palate of a connoisseur, as his pipes were invariably the only pipes fit for the combustion of truly high-class tobacco. Old women, especially charwomen, adored him, and even municipal seigniors admitted that Harry was a smart-looking youth. Fatherless, he was the heir to a tolerable fortune, the bulk of which, during his mother's life, he could not touch save with her consent; but his mother and his sister seemed to exist chiefly for his convenience. His fair hair and his facile smile vanquished them, and vanquished most other people also; and already, when he happened to be crossed, there would appear on his winning face the pouting, hard, resentful lines of the man who has learnt to accept compliance as a right. He had small intellectual power, and no ambition at all. A considerable part of his prospective fortune was invested in the admirable shares of the Birmingham, Sheffield and District Bank, and it pleased him to sit on a stool in the Bursley branch of this bank, since he wanted, *pro tempore*, a dignified avocation without either the anxieties of trade or the competitive tests of a profession. He was a beautiful bank clerk; but he had once thrown a bundle of cheques into the office fire while aiming at a basket on the mantelpiece; the whole banking world would have been agitated and disorganised had not another clerk snatched the bundle from peril at the expense of his own fingers: the incident, still legendary behind the counter of the establishment at the top of St. Luke's Square, kept Harry awake to the seriousness of life for several weeks.

'Well, Harry, ' said Leonora with languid good nature. He paid his homage in form to the mistress of the house; raised his eyebrows at Milly, who returned the gesture; smiled upon Ethel, who feebly waved a hand as if too exhausted to do more; and then sat down on the piano-stool, carefully easing the strain on his trousers at the knees and exposing an inch of fine wool socks above his American boots. He was a familiar of the house, and had had the unconditional *entrée* since he and the Stanway girls first went to the High Schools at Oldcastle.

'I hope I haven't disturbed your beauty sleep—any of you, ' was his opening remark.

'Yes, you have, ' said Ethel.

He continued: 'I just came in to seek a little temporary relief from the excellent Quain. Quain at breakfast, Quain at chapel, Quain at dinner.... I got him to slumber on one side of the hearth and mother on the other, and then I slipped away in case they awoke. If they do, I've told Cissie to say that I've gone out to take a tract to a sick friend—back in five minutes. '

Leonora

'Oh, Harry, you are silly! ' Millicent laughed. Every one, including the narrator, was amused by this elaborate fiction of the managing of those two impressive persons, Mrs. Burgess and the venerable Christian geologist, by a kind, indulgent, bored Harry. Leonora, who had resumed her magazine, looked up and smiled the guarded smile of the mother.

'I'm afraid you're getting worse, ' she murmured, and his candid seductive face told her that while he was on no account not to be regarded as a gay dog, and a sad dog, and a worldly dog, yet nevertheless he and she thoroughly appreciated and understood each other. She did indeed like him, and she found pleasure in his presence; he gratified the eye.

'I wish you'd sing something, Milly, ' he began again after a pause.

'No, ' said Milly, 'I'm not going to sing now. '

'But do. Can't she, Mrs. Stanway? '

'Well, what do you want me to sing? '

'Sing "Love is a plaintive song, " out of the second act. '

Harry was the newly appointed secretary of the Bursley Amateur Operatic Society, of which both Ethel and Millicent were members. In a few weeks' time the Society was to render *Patience* in the Town Hall for the benefit of local charities, and rehearsals were occurring frequently.

'Oh! I'm not Patience, ' Milly objected stiffly; she was only Ella. 'Besides, I mayn't, may I, mamma? '

'Your father might not like it, ' said Leonora.

'The dad has taken Bran out for a walk, so it won't trouble him, ' Ethel interjected sleepily under her breath.

'Well, but look here, Mrs. Stanway, ' said Harry conclusively, 'the organist at the Wesleyan chapel actually plays the sextet from *Patience* for a voluntary. What about that? If there's no harm in that——' Leonora surrendered. 'Come on, Mill, ' he commanded. 'I

41

shall have to return to my muttons directly, ' and he opened the piano.

'But I tell you I'm not Patience. '

'Come *on*! You know the music all right. Then we'll try Ella's bit in the first act. I'll play. '

Millicent arose, shook her hair, and walked to the piano with the mien of a prima donna who has the capitals of Europe at her feet, exultant in her youth, her charm, her voice, revelling unconsciously in the vivacity of her blood, and consciously in her power over Harry, which Harry strove in vain to conceal under an assumed equanimity.

And as Millicent sang the ballad Leonora was beguiled, by her singing, into a mood of vague but overpowering melancholy. It seemed tragic that that fresh and pure voice, that innocent vanity, and that untested self-confidence should change and fade as maturity succeeded adolescence and decay succeeded maturity; it seemed intolerable that the ineffable charm of the girl's youth must be slowly filched away by the thefts of time. 'I was like that once! And Jack too! ' she thought, as she gazed absently at the pair in front of the piano. And it appeared incredible to her that she was the mother of that tall womanly creature, that the little morsel of a child which she had borne one night had become a daughter of Eve, with a magic to mesmerise errant glances and desires. She had a glimpse of the significance of Nature's eternal iterance. Then her mood developed a bitterness against Millicent. She thought cruelly that Millicent's magic was no part of the girl's soul, no talent acquired by loving exertion, but something extrinsic, unavoidable, and unmeritorious. Why was it so? Why should fate treat Milly like a godchild? Why should she have prettiness, and adorableness, and the lyric gift, and such abounding confident youth? Why should circumstances fall out so that she could meet her unacknowledged lover openly at all seasons? Leonora's eyes wandered to the figure of Ethel reclining with shut eyes in the arm-chair. Ethel in her graver and more diffident beauty had already begun to taste the sadness of the world. Ethel might not stand victoriously by her lover in the midst of the drawing-room, nor joyously flip his ear when he struck a wrong note on the piano. Ethel, far more passionate than the active Milly, could only dream of her lover, and see him by stealth. Leonora grieved for Ethel, and envied her too, for her dreams, and for her

42

solitude assuaged by clandestine trysts. Those trysts lay heavy on Leonora's mind; although she had discovered them, she had done nothing to prevent them; from day to day she had put off the definite parental act of censure and interdiction. She was appalled by the serene duplicity of her girls. Yet what could she say? Words were so trivial, so conventional. And though she objected to the match, wishing with ardour that Ethel might marry far more brilliantly, she believed as fully in the honest warm kindliness of Fred Ryley as in that of Ethel. 'And what else matters after all? ' she tried to think.... Her reverie shifted to Rose, unfortunate Rose, victim of peculiar ambitions, of a weak digestion, and of a harsh temperament that repelled the sympathy it craved but was too proud to invite. She felt that she ought to go upstairs and talk to the prostrate Rose in the curt matter-of-fact tone that Rose ostensibly preferred, but she did not wish to talk to Rose. 'Ah well! ' she reflected finally with an inward sigh, as though to whisper the last word and free herself of this preoccupation, 'they will all be as old as me one day. '

'Mr. Twemlow, ' said the parlourmaid.

Milly deliberately lengthened a high full note and then stopped and turned towards the door.

'Bravo! ' Arthur Twemlow answered at once the challenge of her whole figure; but he seemed to ignore the fact that he had caused an interruption, and there was something in his voice that piqued the cantatrice, something that sent her back to the days of short frocks. She glanced nervously aside at Harry, who had struck a few notes and then dropped his hands from the keyboard. Twemlow's demeanour towards the blushing Ethel when Leonora brought her forward was much more decorous and simple. As for Harry, to whom his arrival was a surprise, at first rather annoying, Twemlow treated the young buck as one man of the world should treat another, and Harry's private verdict upon him was extremely favourable. Nevertheless Leonora noticed that the three young ones seemed now to shrink into themselves, to become passive instead of active, and by a common instinct to assume the character of mere spectators.

'May I choose this place? ' said Twemlow, and sat down by Leonora in the other corner of the Chesterfield and looked round. She could see that he was admiring the spacious room and herself in her beautiful afternoon dress, and the pensive and the sprightly comeliness of her daughters. His wandering eyes returned to hers, and their appreciation pleased her and increased her charm.

'I am expecting my husband every minute, ' she said.

'Papa's gone out for a walk with Bran, ' Milly added.

'Oh! Bran! ' He repeated the word in a voice that humorously appealed for further elucidation, and both Ethel and Harry laughed.

'The St. Bernard, you know, ' Milly explained, annoyed.

'I wouldn't be surprised if that was a St. Bernard out there, ' he said pointing to the French window. 'What a fine fellow! And what a fine garden! '

Bran was to be seen nosing low down at the window; and alternately lifting two huge white paws in his futile anxiety to enter the room.

'Then I dare say John is in the garden, ' Leonora exclaimed, with sudden animation, glad to be able to dismiss the faint uneasy suspicion which had begun to form in her mind that John meant after all to avoid Arthur Twemlow. 'Would you like to look at the garden? ' she demanded, half rising, and lifting her brows to a pretty invitation.

'Very much indeed, ' he replied, and he jumped up with the impulsiveness of a boy.

'It's quite warm, ' she said, and thanked Harry for opening the window for them.

'A fine severe garden! ' he remarked enthusiastically outside, after he had descanted to Bran on Bran's amazing perfections, and the dog had greeted his mistress. 'A fine severe garden! ' he repeated.

'Yes, ' she said, lifting her skirt to cross the lawn. 'I know what you mean. I wouldn't have it altered for anything, but many people think it's too formal. My husband does. '

'Why! It's just English. And that old wall! and the yew trees! I tell you——'

She expanded once more to his appreciation, which she took to herself; for none but she, and the gardener who was also the groom, and worked under her, was responsible for the garden. But as she displayed the African marigolds and the late roses and the hardy outdoor chrysanthemums, and as she patted Bran, who dawdled under her hand, she looked furtively about for John. She hoped he might be at the stables, and when in their tour of the grounds they reached the stables and he was not there, she hoped they would find him in the drawing-room on their return. Her suspicion reasserted itself, and it was strengthened, against her reason, by the fact that Arthur Twemlow made no comment on John's invisibility. In the dusk of the spruce stable, where an enamelled name-plate over the manger of a loose box announced that 'Prince' was its pampered tenant, she opened the cornbin, and, entering the loose-box, offered the cob a handful of crushed oats. And when she stood by the cob, Twemlow looking through the grill of the door at this picture which suggested a beast-tamer in the cage, she was aware of her beauty and the beauty of the animal as he curved his neck to her jewelled hand, and of the ravishing effect of an elegant woman seen in a stable. She smiled proudly and yet sadly at Twemlow, who was pulling his heavy moustache. Then they could hear an ungoverned burst of Milly's light laughter from the drawing-room, and presently Milly resumed her interrupted song. Opposite the outer door of the stable was the window of the kitchen, whence issued, like an undertone to the song, the subdued rattle of cups and saucers; and the glow of the kitchen fire could be distinguished. And over all this complex domestic organism, attractive and efficient in its every manifestation, and vigorously alive now in the smooth calm of the English Sunday, she was queen; and hers was the brain that ruled it while feigning an aloof quiescence. 'He is a romantic man; he understands all that, ' she felt with the certainty of intuition. Aloud she said she must fasten up the dog.

When they returned to the drawing-room there was no sign of John.

'Hasn't your father come in? ' she asked Ethel in a low voice; Milly was still singing.

'No, mother, I thought he was with you in the garden. ' The girl seemed to respond to Leonora's inquietude.

Milly finished her song, and Twemlow, who had stationed himself behind her to look at the music, nodded an austere approval.

'You have an excellent voice, ' he remarked, 'and you can use it. ' To Leonora this judgment seemed weighty and decisive.

'Mr. Twemlow, ' said the girl, smiling her satisfaction, 'excuse me asking, but are you married? '

'No, ' he answered, 'are you? '

'*Mr.* Twemlow! ' she giggled, and turning to Ethel, who in anticipation blushed once again: 'There! I told you. '

'You girls are very curious, ' Leonora said perfunctorily.

Bessy came in and set a Moorish stool before the Chesterfield, on the stool an inlaid Sheraton tray with china and a copper kettle droning over a lamp, and near it a cakestand in three storeys. And Leonora, manoeuvring her bangles, commenced the ritual of refection with Harry as acolyte. 'If he doesn't come—well, he doesn't come, ' she thought of her husband, as she smiled interrogatively at Arthur Twemlow, holding a lump of sugar aloft in the tongs.

'The Reverend Simon Quain asked who you were, at dinner to-day, ' said Harry. During the absence of Leonora and her guest, Harry had evidently acquired information concerning Arthur.

'Oh, Mr. Twemlow! ' Milly appealed quickly, 'do tell Harry and Ethel what Dr. Talmage said to you. I think it's so funny—I can't do the accent. '

'What accent? ' he laughed.

She hesitated, caught. 'Yours, ' she replied boldly.

'Very amusing! ' Harry said judicially, after the episode of the Brooklyn collection had been related. 'Talmage must be a caution.... I suppose you're staying at the Five Towns Hotel? ' he inquired, with an implication in his voice that there was no other hotel in the district fit for the patronage of a man of the world. Twemlow nodded.

'What! At Knype? ' Leonora exclaimed. 'Then where did you dine to-day? '

'I had dinner at the Tiger, and not a bad dinner either, ' he said.

'Oh dear! ' Harry murmured, indicating an august sympathy for Arthur Twemlow in affliction.

'If I had only known—I don't know what I was thinking of not to ask you to come here for dinner, ' said Leonora. 'I made sure you would be engaged somewhere. '

'Fancy you eating all alone at the Tiger, on Sunday too! ' remarked Milly.

'Tut! tut! ' Twemlow protested, with a farcical exactness of pronunciation; and Ethel laughed.

'What are you laughing at, my dear? ' Leonora asked mildly.

'I don't know, mother—really I don't. ' Whereupon they all laughed together and a state of absolute intimacy was established.

'I hadn't the least notion of being at Bursley to-day, ' Twemlow explained. 'But I thought that Knype wasn't much of a place—I always did think that, being a native of Bursley. I wouldn't be surprised if you've noticed, Mrs. Stanway, how all the five Five Towns kind of sit and sniff at each other. Well, I felt dull after breakfast, and when I saw the advertisement of Dr. Quain at the old chapel, I came right away. And that's all, except that I'm going to sup with a man at Knype to-night. '

There were sounds in the hall, and the door of the drawing-room opened; but it was only Bessie coming to light the gas.

'Is that your master just come in? ' Leonora asked her.

'Yes, ma'am. '

'At last, ' said Leonora, and they waited. With noiseless precision Bessie lit the gas, made the fire, drew the curtains, and departed. Then they could hear John's heavy footsteps overhead.

Leonora began nervously to talk about Rose, and Twemlow showed a polite interest in Rose's private trials; Ethel said that she had just visited the patient, who slept. Harry asseverated that to remain a moment longer away from his mother's house would mean utter ruin for him, and with extraordinary suddenness he made his adieux and went, followed to the front door by Millicent. The conversation in the room dwindled to disconnected remarks, and was kept alive by a series of separate little efforts. Footsteps were no longer audible overhead. The clock on the mantelpiece struck five, emphasising a silence, and amid growing constraint several minutes passed. Leonora wanted to suggest that John, having lost the dog, must have been delayed by looking for him, but she felt that she could not infuse sufficient conviction into the remark, and so said nothing. A thousand fears and misgivings took possession of her, and, not for the first time, she seemed to discern in the gloom of the future some great catastrophe which would swallow up all that was precious to her.

At length John came in, hurried, fidgetty, nervous, and Ethel slipped out of the room.

'Ah! Twemlow! ' he broke forth, 'how d'ye do? How d'ye do? Glad to see you. Hadn't given me up, had you? How d'ye do? '

'Not quite, ' said Twemlow gravely as they shook hands.

Leonora took the water-jug from the tray and went to a chrysanthemum in the farthest corner of the room, where she remained listening, and pretending to be busy with the plant. The men talked freely but vapidly with the most careful politeness, and it seemed to her that Twemlow was annoyed, while Stanway was determined to offer no explanation of his absence from tea. Once, in a pause, John turned to Leonora and said that he had been upstairs to see Rose. Leonora was surprised at the change in Twemlow's demeanour. It was as though the pair were fighting a duel and Twemlow wore a coat of mail. 'And these two have not seen each other for twenty-five years! ' she thought. 'And they talk like this! ' She knew then that something lay between them; she could tell from a peculiar well-known look in her husband's eyes.

When she summoned decision to approach them where they stood side by side on the hearthrug, both tall, big, formal, and preoccupied, Twemlow at once said that unfortunately he must go; Stanway made none but the merest perfunctory attempt to detain him. He thanked Leonora stiffly for her hospitality, and said good-bye with scarcely a smile. But as John opened the door for him to pass out, he turned to glance at her, and smiled brightly, kindly, bowing a final adieu, to which she responded. She who never in her life till then had condescended to such a device softly stepped to the unlatched door and listened.

'This one yours? ' she heard John say, and then the sound of a hat bouncing on the tiled floor.

'My fault entirely, ' said Twemlow's voice. 'By the way, I guess I can see you at your office one day soon? '

'Yes, certainly, ' John answered with false glib lightness. 'What about? Some business? '

'Well, yes—business, ' drawled Twemlow.

They walked away towards the outer hall, and she heard no more, except the indistinct murmur of a sudden brief dialogue between the visitor and the two girls, who must have come in from the garden. Then the front door banged heavily. He was gone. The vast and arid tedium of her life closed in upon her again; she seemed to exist in a colourless void peopled only by ominous dim elusive shapes of disaster.

But as involuntarily she clenched her hands the formidable thought swept through her brain that Arthur Twemlow was not so calm, nor so impassive, nor so set apart, but that her spell over him, if she chose to exert it, might be a shield to the devious man her husband.

CHAPTER IV

AN INTIMACY

'Does father really mean it about me going to the works to-morrow? ' Ethel asked that night.

'I suppose so, my dear, ' replied Leonora, and she added: 'You must do all you can to help him. '

Ethel's clear gift of interpreting even the most delicate modulations in her mother's voice, instantly gave her the first faint sense of alarm.

'Why, mamma! what do you mean? '

'What I say, dear, ' Leonora murmured with neutral calm. 'You must do all you can to help him. We look on you as a woman now. '

'You don't, you don't! ' Ethel thought passionately as she went upstairs. 'And you never will. Never! '

The profound instinctive sympathy which existed between her mother and herself was continually being disturbed by the manifest insincerity of that assertion contained in Leonora's last sentence. The girl was in arms, without knowing it, against a whole order of things. She could scarcely speak to Millicent in the bedroom. She was disgusted with her father, and she was disgusted with Leonora for pretending that her father was sagacious and benevolent, for not admitting that he was merely a trial to be endured. She was disgusted with Fred Ryley because he was not as other young men were—Harry Burgess for instance. The startling hint from Leonora that perhaps all was not well at the works exasperated her. She held the works in abhorrence. With her sisters, she had always regarded the works as a vague something which John Stanway went to and came away from, as the mysterious source of food, raiment, warmth. But she was utterly ignorant of its mechanism, and she wished to remain ignorant. That its mechanism should be in danger of breaking down, that it should even creak, was to her at first less a disaster than a matter for resentment. She hated the works as one is sometimes capable of unreasonably hating a benefactor.

On Monday morning, rising a little earlier than usual, she was surprised to find her mother alone at a disordered breakfast-table.

'Has dad finished his breakfast already? ' she inquired, determined to be cheerful. Sleep, and her fundamental good-nature, had modified her mood, and for the moment she meant to play the rôle of dutiful daughter as well as she could.

'He has had to go off to Manchester by the first train, ' said Leonora. 'He'll be away all day. So you won't begin till to-morrow. ' She smiled gravely.

'Oh, good! ' Ethel exclaimed with intense momentary relief.

But now again in Leonora's voice, and in her eye, there was the soft warning, which Ethel seized, and which, without a relevant word spoken, she communicated to her sisters. John Stanway's young women began to reflect apprehensively upon the sudden irregularities of his recent movements, his conferences with his lawyer, his bluffing air; a hundred trifles too insignificant for separate notice collected themselves together and became formidable. A certain atmosphere of forced and false cheerfulness spread through the house.

'Not gone to bed! ' said Stanway briskly, when he returned home by the late train and discovered his three girls in the drawing-room. They allowed him to imagine that his jaunty air deceived them; they were jaunty too; but all the while they read his soul and pitied him with the intolerable condescension of youth towards age.

The next day Ethel had a further reprieve of several hours, for Stanway said that he must go over to Hanbridge in the morning, and would come back to Hillport for dinner, and escort Ethel to the works immediately afterwards. None asked a question, but everyone knew that he could only be going to Hanbridge to consult with David Dain. This time the programme was in fact executed. At two o'clock Ethel found herself in her father's office.

As she took off her hat and jacket in the hard sinister room, she looked like a violet roughly transplanted and bidden to blossom in the mire. She knew that amid that environment she could be nothing but incapable, dull, stupid, futile, and plain. She knew that she had no brains to comprehend and no energy to prevail. Every detail repelled her—the absence of fire-irons in the hearth, the business almanacs on the discoloured walls, the great flat table-desk, the dusty samples of tea-pots in the window, the vast green safe in the corner, the glimpses of industrial squalor in the yard, the sound of uncouth voices from the clerks' office, the muffled beat of machinery under the floor, and the strange uninhabited useless appearance of a small room seen through a half-open door near the safe. She would have given a year of life, in that first moment, to be helping her mother in some despised monotonous household task at Hillport.

She felt that she was being outrageously deprived of a natural right, hitherto enjoyed without let, to have the golden fruits of labour brought to her in discreet silence as to their origin.

Stanway struck a bell with determination, and the manager appeared, a tall, thin, sandy-haired man of middle age, who wore a grey tailed-coat and a white apron.

'Ha! Mayer! That you? '

'Yes, sir.... Good afternoon, miss. '

'Good afternoon, ' Ethel simpered foolishly, and she had it in her to have slain both men because she felt such a silly schoolgirl.

'I wanted Ryley. Where is he? '

'He's somewhere on the bank, [3] sir—speaking to the mouldmaker, I think. '

> [3] Bank = earthenware manufactory. But here the word is used in a limited sense, meaning the industrial, as distinguished from the bureaucratic, part of the manufactory.

'Well, just bring me in that letter from Paris that came on Saturday, will you? ' Stanway requested.

'I've several things to speak to you about, ' said Mr. Mayer, when he had brought the letter.

'Directly, ' Stanway answered, waving him away, and then turning to Ethel: 'Now, young lady, I want this letter translating. ' He placed it before her on the table, together with some blank paper.

'Yes, father, ' she said humbly.

Three hours a week for seven years she had sat in front of French manuals at the school at Oldcastle; but she knew that, even if the destiny of nations turned on it, she could not translate that letter of ten lines. Nevertheless she was bound to make a pretence of doing so.

'I don't think I can without a dictionary, ' she plaintively murmured, after a few minutes.

'Oh! Here's a French dictionary, ' he replied, producing one from a drawer, much to her chagrin; she had hoped that he would not have a dictionary.

Then Stanway began to look through a pile of correspondence, and to scribble in a large saffron-coloured diary. He went out to Mr. Mayer; Mr. Mayer came in to him; they called to each other from room to room. The machinery stopped beneath and started again. A horse fell down in the yard, and Stanway, watching from the window, exclaimed: 'Tsh! That carter! '

Various persons unceremoniously entered and asked questions, all of which Stanway answered with equal dryness and certainty. At intervals he poked the fire with an old walking-stick, Ethel never glanced up. In a dream she handled the dictionary, the letter, the blank paper, and wrote unfinished phrases with the thick office pen.

'Done it? ' he inquired at last.

'I—I—can't make out the figures, ' she stammered. 'Is that a 5 or a 7? ' She pushed the letter across.

'Oh! That's a French 7, ' he replied, and proceeded to make shots at the meaning of sentences with a *flair* far surpassing her own skill, though it was notorious that he knew no French whatever. She had a sudden perception of his cleverness, his capacity, his force, his mysterious hold on all kinds of things which eluded her grasp and dismayed her.

'Let's see what you've done, ' he demanded. She sighed in despair, hesitating to give up the paper.

'Mr. Twemlow, by appointment, ' announced a clerk, and Arthur Twemlow walked into the office.

'Hallo, Twemlow! ' said Stanway, meeting him gaily. 'I was just expecting you. My new confidential clerk. Eh? ' He pointed to Ethel, who flushed to advantage. 'You've plenty of them over there, haven't you—girl-clerks? '

Twemlow assented, and remarked that he himself employed a 'lady secretary. '

'Yes, ' Stanway eagerly went on. 'That's what I mean to do. I mean to buy a type-writer, and Miss shall learn shorthand and type-writing. '

Ethel was astounded at the glibness of invention which could instantly bring forth such an idea. She felt quite sure that until that moment her father had had no plan at all in regard to her attendance at the office.

'I'm sure I can't learn, ' she said with genuine modesty, and as she spoke she became very attractive to Twemlow, who said nothing, but smiled at her sympathetically, protectively. She returned the smile. By a swift miracle the violet was back again in its native bed.

'You can go in there and finish your work, we shall disturb you, ' said her father, pointing to the little empty room, and she meekly disappeared with the letter, the dictionary, and the piece of paper.

* * * * *

'Well, how's business, Twemlow? By the way, have a cigar. '

Ethel, at the dusty table in the little room, could just see her father's broad back through the door which, in her nervousness, she had forgotten to close. She felt that the door ought to have been latched, but she could not find courage deliberately to get up and latch it now.

'Thanks, ' said Arthur Twemlow. 'Business is going right along. '

She heard the striking of a match, and the pleasant twang of cigar-smoke greeted her nostrils. The two men seemed splendidly masculine, important, self-sufficient. The triviality of feminine atoms like herself, Rose, and Millicent, occurred to her almost as a new fact, and she was ashamed of her existence.

'Buying much this trip? ' asked Stanway.

'Not much, and not your sort, ' said Twemlow. 'The truth is, I'm fixing up a branch in London. '

'But, my dear fellow, surely there's no American business done through London in English goods? '

'No, perhaps not, ' said Twemlow. 'But that don't say there isn't going to be. Besides, I've got a notion of coming in for a share of your colonial shipping trade. And let me tell you there's a lot of business done through London between the United States and the Continent, in glass and fancy goods. '

'Oh, yes, I know there is, ' Stanway conceded. 'And so you think you're going to teach the old country a thing or two? '

'That depends. '

'On what? '

'On whether the old country's made up her mind yet to sit down and learn. ' He laughed.

Ethel saw by the change of colour in her father's neck that the susceptibilities of his patriotism had been assailed.

'What do you mean? ' Stanway asked pugnaciously.

'I mean that you are falling behind here, ' said Twemlow with cold, nonchalant firmness. 'Every one knows that. You're getting left. Look how you're being cut out in cheap toilet stuff. In ten years you won't be shipping a hundred dollars' worth per annum of cheap toilet to the States. '

'But listen, Twemlow, ' said Stanway impressively.

Twemlow continued, imperturbable: 'You in the Five Towns stick to old-fashioned methods. You can't cut it fine enough. '

'Old-fashioned? Not cut it fine enough? ' Stanway exclaimed, rising.

Twemlow laughed with real mirth. 'Yes, ' he said.

'Give me one instance—one instance, ' cried Stanway.

'Well, ' said Twemlow, 'take firing. I hear you still pay your firemen by the oven, and your placers by the day, instead of settling all oven-work by scorage. '

'Tell me about that—the Trenton system. I'd like to hear about that. It's been mentioned once or twice, ' said Stanway, resuming his chair.

'Mentioned! '

Ethel perceived vaguely that the forceful man who held her in the hollow of his hand had met more than his match. Over that spectacle she rejoiced like a small child; but at the same time Arthur Twemlow's absolute conviction that the Five Towns was losing ground frightened her, made her feel that life was earnest, and stirred faint longings for the serious way. It seemed to her that she was weighed down by knowledge of the world, whereas gay Millicent, and Rose with her silly examinations.... She plunged again into the actuality of the letter from Paris....

'I called really to speak to you about my father's estate. '

Ethel was startled into attention by the sudden careful politeness in Arthur Twemlow's manner and by a quivering in his voice.

'What of it? ' said Stanway. 'I've forgotten all the details. Fifteen years since, you know. '

'Yes. But it's on behalf of my sister, and I haven't been over before. Besides, it wasn't till she heard I was coming to England that she—asked me. '

'Well, ' said Stanway. 'Of course I was the sole executor, and it's my duty——'

'That's it, ' Twemlow broke in. 'That's what makes it a little awkward. No one's got the right to go behind you as executor. But the fact is, my sister—we—my sister was surprised at the smallness of the estate. We want to know what he did with his money, that is, how much he really received before he died. Perhaps you won't mind letting me look at the annual balance-sheets of the old firm, say for 1875, 6, and 7. You see——'

Twemlow stopped as Stanway half-turned to look at the door between the two rooms.

'Go on, go on, ' said Stanway in his grandiose manner. 'That's all right. '

Ethel knew in a flash that her father would have given a great deal to have had the door shut, and equally that nothing on earth would have induced him to shut it.

'That's all right, ' he repeated. 'Go on. '

Twemlow's voice regained steadiness. 'You can perhaps understand my sister's feelings. ' Then a long pause. 'Naturally, if you don't care to show me the balance-sheets——'

'My dear Twemlow, ' said John stiffly, 'I shall be delighted to show you anything you wish to see. '

'I only want to know——'

'Certainly, certainly. Quite justifiable and proper. I'll have them looked up. '

'Any time will do. '

'Well, we're rather busy. Say a week to-day—if you're to be here that long. '

'I guess that'll suit me, ' said Twemlow.

His tone had a touch of cynical cruel patience.

The intangible and shapeless suspicions which Ethel had caught from Leonora took a misty form and substance, only to be immediately dispelled in that inconstant mind by the sudden refreshing sound of Milly's voice: 'We've called to take Ethel home, papa—oh, mother, here's Mr. Twemlow! '

In another moment the office was full of chatter and scent, and Milly had run impulsively to Ethel: 'What *has* father given you to do? '

'Oh dear! ' Ethel sighed, with a fatigued gesture of knowing nothing whatever.

'It's half-past five, ' said Leonora, glancing into the inner room, after she had spoken to Mr. Twemlow.

Three hours and a half had Ethel been in thrall! It was like a century to her. She could have dropped into her mother's arms.

'What have you come in, Nora? ' asked Stanway, 'the trap? '

'No, the four-wheeled dog-cart, dear. '

'Well, Twemlow, drive up and have tea with us. Come along and have a Five Towns high-tea. '

'Oh, Mr. Twemlow, do! ' said Milly, nearly drowning Leonora's murmured invitation.

Arthur hesitated.

'Come *along*, ' Stanway insisted genially. 'Of course you will. '

'Thank you, ' was the rather feeble answer. 'But I shall have to leave pretty early. '

'We'll see about that, ' said Stanway. 'You can take Mr. Twemlow and the girls, Nora, and I'll follow as quick as I can. I must dictate a letter or two. '

The three women, Twemlow in the midst, escaped like a pretty cloud out of the rude, dingy office, and their bright voices echoed *diminuendo* down the stair. Stanway rang his bell fiercely. The dictionary and the letter and Ethel's paper lay forgotten on the dusty table of the inner room.

* * * * *

Arthur Twemlow felt that he ought to have been annoyed, but he could do no more than keep up a certain reserve of manner. Neither the memory of his humiliating clumsy lies about his sister in broaching the matter of his father's estate to Stanway, nor his clear perception that Stanway was a dishonest and a frightened man, nor his strong theoretical objection to Stanway's tactics in so urgently inviting him to tea, could overpower the sensation of spiritual comfort and complacency which possessed him as he sat between Leonora and Ethel at Leonora's splendidly laden table. He fought doggedly against this sensation. He tried to assume the attitude of a philosopher observing humanity, of a spider watching flies; he tried to be critical, cold, aloof. He listened as one set apart, and answered in monosyllables. But despite his own volition the monosyllables were accompanied by a smile that destroyed the effect of their curtness. The intimate charm of the domesticity subdued his logical antipathies. He knew that he was making a good impression among these women, that for them there was something romantic and exciting about his history and personality. And he liked them all. He liked even Rose, so pale, strange, and contentious. In regard to Milly, whom he had begun by despising, he silently admitted that a girl so vivacious, supple, sparkling, and pretty, had the right to be as pertly foolish as she chose. He took a direct fancy to Ethel. And he decided once for ever that Leonora was a magnificent creature.

In the play of conversation on domestic trifles, the most ordinary phrases seemed to him to be charged with a peculiar fascination. The little discussions about Milly's attempts at housekeeping, about the austere exertions of Rose, Ethel's first day at the office, Bran's new biscuits, the end of the lawn-tennis season, the propriety of hockey for girls, were so mysteriously pleasant to his ears that he felt it a sort of privilege to have been admitted to them. And yet he clearly perceived the shortcomings of each person in this little world of which the totality was so delightful. He knew that Ethel was languidly futile, Rose cantankerous, Milly inane, Stanway himself crafty and meretricious, and Leonora often supine when she should not be. He dwelt specially on the more odious aspects of Stanway's character, and swore that, had Stanway forty womenfolk instead of four, he, Arthur Twemlow, should still do his obvious duty of finishing what he had begun. In chatting with his host after tea, he marked his own attitude with much care, and though Stanway pretended not to observe it, he knew that Stanway observed it well enough.

The three girls disappeared and returned in street attire. Rose was going to the science classes at the Wedgwood Institution, Ethel and Millicent to the rehearsal of the Amateur Operatic Society. Again, in this distribution of the complex family energy, there reappeared the suggestion of a mysterious domestic charm.

'Don't be late to-night, ' said Stanway severely to Millicent.

'Now, grumbler, ' retorted the intrepid child, putting her gloved hand suddenly over her father's mouth; Stanway submitted. The picture of the two in this delicious momentary contact remained long in Twemlow's mind; and he thought that Stanway could not be such a brute after all.

'Play something for us, Nora, ' said the august paterfamilias, spreading at ease in his chair in the drawing-room, when the girls were gone. Leonora removed her bangles and began to play 'The Bees' Wedding. ' But she had not proceeded far before Milly ran in again.

'A note from Mr. Dain, pa. '

Milly had vanished in an instant, and Leonora continued to play as if nothing had happened, but Arthur was conscious of a change in the atmosphere as Stanway opened the letter and read it.

'I must just go over the way and speak to a neighbour, ' said Stanway carelessly when Leonora had struck the final chord. 'You'll excuse me, I know. Sha'n't be long. '

'Don't mention it, ' Arthur replied with politeness, and then, after Stanway had gone, leaving the door open, he turned to Leonora at the piano, and said: 'Do play something else. '

Instead of answering, she rose, resumed her jewellery, and took the chair which Stanway had left. She smiled invitingly, evasively, inscrutably at her guest.

'Tell me about American women, ' she said: 'I've always wanted to know. '

He thought her attitude in the great chair the most enchanting thing he had ever seen.

* * * * *

Leonora had watched Twemlow's demeanour from the moment when she met him in her husband's office. She had guessed, but not certainly, that it was still inimical at least to John, and the exact words of Uncle Meshach's warning had recurred to her time after time as she met his reluctant, cautious eyes. Nevertheless, it was by the sudden uprush of an instinct, rather than by a calculated design, that she, in her home and surrounded by her daughters, began the process of enmeshing him in the web of influences which she spun ceaselessly from the bright threads of her own individuality. Her mind had food for sombre preoccupation—the lost battle with Milly during the day about Milly's comic-opera housekeeping; the tale told by John's nervous, effusive, guilty manner; and especially the episode of the letter from Dain and John's disappearance: these things were grave enough to the mother and wife. But they receded like negligible trifles into the distance as she rose so suddenly and with such a radiant impulse from the piano. In the new enterprise of consciously arousing the sympathy of a man, she had almost forgotten even the desperate motive which had decided her to undertake it should she get the chance.

'Tell me about American women, ' she said. All her person was a challenge. And then: 'Would you mind shutting the door after Jack? ' She followed him with her gaze as he crossed and recrossed the room.

'What about American women? ' he said, dropping all his previous reserve like a garment. 'What do you want to know? '

'I've never seen one. I want to know what makes them so charming. '

The fresh desirous interest in her voice flattered him, and he smiled his content.

'Oh! ' he drawled, leaning back in his chair, which faced hers by the fire. 'I never noticed they were so specially charming. Some of them are pretty nice, I expect, but most of the young ones put on too much lugs, at any rate for an Englishman. '

'But they're always marrying Englishmen. So how do you explain that? I did think you'd be able to tell me about the American women.'

'Perhaps I haven't met enough of just the right sort, ' he said.

'You're too critical, ' she remarked, as though his case was a peculiarly interesting one and she was studying it on its merits.

'You only say that because I'm over forty and unmarried, Mrs. Stanway. I'm not at all critical. '

'Over forty! ' she exclaimed, and left a pause. He nodded. 'But you are too critical, ' she went on. 'It isn't that women don't interest you—they do——'

'I should think they did, ' he murmured, gratified.

'But you expect too much from them. '

'Look here! ' he said, 'how do you know? '

She smiled with an assumption of the sadness of all knowledge; she made him feel like a boy again: 'If you didn't expect too much from them, you would have married long ago. It isn't as if you hadn't seen the world. '

'Seen the world! ' he repeated. 'I've never seen anything half so charming as your home, Mrs. Stanway. '

Both were extremely well satisfied with the course of the conversation. Both wished that the interview might last for indefinite hours, for they had slipped, as into a socket, into the supreme topic, and into intimacy. They were happy and they knew it. The egotism of each tingled sensitively with eager joy. They felt that this was 'life, ' one of the justifications of existence.

She shook her head slowly.

'Yes, ' he continued, 'it's you who stay quietly at home that are to be envied. '

'And you, a free bachelor, say that! Why, I should have thought——'

'That's just it. You're quite wrong, if you'll let me say so. Here am I, a free bachelor, as you call it. Can do what I like. Go where I like. And yet I would sell my soul for a home like this. Something... you know. No, you don't. People say that women understand men and what men feel, but they can't—they can't. '

'No, ' said Leonora seriously, 'I don't think they can—still, I have a notion of what you mean. ' She spoke with modest sympathy.

'Have you? ' he questioned.

She nodded. For a fraction of an instant she thought of her husband, stolid with all his impulsiveness, over at David Dain's.

'People say to me, "Why don't you get married? "' Twemlow went on, drawn by the subtle invitation of her manner. 'But how can I get married? I can't get married by taking thought. They make me tired. I ask them sometimes whether they imagine I keep single for the fun of the thing.... Do you know that I've never yet been in love—no, not the least bit. '

He presented her with this fact as with a jewel, and she so accepted it.

'What a pity! ' she said, gently.

'Yes, it's a pity, ' he admitted. 'But look here. That's the worst of me. When I get talking about myself I'm likely to become a bore. '

Offering him the cigarette cabinet she breathed the old, effective, sincere answer: 'Not at all, it's very interesting. '

'Let me see, this house belongs to you, doesn't it? ' he said in a different casual tone as he lighted a cigarette.

Shortly afterwards he departed. John had not returned from Dain's, but Twemlow said that he could not possibly stay, as he had an appointment at Hanbridge. He shook hands with restrained ardour. Her last words to him were: 'I'm so sorry my husband isn't back, ' and even these ordinary words struck him as a beautiful phrase. Alone in the drawing-room, she sighed happily and examined herself in the large glass over the mantelpiece. The shaded lights left her loveliness unimpaired; and yet, as she gazed at the mirror, the worm gnawing at the root of her happiness was not her husband's precarious situation, nor his deviousness, nor even his mere existence, but the one thought: 'Oh! That I were young again! '

* * * * *

'Mother, whatever do you think? ' cried Millicent, running in eagerly in advance of Ethel at ten o'clock. 'Lucy Turner's sister died to-day, and so she can't sing in the opera, and I am to have her part if I can learn it in three weeks. '

'What is her part? ' Leonora asked, as though waking up.

'Why, mother, you know! Patience, of course! Isn't it splendid? '

'Where are father and Mr. Twemlow? Ethel inquired, falling into a chair.

CHAPTER V

THE CHANCE

Leonora was aware that she had tamed one of the lions which menaced her husband's path; she could not conceive that Arthur Twemlow, whatever his mysterious power over John, would find himself able to exercise it now; Twemlow was a friend of hers, and so disarmed. She wished to say proudly to John: 'I neither know nor wish to know the nature of the situation between you and Arthur Twemlow. But be at ease. He is no longer dangerous. I have arranged it. ' The thing was impossible to be said; she was bound to leave John in ignorance; she might not even hint. Nevertheless, Leonora's satisfaction in this triumph, her pleasure in the mere memory of the intimate talk by the fire, her innocent joyous desire to see Twemlow again soon, emanated from her in various subtle ways, and the household was thereby soothed back into a feeling of security about John. Leonora ignored, perhaps deliberately, that Stanway had still before him the peril of financial embarrassment, that he was mortgaging the house, and that his colloquies with David Dain continued to be frequent and obviously disconcerting. When she saw him nervous, petulant, preoccupied, she attributed his condition solely to his thought of the one danger which she had secretly removed. She had a strange determined impulse to be happy and gay.

An episode at an extra Monday night rehearsal of the Amateur Operatic Society seemed to point to the prevalence of certain sinister rumours about Stanway's condition. Milly, inspired by dreams of the future, had learnt her part perfectly in five days. She sang and acted with magnificent assurance, and with a vivid theatrical charm which awoke enthusiasm in the excitable breasts of the male chorus. Harry Burgess lost his air of fatigued worldliness, and went round naïvely demanding to be told whether he had not predicted this miracle. Even the conductor was somewhat moved.

'She'll do, by gad! ' said that man of few illusions to his crony the accompanist.

But it is not to be imagined that such a cardinal event as the elevation of a chit like Millicent Stanway to the principal r'le could achieve itself without much friction and consequent heat. Many ladies of the chorus thought that the committee no longer deserved the confidence of the society. At least three suspected that the conductor had a private spite against themselves. And one, aged thirty-five, felt convinced that she was the victim of an elaborate and scandalous plot. To this maid had been offered Milly's old part of Ella; it was a final insult—but she accepted it. In the scene with Angela and Bunthorne in the first act, the new Ella made the same mistake three times at the words, 'In a doleful train, ' and the conductor grew sarcastic.

'May I show you how that bit goes, Miss Gardner? ' said Milly afterwards with exquisite pertness.

'No, thank you, Milly, ' was the freezing emphasised answer; 'I dare say I shall be able to manage without *your* assistance. '

'Oh, ho! ' sang Milly, delighted to have provoked this exhibition, and she began a sort of Carmen dance of disdain.

'Girls grow up so quick nowadays! ' Miss Gardner exclaimed, losing control of herself; 'who are *you*, I should like to know! ' and she proceeded with her irrelevant inquiries: 'who's *your* father? Doesn't every one know that he'll have gone smash before the night of the show? ' She was shaking, insensate, brutal.

Millicent stood still, and went very white.

'Miss Gardner! '

'*Miss* Stanway! '

The rival divas faced each other, murderous, for a few seconds, and then Milly turned, laughing, to Harry Burgess, who, consciously secretarial, was standing near with several others.

'Either Miss Gardner apologises to me at once, ' she said lightly, 'at *once*, or else either she or I leave the Society. '

Milly tapped her foot, hummed, and looked up into Miss Gardner's eyes with serene contempt. Ethel was not the only one who was amazed at the absolute certitude of victory in little Millicent's demeanour. Harry Burgess spoke apart with the conductor upon this astonishing contretemps, and while he did so Milly, still smiling, hummed rather more loudly the very phrase of Ella's at which Miss Gardner had stumbled. It was a masterpiece of insolence.

'We think Miss Gardner should withdraw the expression, ' said Harry after he had coughed.

'Never! ' said Miss Gardner. 'Good-bye all! '

Thus ended Miss Gardner's long career as an operatic artist—and not without pathos, for the ageing woman sobbed as she left the room from which she had been driven by a pitiless child.

* * * * *

According to custom Harry Burgess set out from the National School, where the rehearsals were held, with Ethel and Milly for Hillport. But at the bottom of Church Street Ethel silently fell behind and joined a fourth figure which had approached. The two couples walked separately to Hillport by the field-path. As Harry and Milly opened the wicket at the foot of Stanway's long garden, Ethel ran up, alone again.

'That you? ' cried a thin voice under the trees by the gate. It was Rose, taking late exercise after her studies.

'Yes, it's us, ' replied Harry. 'Shall you give me a whisky if I come in?'

And he entered the house with the three girls.

'I'm certain Rose saw you with Fred in the field, and if she did she's sure to split to mother, ' Milly whispered as she and Ethel ran upstairs. They could hear Harry already strumming on the piano.

'I don't care! ' said Ethel callously, exasperated by three days of futility at the office, and by the manifest injustice of fate.

'My dear, I want to speak to you, ' said Leonora to Ethel, when the informal supper was over, and Harry had buckishly departed, and Rose and Milly were already gone upstairs. Not a word had been mentioned as to the great episode of the rehearsal.

'Well, mother? ' Ethel answered in a tone of weary defiance.

Leonora still sat at the supper-table, awaiting John, who was out at a meeting; Ethel stood leaning against the mantelpiece like a boy.

'How often have you been seeing Fred Ryley lately? ' Leonora began with a gentle, pacific inquiry.

'I see him every day at the works, mother. '

'I don't mean at the works; you know that, Ethel. '

'I suppose Rose has been telling you things. '

'Rose told me quite innocently that she happened to see Fred in the field to-night. '

'Oh, yes! ' Ethel sneered with cold irony. 'I know Rose's innocence! '

'My dear girl, ' Leonora tried to reason with her. 'Why will you talk like that? You know you promised your father——'

'No, I didn't, ma, ' Ethel interrupted her sharply. 'Milly did; I never promised father anything. '

Leonora was astonished at the mutinous desperation in Ethel's tone. It left her at a loss.

'I shall have to tell your father, ' she said sadly.

'Well, of course, mother, ' Ethel managed her voice carefully. 'You tell him everything. '

'No, I don't, my dear, ' Leonora denied the charge like a girl. 'A week last night I heard Fred Ryley talking to you at your window. And I have said nothing. '

Ethel flushed hotly at this disclosure.

'Then why say anything now? ' she murmured, half daunted and half daring.

'Your father must know. I ought to have told him before. But I have been wondering how best to act. '

'What's the matter with Fred, mother? ' Ethel demanded, with a catch in her throat.

'That isn't the point, Ethel. Your father has distinctly said that he won't permit any'—she stopped because she could not bring herself to say the words; and then continued: 'If he had the slightest suspicion that there was anything between *you* and Fred Ryley he would never have allowed you to go to the works at all. '

'Allowed me to go! I like that, mother! As if I wanted to go to the works! I simply hate the place—father knows that. And yet—and yet——' She almost wept.

'Your father must be obeyed, ' Leonora stated simply.

'Suppose Fred *is* poor, ' Ethel ran on, recovering herself. 'Perhaps he won't be poor always. And perhaps we shan't be rich always. The things that people are saying——' She hesitated, afraid to proceed.

'What do you mean, dear? '

'Well! ' the girl exclaimed, and then gave a brief account of the Gardner incident.

'My child, ' was Leonora's placid comment, 'you ought to know that Florence Gardner will say anything when she is in a temper. She is the worst gossip in Bursley. I only hope Milly wasn't rude. And really this has got nothing to do with what we are talking about. '

'Mother! ' Ethel cried hysterically, 'why are you always so calm? Just imagine yourself in my place—with Fred. You say I'm a woman, and I am, I am, though you don't think so, truly. Just imagine——No, you can't! You've forgotten all that sort of thing, mother. ' She burst into gushing tears at last. 'Father can kill me if he likes! I don't care! '

She fled out of the room.

'So I've forgotten, have I! ' Leonora said to herself, smiling faintly, as she sat alone at the table waiting for John.

She was not at all hurt by Ethel's impassioned taunt, but rather amused, indulgently amused, that the girl should have so misread her. She felt more maternal, protective, and tender towards Ethel than she had ever felt since the first year of Ethel's existence. She seemed perfectly to comprehend, and she nobly excused, the sudden outbreak of violence and disrespect on the part of her languid, soft-eyed daughter. She thought with confidence that all would come right in the end, and vaguely she determined that in some undefined way she would help Ethel, would yet demonstrate to this child of hers that she understood and sympathised. The interview which had just terminated, futile, conflicting, desultory, muddled, tentative, and abrupt as life itself, appeared to her in the light of a positive achievement. She was not unhappy about it, nor about anything. Even the scathing speech of Florence Gardner had failed to disturb her.

'I want to tell you something, Jack, ' she began, when her husband at length came home.

'Who's been drinking whisky? ' was Stanway's only reply as he glanced at the table.

'Harry brought the girls home. I dare say he had some. I didn't notice, ' she said.

'H'm! ' Stanway muttered gloomily, 'he's young enough to start that game. '

'I'll see it isn't offered to him again, if you like, ' said Leonora. 'But I want to tell you something, Jack. '

'Well? ' He was thoughtlessly cutting a piece of cheese into small squares with the silver butter-knife.

'Only you must promise not to say a word to a soul. '

'I shall promise no such thing, ' he said with uncompromising bluntness.

She smiled charmingly upon him. 'Oh yes, Jack, you will, you must. '

He seemed to be taken unawares by her sudden smile. 'Very well, ' he said gruffly.

She then told him, in the manner she thought best, of the relations between Ethel and Fred Ryley, and she pointed out to him that, if he had reflected at all upon the relations between Harry Burgess and Millicent, he would not have fallen into the error of connecting Milly, instead of her sister, with Fred.

'What relations between Milly and young Burgess? ' he questioned stolidly.

'Why, Jack, ' she said, 'you know as much as I do. Why does Harry come here so often? '

'He'd better not come here so often. What's Milly? She's nothing but a child. '

Leonora made no attempt to argue with him. 'As for Ethel, ' she said softly, 'she's at a difficult age, and you must be careful——'

'As for Ethel, ' he interrupted, 'I'll turn Fred Ryley out of my office to-morrow. '

She tried to look grave and sympathetic, to use all her tact. 'But won't that make difficulties with Uncle Meshach? And people might say you had dismissed him because Uncle Meshach had altered his will. '

'D——n Fred Ryley! ' he swore, unable to reply to this. 'D——n him!'

He walked to and fro in the room, and all his secret, profound resentment against Ryley surged up, loose and uncontrolled.

'Wouldn't it be better to take Ethel away from the works? ' Leonora suggested.

'No, ' he answered doggedly. 'Not for a moment! Can't I have my own daughter in my own office because Fred Ryley is on the place? A pretty thing! '

'It is awkward, ' she admitted, as if admitting also that what puzzled his sagacity was of course too much for hers.

'Fred Ryley! ' he repeated the hateful syllables bitterly. 'And I only took him out of kindness! Simply out of kindness! I tell you what, Leonora! ' He faced her in a sort of bravado. 'It would serve 'em d——n well right if Uncle Meshach died to-morrow, and Aunt Hannah the day after. I should be safe then. It would serve them d——n well right, all of 'em—Ryley and Uncle Meshach; yes, and Aunt Hannah too! She hasn't altered her will, but she'd no business to have let uncle alter his. They're all in it. She's bound to die first, and they know it.... Well, well! ' He was a resigned martyr now, and he turned towards the hearth.

'Jack! ' she exclaimed, 'what's the matter? '

'Ruin's the matter, ' he said. 'That's what's the matter. Ruin! '

He laughed sourly, undecided whether to pretend that he was not quite serious, or to divulge his real condition.

Her calm confident eyes silently invited him to relieve his mind, and he could not resist the temptation.

'You know that mortgage on the house, ' he said quickly. 'I got it all arranged at once. Dain was to have sent the deed in last Tuesday night for you to sign, but he sent in a letter instead. That's why I had to go over and see him. There was some confounded hitch at the last moment, a flaw in the title——'

'A flaw in the title! ' It was the phrase only that alarmed her.

'Oh! It's all *right*, ' said Stanway, wondering angrily why women should always, by the trick of seizing on trifles, destroy the true perspective of a business affair. 'The title's all right, at least it will be put right. But it means delay, and I can't wait. I must have money at once, in three days. Can you understand that, my girl? '

By an effort she conquered the impulses to ask why, and why, and why; and to suggest economy in the house. Something came to her mysteriously out of her memory of her own father's affairs, a sudden inspiration; and she said:

'Can't you deposit my deeds at the bank and get a temporary advance? ' She was very proud of this clever suggestion.

He shook his head: 'No, the bank won't. '

The fact was that the bank had long been pressing him to deposit security for his over-draft.

'I tell you what might be done, ' he said, brightening as her idea gave birth to another one in his mind. 'Uncle Meshach might lend some money on the deeds. You shall go down to-morrow morning and ask him, Nora. '

'Me! ' She was scared at this result.

'Yes, you, ' he insisted, full of eagerness. 'It's your house. Ask him to let you have five hundred on the house for a short while. Tell him we want it. You can get round him easily enough. '

'Jack, I can't do it, really. '

'Oh yes, you can, ' he assured her. 'No one better. He likes you. He doesn't like me—never did. Ask him for five hundred. No, ask him for a thousand. May as well make it a thousand. It'll be all the same to him. You go down in the morning, and do it for me. '

Stanway's animation became quite cheerful.

'But about the title—the flaw? ' she feebly questioned.

'That won't frighten uncle, ' said Stanway positively. 'He knows the title is good enough. That's only a technical detail. '

'Very well, ' she agreed, 'I'll do what I can, Jack. '

'That's good, ' he said.

And even now, the resolve once made, she did not lose her sense of tranquil optimism, her mild happiness, her widespreading benevolence. The result of this talk with John aroused in her an innocent vanity, for was it not indirectly due to herself that John had been able to see a way out of his difficulties?

They soon afterwards dismissed the subject, put it with care away in a corner; and John finished his supper.

'Is Mr. Twemlow still in the district? ' she asked vivaciously.

'Yes, ' said John, and there was a pause.

'You're doing some business together, aren't you, Jack? ' she hazarded.

John hesitated. 'No, ' he said, 'he only wanted to see me about old Twemlow's estate—some details he was after. '

'I felt it, ' she mused. 'I felt all the time it was that that was wrong. And John is worrying over it! But he needn't—he needn't—and he doesn't know! '

She exulted.

She could read plainly the duplicity in his face. She knew that he had done some wicked thing, and that all his life was a maze of more or less equivocal stratagems. But she was so used to the character of her husband that this aspect of the situation scarcely impressed her. It was her new active beneficent interference in John's affairs that seemed to occupy her thoughts.

'I told you I wouldn't say anything about Ethel's affair, ' said John later, 'and I won't. ' He was once more judicial and pompous. 'But, of course, you will look after it. I shall leave it to you to deal with. You'll have to be firm, you know. '

'Yes, ' she said.

* * * * *

Not till after breakfast the next day did Leonora realise the utter repugnance with which she shrank from the mission to Uncle Meshach. She had declined to look the project fairly in the face, to examine her own feelings concerning it. She had said to herself when she awoke in the dark: 'It is nothing. It is a mere business matter. It isn't like begging. ' But the idea, the absurd indefensible idea, of its similarity to begging was precisely what troubled her as the moment approached for setting forth. She pondered, too, upon the intolerable fact that such a request as she was about to prefer to Uncle Meshach was a tacit admission that John, with all his ostentations, had at last come to the end of the tether. She felt that she was a living part of John's meretriciousness. She had the fancy that she should have dressed for the occasion in rusty black. Was it not somehow shameful that she, a suppliant for financial aid, should outrage the ugly modesty of the little parlour in Church Street by the arrogant and expensive perfection of her beautiful skirt and street attire?

Moreover, she would fail.

The morning was fine, and with infantile pusillanimity she began to hope that Uncle Meshach would be taking his walks abroad. In order to give him every chance of being out she delayed her departure, upon one domestic excuse or another, for quite half an hour. 'How silly I am! ' she reflected. But she could not help it, and when she had started down the hill towards Bursley she felt sick. She had a suspicion that her feet might of their own accord turn into a by-road and lead her away from Uncle Meshach's. 'I shall never get there! ' she exclaimed. She called at the fishmonger's in Oldcastle Street, and was delighted because the shop was full of customers and she had to wait. At last she was crossing St. Luke's Square and could distinguish Uncle Meshach's doorway with its antique fanlight. She wished to stop, to turn back, to run, but her traitorous feet were inexorable. They carried her an unwilling victim to the house. Uncle Meshach, by some strange accident, was standing at the window and saw her. 'Ah! ' she thought, 'if he had not been at the window, if he had not caught sight of me, I should have walked past! ' And that chance of escape seemed like a lost bliss.

Uncle Meshach himself opened the door.

'Come in, lass, ' he said, looking her up and down through his glasses. 'You're the prettiest thing I've seen since I saw ye last. Your aunt's out, with the servant too; and I'm left here same as a dog on the chain. That's how they leave me. '

She was thankful that Aunt Hannah was out: that made the affair simpler.

'Well, uncle, ' she said, 'I haven't seen you since you came back from the Isle of Man, have I? '

Some inspiration lent her a courage which rose far beyond embarrassment. She saw at once that the old man was enchanted to have her in the house alone, and flattered by the apparatus of feminine elegance which she always displayed for him at its fullest. These two had a sort of cult for each other, a secret sympathy, none the less sincere because it seldom found expression. His pale blue eyes, warmed by her presence, said: 'I'm an old man, and I've seen the world, and I keep a few of my ideas to myself. But you know that no one understands a pretty woman better than I do. A glance is enough. ' And in reply to this challenge she gave the rein to her profoundest instincts. She played the simple feminine to his masculine. She dared to be the eternal beauty who rules men, and will ever rule them, they know not why.

'My lass, ' he said in a tone that granted all requests in advance, after they had talked a while, 'you're after something. '

His wrinkled features, ironic but benevolent, intimated that he knew she wished to take an unfair advantage of the gifts which Nature had bestowed on her, and that he did not object.

She allowed herself to smile mysteriously, provocatively at him.

'Yes, ' she admitted frankly, 'I am. '

'Well? ' He waited indulgently for the disclosure.

She paused a moment, smiling steadily at him. The contrast of his wizened age made her feel deliciously girlish.

'It's about my house, at Hillport, ' she began with assurance. 'I want you——'

And she told him, with no more than a sufficiency of detail, what she wanted. She did not try to conceal that the aim was to help John, that, in crude fact, it was John who needed the money. But she emphasised '*my* house, ' and '*I* want you to lend *me*. ' The thing was well done, and she knew it was well done, and felt satisfied accordingly. As for Meshach, he was decidedly caught unawares. He might, perhaps, have suspected from the beginning that she was only an emissary of John's, but the form and magnitude of her proposal were a violent surprise to him. He hesitated. She could see clearly that he sought reasons by which to justify himself in acquiescence.

'It's your affair? ' he questioned meditatively.

'Quite my own, ' she assured him.

'Let me see— —'

'I shall get it! ' she said to herself, and she was astounded at the felicitous event of the enterprise. She could scarcely believe her good luck, but she knew beyond any doubt that she was not mistaken in the signs of Meshach's demeanour. She thought she might even venture to ask him for an explanation of his warning letter about Arthur Twemlow.

At that moment Aunt Hannah and the middle-aged servant re-entered the house, and the servant had to pass through the parlour to reach the kitchen. The atmosphere which Meshach and Leonora had evolved in solitude from their respective individualities was dissipated instantly. The parlour became nothing but the parlour, with its glass partition, its antimacassars, its Meshach by the hob, and its diminutive Hannah uttering fatuous, affectionate exclamations of pleasure.

Leonora's heart was pierced by a sudden stab of doubt, as she waited for the result.

'Sister, ' said Meshach, 'what dost think? Here's your nephew been speculating in stocks and shares till he can't hardly turn round— —'

'Uncle! ' Leonora exclaimed horrified, 'I never said such a thing! '

'Sh! ' said Hannah in an awful whisper, as she shut the kitchen door.

'Till he can't hardly turn round, ' Meshach continued; 'and now he wants Leonora here to mortgage her house to get him out of his difficulties. Haven't I always told you as John would find himself in a rare fix one of these days? '

Few human beings could dominate another more completely than Meshach dominated his sister. But here, for Leonora's undoing, was just a case where, without knowing it, Hannah influenced her brother. He had a reputation to keep up with Hannah, a great and terrible reputation, and in several ways a loan by him through Leonora to John would have damaged it. A few minutes later, and he would have been committed both to the loan and to the demonstration of his own consistency in the humble eyes of Hannah; but the old spinster had arrived too soon. The spell was broken. Meshach perceived the danger of his position, and retired.

'Nay, nay! ' Hannah protested. 'That's very wrong of John. Eh, this speculation! '

'But, really, uncle, ' Leonora said as convincingly as she could. 'It's capital that John wants. '

She saw that all was lost.

'Capital! ' Meshach sarcastically flouted the word, and he turned with a dubious benevolence to Leonora. 'No, my lass, it isn't, ' he said, pausing. 'John'll get out of this mess as he's gotten out of many another. Trust him. He's your husband, and he's in the family, and I'm saying nothing against him. But trust him for that. '

'No, ' Hannah inserted, 'John's always been a good nephew.... If it wasn't— —'

Meshach quelled her and proceeded: 'I'll none consent to John raising money on your property. It's not right, lass. Happen this'll be a lesson to him, if anything will be. '

'Five hundred would do, ' Leonora murmured with mad foolishness.

Of what use to chronicle the dreadful shame which she endured before she could leave the house, she who for a quarter of an hour had been a queen there, and who left as the pitied wife of a wastrel nephew?

'You're not *short*, my dear? ' Hannah asked at the end in an anxious voice.

'Not he! ' Uncle Meshach testily ejaculated, fastening the button of that droll necktie of his.

'Oh dear no! ' said Leonora, with such dignity as she could assume.

As she walked home she wondered what 'speculation' really was. She could not have defined the word. She possessed but a vague idea of its meaning. She had long apprehended, ignorantly and indifferently and uneasily, that John was in the habit of tampering with dangerous things called stocks and shares. But never before had the vital import of these secret transactions been revealed to her. The dramatic swiftness of the revelation stunned her, and yet it seemed after all that she only knew now what she had always known.

When she reached home John was already in the hall, taking off his overcoat, though the hour of one had not struck. Was this a coincidence, or had he been unable to control his desire to learn what she had done?

In silence she smiled plaintively at him, shaking her head.

'What do you mean? ' he asked harshly.

'I couldn't arrange it, ' she said. 'Uncle Meshach refused. '

John gave a scarcely perceptible start. 'Oh! That! ' he exclaimed. 'That's all right. I've fixed it up. '

'This morning? '

'Eh? Yes, this morning. '

During dinner he showed a certain careless amiability.

'You needn't go to the works any more to-day, ' he said to Ethel.

To celebrate this unexpected half-holiday, Ethel and Millicent decided that they would try to collect a scratch team for some hockey practice in the meadow.

'And, mother, you must come, ' said Millicent. 'You'll make one more anyway. '

'Yes, ' John agreed, 'it will do your mother good. '

'He will never know, and never guess, and never care, what I have been through! ' she thought.

Before leaving for the works John helped the girls to choose some sticks.

When he reached his office, the first thing he did was to build up a good fire. Next he looked into the safe. Then he rang the bell, and Fred Ryley responded to the summons.

This family connection, whom he both hated and trusted, was a rather thickset, very neatly dressed man of twenty-three, who had been mature, serious, and responsible for eight years. His fair, grave face, with its short thin beard, showed plainly his leading qualities of industry, order, conscientiousness, and doggedness. It showed, too, his mild benevolence. Ryley was never late, never neglectful, never wrong; he never wasted an hour either of his own or his employer's time. And yet his colleagues liked him, perhaps because he was unobtrusive and good-natured. At the beginning of each year he laid down a programme for himself, and he was incapable of swerving from it. Already he had acquired a thorough knowledge of both the manufacturing and the business sides of earthenware manufacture, and also he was one of the few men, at that period, who had systematically studied the chemistry of potting. He could not fail to 'get on, ' and to win universal respect. His chances of a truly striking success would have been greater had he possessed imagination, humour, or any sort of personal distinction. In appearance, he was common, insignificant; to be appreciated, he 'wanted knowing'; but he was extremely sensitive and proud, and he could resent an affront like a Gascon. He had apparently no humour whatever. The sole spark of romance in him had been fanned into a small steady flame by his passion for Ethel. Ryley was a man who could only love once for all.

'Did you find that private ledger for me out of the old safe? ' Stanway demanded.

'Yes, ' said Ryley, 'and I put it in your safe, at the front, and gave you the key back this morning. '

'I don't see it there, ' Stanway retorted.

'Shall I look? ' Ryley suggested quietly, approaching the safe, of which the key was in the lock.

'Never mind, now! Never mind, now! ' Stanway stopped him. 'I don't want to be bothered now. Later on in the afternoon, before Mr. Twemlow comes.... Did you write and ask him to call at four thirty? '

'Yes, ' said Ryley, departing without a sign on his face, the model clerk.

'Fool! ' whispered Stanway. It would have been impossible for Ryley to breathe without irritating his employer, and the fact that his plebeian cousin's son was probably the most reliable underling to be got in the Five Towns did not in the slightest degree lessen Stanway's dislike of him; it increased it.

Stanway had been perfectly aware that the little ledger was in his safe, and as soon as Ryley had shut the door he jumped up, unlatched the safe, removed the book, and after tearing it in two stuck first one half and then the other into the midst of the fire.

'That ends it, anyhow! ' he thought, when the leaves were consumed.

Then he selected some books of cheque counterfoils, a number of prospectuses of companies, some share certificates (exasperating relic of what rich dreams!), and a lot of letters. All these he burnt with much neatness and care, putting more coal on the fire so as to hide every trace of their destruction. Then he opened a drawer in the desk, and took out a revolver which he unloaded and loaded again.

'I'm pretty cool, ' he flattered himself.

He was the sort of flamboyant man who keeps a loaded revolver in obedience to the theory that a loaded revolver is a necessary and proper part of the true male's outfit, like a gold watch and chain, a gold pencil case, a razor for every day in the week, and a cigar-holder with a bit of good amber to it. He had owned that revolver for years, with no thought of utilising the weapon. But in justice to him, it must be said that when any of his contemporaries—Titus Price, for instance—had made use of revolvers or ropes in a particular way, he had always secretly justified and commended them.

He put the revolver in his hip-pocket, the correct location, and donned his 'works' hat. He did not reflect. Memories of his past life did not occur to him, nor visions of that which was to come. He did not feel solemn. On the contrary he felt cross with everyone, and determined to pay everyone out; in particular he was vexed, in a mean childish way, with Uncle Meshach, and with himself for having fancied for a moment that an appeal to Uncle Meshach could be successful. One other idea struck him forcibly by reason of its strangeness: namely, that the works was proceeding exactly as usual, raw material always coming in, finished goods always going out, the various shops hot and murmurous with toil, money tinkling in the petty cash-box, the very engine beneath his floor beating its customary monotonous stroke; and his comfortable home was proceeding exactly as usual, the man hissing about the stable yard, the servants discreetly moving in the immaculate kitchens, Leonora elegant with sovereigns in her purse, the girls chattering and restless; not a single outward sign of disaster; and yet he was at the end, absolutely at the end at last. There was going to be a magnificent and unparalleled sensation in the town of Bursley... He seemed for an instant dimly to perceive ways, or incomplete portions of ways, by which he might still escape... Then with a brusque gesture he dismissed such futile scheming and yielded anew to the impulse which had suddenly and piquantly seized him, three hours before, when Leonora said: 'Uncle Meshach won't, ' and he replied, 'I've fixed it up. ' His dilemma was too complicated. No one, not even Dain, was aware of its intricacies; Dain knew a lot, Leonora a little, and sundry other persons odd fragments. But he himself could scarcely have drawn the outlines of the whole sinister situation without much reference to books and correspondence. No, he had finished. He was bored, and he was irritable. The impulse hurried him on.

'In half an hour that ass Twemlow will be here, ' he thought, looking at the office dial over the mantelpiece.

And then he left his room, calling out to the clerks' room as he passed: 'Just going on to the bank. I shall be back in a minute or two.'

At the south-western corner of the works was a disused enamel-kiln which had been built experimentally and had proved a failure. He walked through the yard, crept with some difficulty into the kiln, and closed the iron door. A pale silver light came down the open chimney. He had decided as he crossed the yard that he should place the mouth of the revolver between his eyes, so that he had nothing to do in the kiln but to put it there and touch the trigger. The idea of this simple action preoccupied him. 'Yes, ' he reflected, taking the revolver from his pocket, 'that is where I must put it, and then just touch the trigger. ' He thought neither of his family, nor of his sins, nor of the grand fiasco, but solely of this physical action. Then, as he raised the revolver, the fear troubled him that he had not burnt a particular letter from a Jew in London, received on the previous day. 'Of course I burnt it, ' he assured himself. 'Did I, though? ' He felt that a mysterious volition over which he had no control would force him to return to his office in order to make sure. He gave a weary curse at the prospect of having to put back the revolver, leave the kiln, enter the kiln again, and once more raise the revolver.

As he passed by the archway near the packing house the afternoon postman appeared and gave him a letter. Without thinking he halted on the spot and opened it. It was written in haste, and ran: 'My Dear Stanway, —I am called away to London and *may* have to sail for New York at once. Sorry to have to break the appointment. We must leave that affair over. In any case it could only be a mere matter of form. As I told you, I was simply acting on behalf of my sister. My kindest regards to your wife and your daughters. Believe me, yours very truly, —ARTHUR TWEMLOW. '

He read the letter a second time in his office, standing up against the shut door. Then his eye wandered to the desk and he saw that an envelope had been placed with mathematical exactitude in the middle of his blotting-pad. 'Ryley! ' he thought. This other letter was marked private, and as the envelope said 'John Stanway, Esq., ' without an address, it must have been brought by special messenger. It was from David Dain, and stated that the difficulty as to the title of the house had been settled, that the mortgage would be sent in for Mrs. Stanway to sign that night, and that Stanway might safely draw against the money to-morrow.

'My God! ' he exclaimed, pushing his hat back from his brow. 'What a chance! '

In five minutes he was drawing cheques, and simultaneously planning how to get over the disappearance of the old private ledger in case Twemlow should after all, at some future date, ask to see original documents.

'What a chance! ' The thought ran round and round in his brain.

As he left the works by the canal side, he paused under Shawport Bridge and furtively dropped the revolver into the water. 'That's done with! ' he murmured.

He saw now that his preparations for departure, which at the moment he had deemed to be so well designed and so effective, were after all ridiculous. No amount of combustion could have prevented the disclosure at an inquest of the ignominious facts.

* * * * *

During tea he laughed loudly at Milly's descriptions of the hockey match, which had been a great success. Leonora had kept goal with distinction, and admitted that she rather enjoyed the game.

'So it is arranged? ' said Leonora, with a hint of involuntary surprise, when he handed her the mortgage to sign.

'Didn't I tell you so this morning? ' he answered loftily. There is always a despicable joy in resuscitating a lie which events have changed into a truth.

He insisted on retiring early that night. In the bedroom he remarked: 'Your friend Twemlow's had to go to London to-day, and may return straight from there to New York. I had a note from him. He sent you his kindest regards and all that sort of thing. '

'Then we mayn't see him again? ' she said, delicately fingering her hair in front of the pier-glass.

CHAPTER VI

COMIC OPERA

Early one evening a few weeks later, Leonora, half attired for the gala night of the operatic performance, was again delicately fingering her hair in that large bedroom whose mirrors daily reflected the leisured process of her toilette. Her black skirt trimmed with yellow made a sudden sharp contrast with the pale tints of her corset and her long bare arms. The bodice lay like a trifling fragment on the blue-green eiderdown of her bed, a pair of satin shoes glistened in front of the fire, and two chairs bore the discarded finery of the day. The dressing-table was littered with silver and ivory. A faint and charming odour of violets mingled mysteriously with the warmth of the fire as Leonora moved away from the pier-glass between the two curtained windows where the light was centred, and with accustomed hands picked up the bodice apparently so frail that a touch might have ruined it.

The door was brusquely opened, and some one entered.

'Not dressed, Rose? ' said Leonora, a little startled. 'We ought to be going in ten minutes. '

'Oh, mother! I mustn't go. I mustn't really! '

The tall slightly-stooping girl, with her flat figure, her plain shabby serge frock, her tired white face, and the sinister glance of the idealist in her great, fretful eyes, seemed to stand there and accuse the whole of Leonora's existence. Utterly absorbed in the imminent examination, her brain a welter of sterile facts, Rose found all the seriousness of life in dates, irregular participles, algebraic symbols, chemical formulas, the altitudes of mountains, and the areas of inland seas. To the cruelty of the too earnest enthusiast she added the cruelty of youth, and it was with a merciless justice that she judged everyone with whom she came into opposition.

'But, my dear, you'll be ill if you keep on like this. And you know what your father said. '

Rose smiled, bitterly superior, at the misguided creature whose horizons were bounded by domesticity on one side and by dress on the other.

'I shall not be ill, mother, ' she said firmly, sniffing at the scent in the room. 'I can't help it. I must work at my chemistry again to-night. Father knows perfectly well that chemistry is my weak point. I must work. I just came in to tell you. '

She departed slowly, as it were daring her mother to protest further.

Leonora sighed, overpowered by a feeling of impotence. What could she do, what could any person do, when challenged by an individuality at once so harsh and so impassioned? She finished her toilette with minute care, but she had lost her pleasure in it. The sense of the contrariety of things deepened in her. She looked round the circle of her environment and saw hope and gladness nowhere. John's affairs were perhaps running more smoothly, but who could tell? The shameful fact that the house was mortgaged remained always with her. And she was intimately conscious of a soilure, a moral stain, as the result of her recent contacts with the man of business in her husband. Why had she not been able to keep femininely aloof from those puzzling and repellent matters, ignorant of them, innocent of them? And Ethel, too! Twelve days of the office had culminated for Ethel in a slight illness, which Doctor Hawley described as lack of tone. Her father had said airily that she must resume her clerkship in due season, but the entire household well knew that she would not do so, and that the experiment was one of the failures which invariably followed John's interference in domestic concerns. As for Milly's housekeeping, it was an admitted absurdity. Millicent had lived of late solely for the opera, and John resented any preoccupation which detached the girls' interest from their home. When Ethel recovered in the nick of time to attend the final rehearsals, he grew sarcastic, and irrelevantly made cutting remarks about the letter from Paris which Ethel had never translated and which she thought he had forgotten. Finally he said he probably could not go to the opera at all, and that at best he might look in at it for half an hour. He was careful to disclaim all interest in the performance.

Carpenter had driven the two girls to the Town Hall at seven o'clock, and at a quarter to eight he returned to fetch his mistress. Enveloped in her fur cloak, Leonora climbed silently into the cart.

'I did hear, ' said Carpenter, respectfully gossiping, 'as Mr. Twemlow was gone back to America; but I seed him yesterday as I was coming back from taking the mester to that there manufacturers' meeting at Knype.... Wonderful like his mother he is, mum. '

'Oh, indeed! ' said Leonora.

Her first impatient querulous thought was that she would have preferred Mr. Twemlow to be in America.

The illuminated windows of the Town Hall, and the knot of excited people at the principal portico, gave her a sort of preliminary intimation that the eternal quest for romance was still active on earth, though she might have abandoned it. In the corridor she met Uncle Meshach, wearing an antique frock-coat. His eye caught hers with quiet satisfaction. There was no sign in his wrinkled face of their last interview.

'Your aunt's not very well, ' he answered her inquiry. 'She wasn't equal to coming, she said. I bid her go to bed. So I'm all alone. '

'Come and sit by me, ' Leonora suggested. 'I have two spare tickets. '

'Nay, I think not, ' he faintly protested.

'Yes, do, ' she said, 'you must. '

As his trembling thin hands stole away her cloak, disclosing the perfection and dark magnificence of her toilette, and as she perceived in his features the admiration of a connoisseur, and in the eyes of other women envy and astonishment, she began to forget her despondencies. She lived again. She believed again in the possibility of joy. And perhaps it was not strange that her thought travelled at once to Ethel—Ethel whom she had not questioned further about her lover, Ethel whom till then she had figured as the wretched victim of love, but whom now she saw wistfully as love's elect.

* * * * *

The front seats of the auditorium were filled with all that was dashing, and much that was solidly serious, in Bursley. Hoarded wealth, whose religion was spotless kitchens and cash down, sat side by side with flightiness and the habit of living by credit on rather

87

more than one's income. The members of the Society had exerted themselves in advance to impress upon the public mind that the entertainment would be nothing if not fashionable and brilliant; and they had succeeded. There was not a single young man, and scarcely an old one, but wore evening-dress, and the frocks of the women made a garden of radiant blossoms. Supreme among the eminent dandies who acted as stewards in that part of the house was Harry Burgess, straight out of Conduit Street, W., with a mien plainly indicating that every reserved seat had been sold two days before. From the second seats the sterling middle classes, half envy and half disdain, examined the glittering ostentation in front of them; they had no illusions concerning it; their knowledge of financial realities was exact. Up in the gloom of the balcony the crowded faces of the unimportant and the obscure rose tier above tier to the organ-loft. Here was Florence Gardner, come incognito to deride; here was Fred Ryley, thief of an evening's time; and here were sundry dressmakers who experienced the thrill of the creative artist as they gazed at their confections below.

The entire audience was nervous, critical, and excited: partly because nearly every unit of it boasted a relative or an intimate friend in the Society, and partly because, as an entity representing the town, it had the trepidations natural to a mother who is about to hear her child say a piece at a party. It hoped, but it feared. If any outsider had remarked that the youthful Bursley Operatic Society could not expect even to approach the achievements of its remarkable elder sister at Hanbridge, the audience would have chafed under that invidious suggestion. Nevertheless it could not believe that its native talent would be really worth hearing. And yet rumours of a surprising excellence were afloat. The excitement was intensified by the tuning of instruments in the orchestra, by certain preliminary experiments of a too anxious gasman, and most of all by a delay in beginning.

At length the Mayor entered, alone; the interesting absence of the Mayoress had some connection with a silver cradle that day ordered from Birmingham as a civic gift.

'Well, Burgess, ' the Mayor whispered benevolently, 'what sort of a show are we to have? '

'You will see, Mr. Mayor, ' said Harry, whose confident smile expressed the spirit of the Society.

Then the conductor—the man to whom twenty instrumentalists and thirty singers looked for guidance, help, encouragement, and the nullifying of mistakes otherwise disastrous; the man on whose nerve and animating enthusiasm depended the reputation of the Society and of Bursley—tapped his baton and stilled the chatter of the audience with a glance. The footlights went up, the lights of the chandelier went down, and almost before any one was aware of the fact the overture had commenced. There could be no withdrawal now; the die was cast; the boats were burnt. In the artistic history of Bursley a decisive moment had arrived.

In a very few seconds people began to realise, slowly, timidly, but surely, that after all they were listening to a real orchestra. The mere volume of sound startled them; the verve and decision of the players filled them with confidence; the bright grace of the well-known airs laid them under a spell. They looked diffidently at each other, as if to say: 'This is not so bad, you know. ' And when the finale was reached, with its prodigious succession of crescendos, and its irresistible melody somehow swimming strongly through a wild sea of tone, the audience forgot its pose of critical aloofness and became unaffectedly human. The last three bars of the overture were smothered in applause.

The conductor, as pale as though he had seen a ghost, turned and bowed stiffly. 'Put that in your pipe and smoke it, ' his unrelaxing features said to the audience; and also: 'If you have ever heard the thing better played in the Five Towns, be good enough to inform me where! '

There was a hesitation, the brief murmur of a hidden voice, and the curtains of the fit-up stage swung apart and disclosed the roseate environs of Castle Bunthorne, ornamented by those famous maidens who were dying for love of its æsthetic owner. The audience made no attempt to grasp the situation of the characters until it had satisfactorily settled the private identity of each. That done, it applied itself to the sympathetic comprehension of the feelings of a dozen young women who appeared to spend their whole existence in statuesque poses and plaintive but nonsensical lyricism. It failed, honestly; and even when the action descended from song to banal dialogue, it was not reassured. 'Silly' was the unspoken epithet on a hundred tongues, despite the delicate persuasion of the music, the virginal charm of the maidens, and the illuminated richness of costumes and scene. The audience understood as little of the operatic convention as of the æstheticism caricatured in the roseate environs of Castle Bunthorne. A number of people present had never been in a theatre, either for lack of opportunity or from a moral objection to theatres. Many others, who seldom missed a melodrama at the Hanbridge Theatre Royal, avoided operas by virtue of the infallible instinct which caused them to recoil from anything exotic enough to disturb the calm of their lifelong mental lethargy. As for the minority which was accustomed to opera, including the still smaller minority which had seen *Patience* itself, it assumed the right that evening critically to examine the convention anew, to reconsider it unintimidated by the crushing prestige of the Savoy or of D'Oyly Carte's No. 1 Touring Company. And for the most part it found in the convention small basis of common sense.

Then Patience appeared on the eminence. She was a dairymaid, and she could not understand the philosophy prevalent in the roseate environs of Castle Bunthorne. The audience hailed her with joy and relief. The dairymaid and her costume were pretty in a familiar way which it could appreciate. She was extremely young, adorably impudent, airy, tripping, and supple as a circus-rider. She had marvellous confidence. 'We are friends, are we not, you and I? ' her gestures seemed to say to the audience. And with the utmost complacency she gazed at herself in the eyes of the audience as in a mirror. Her opening song renewed the triumph of the overture. It was recognisably a ballad, and depended on nothing external for its effectiveness. It gave the bewildered listeners something to take hold of, and in return for this gift they acclaimed and continued to acclaim. Milly glanced coolly at the conductor, who winked back his permission, and the next moment the Bursley Operatic Society tasted the delight of its first encore. The pert fascinations of the heroine, the bravery of the Colonel and his guards, the clowning of Bunthorne, combined with the continuous seduction of the music and the scene, very quickly induced the audience to accept without reserve this amazing intrigue of logical absurdities which was being unrolled before it. The opera ceased to appear preposterous; the convention had won, and the audience had lost. Small slips in delivery were unnoticed, big ones condoned, and nervousness encouraged to depart. The performance became a homogeneous whole, in which the excellence of the best far more than atoned for the clumsy mediocrity of the worst. When the curtains fell amid storms of applause and cut off the stage, the audience perceived suddenly, like a revelation, that the young men and women whom it knew so well in private life had been creating something—an illusion, an ecstasy, a mood—which transcended the sum total of their personalities. It was this miracle, but dimly apprehended perhaps, which left the audience impressed, and eager for the next act.

* * * * *

'That madam will go her own road, ' said Uncle Meshach under cover of the clapping.

Leonora's smile was embarrassed. 'What do you mean? ' she asked him.

He bent his head towards her, looking into her face with a sort of generous cynicism.

'I mean she'll go her own road, ' he repeated.

And then, observing that most of the men were leaving their seats, he told Leonora that he should step across to the Tiger if she would let him. As he passed out, leaning forward on a stick lightly clutched in the left hand, several people demanded his opinion about the spectacle. 'Nay, nay——' he replied again and again, waving one after another out of his course.

In the bar-parlour of the Tiger, the young blades, the genuine fast men, the deliberate middle-aged persons who took one glass only, and the regular nightly customers, mingled together in a dense and noisy crowd under a canopy of smoke. The barmaid and her assistant enjoyed their brief minutes of feverish contact with the great world. Behind the counter, walled in by a rampart of dress-shirts, they conjured with bottles, glasses, and taps, heard and answered ten men at once, reckoned change by a magic beyond arithmetic, peered between shoulders to catch the orders of their particular friends, and at the same time acquired detailed information as to the progress of the opera. Late comers who, forcing a way into the room, saw the multitude of men drinking and smoking, and the unapproachable white faces of these two girls distantly flowering in the haze and the odour, had that saturnalian sensation of seeing life which is peculiar to saloons during the entr'actes of theatrical entertainments. The success of the opera, and of that chit Millicent Stanway, formed the staple of the eager conversation, though here and there a sober couple would be discussing the tramcars or the quinquennial assessment exactly as if Gilbert and Sullivan had never been born. It appeared that Milly had a future, that she was the best Patience yet seen in the district amateur *or* professional, that any burlesque manager would jump at her, that in five years, if she liked, she might be getting a hundred a week, and that Dolly Chose, the idol of the Tivoli and the Pavilion, had not half her style. It also appeared that Milly had no brains of her own, that the leading man had taught her all her business, that her voice was thin and a trifle throaty, that she was too vulgar for the true Savoy tradition, and that in five years she would have gone off to nothing. But the optimists carried the argument. Sundry men who had seen Meshach in the second row of the stalls expressed a keen desire to ask the old bachelor point-blank what he thought of his nephew's daughter; but Meshach did not happen to come into the Tiger.

When the crowd had thinned somewhat, Harry Burgess entered hurriedly and called for a whisky and potass, which the barmaid, who fancied him, served on the instant.

'I wanted to get a wreath, ' he confided to her. 'But Pointon's is closed. '

'Why, Mr. Burgess, ' she said smiling, 'there's a lot of flowers in the coffee-room, and with them and the leaves off that laurel down the yard, and a bit of wire, I could make you one in no time. '

'Can you? ' He seemed doubtful.

'Can I! ' she exclaimed. 'I should think I could, and a beauty! As soon as these gentleman are gone— —'

'It's awfully kind of you, ' said Harry, brightening. 'Can you send it round to me at the artists' entrance in half an hour? '

She nodded, beaming at the prospect. The manufacture of that wreath would be a source of colloquial gratification to her for days.

Harry politely responded to such remarks as 'Devilish good show, Burgess, ' drank in one gulp another whisky and potass, and hastened away. The remainder of the company soon followed; the barmaid disappeared from the bar, and her assistant was left languidly to watch a solitary pair of topers who would certainly not leave till the clock showed eleven.

* * * * *

The auditorium during the entr'acte was more ceremonious, but not less noisy, than the bar-parlour of the Tiger. The pleasant warmth, the sudden increase of light after the fall of the curtain, the certainty of a success, and the consciousness of sharing in the brilliance of that success—all these things raised the spirits, and produced the loquacity of an intoxication. The individuality of each person was set free from its customary prison and joyously displayed its best side to the company. The universal chatter amounted to a din.

But Leonora, cut off by empty seats on either hand, sat silent. She was glad to be able to do so. She would have liked to be at home in solitude, to think. For she was, if not unhappy, at any rate disturbed and dubious. She felt embarrassed amid this glare and this bright murmur of conversation, as though she were being watched, discussed, and criticised. She was the mother of the star, responsible for the star, guilty of all the star's indiscretions. And it was a timorous, reluctant pride which she took in her daughter's success. The truth was that Milly had astonished and frightened her. When Ethel and Milly were allowed to join the Society, the possible results of the permission had not been foreseen. Both Leonora and John had thought of the girls as modest members of the chorus in an affair unmistakably and confessedly amateur. Ethel had kept within the anticipation. But here was Milly an actress, exploiting herself with unconstrained gestures and arch glances and twirlings of her short skirt, to a crowded and miscellaneous audience. Leonora did not like it; her susceptibilities were outraged. She blushed at this amazing public contradiction of Milly's bringing-up. It seemed to her as if she had never known the real Milly, and knew her now for the first time. What would the other mothers think? What would all Hillport think secretly, and say openly behind the backs of the Stanways? The girl was as innocent as a fawn, she had the free grace of extreme youth; no one could utter a word against her. But she was rouged, her lips were painted, several times she had shown her knees, and she seemed incapable of shyness. She was at home on the stage, she faced a thousand people with a pert, a brazen attitude, and said, 'Look at me; enjoy me, as I enjoy your fervent glances; I am here to tickle your fancy.' Patience! She was no more Patience than she was Sister Dora or a heroine of Charlotte Yonge's. She was the eternal unashamed doll, who twists 'men' round her little finger, and smiles on them, always with an instinct for finance.

'Quite a score for Milly!' said a polite voice in Leonora's ear. It was Mrs. Burgess, who sat in the next row.

'Do you think so? ' Leonora replied, perceptibly reddening.

'Oh, yes! ' said Mrs. Burgess with smooth insistence. 'And dear Ethel is very sweet in the chorus, too. '

Leonora tried to fix her thoughts on the grateful figure of mild, nervous, passionate Ethel, the child of her deepest affection.

She turned sharply. Arthur Twemlow was standing in the shadow of the side-aisle near the door. She knew he was there before her eyes saw him. He was evidently rather at a loss, unnoticed, and irresolute. He caught sight of her and bowed. She said to herself that she wished to be alone in her embarrassment, that she could not bear to talk to any one; nevertheless, she raised her finger, and beckoned to him, while striving hard to refrain from doing so. He approached at once. 'He is not in America, ' she reflected in sudden agitation, 'He is here, actually here. In an instant we shall speak. '

'I quite understood you had gone back to New York, ' she said, looking at him, as he stood in front of her, with the upward feminine appealing gesture that men love.

'What! ' he exclaimed. 'Without saying good-bye? No! And how are you all? It seems just about a year since I saw you last. '

'All well, thanks, ' she said, smiling. 'Won't you sit here? It's John's seat, but he isn't coming. '

'Then you are alone? ' He seemed to apologise for the rest of his sex.

She told him that Uncle Meshach was with her, and would return directly. When he asked how the opera was going, and she learnt that, being detained at Knype, he had not seen the first act, she was relieved. He would make the discovery concerning Millicent gradually, and by her side; it was better so, she thought—less disconcerting. In a slight pause of their talk she was startled to feel her heart beating like a hammer against her corsage. Her eyes had brightened. She conversed rapidly, pleased to be talking, pleased at his sympathetic responsiveness, ignoring the audience, and also forgetting the uneasy preoccupations of her recent solitude. The men returned from the Tiger and elsewhere, all except Uncle Meshach. The lights were lowered. The conductor's stick curtly demanded silence and attention. She sank back in her seat.

'A peremptory conductor! ' remarked Twemlow in a whisper.

'Yes, ' she laughed. And this simple exchange of thought, effected, as it were, surreptitiously in the gloom and contrary to the rules, gave her a distinct sensation of joy.

Then began, in Bursley Town Hall, a scene similar to the scenes which have rendered famous the historic stages of European capitals. The verve and personal charm of a young *débutante* determined to triumph, and the enthusiasm of an audience proudly conscious that it was making a reputation, reacted upon and intensified each other to such a degree that the atmosphere became electric, delirious, magical. Not a soul in the auditorium or on the stage but what lived consummately during those minutes—some creatively, like the conductor and Millicent; some agonised with jealousy, like Florence Gardner and a few of the chorus; one maternally in tumultuous distress of spirit; and the great naïve mass yielding with rapture to a sensuous spell.

The outstanding defect in the libretto of *Patience* is the decentralisation of interest in the second act. The alert ones who remembered that in that act the heroine has only one song, and certain passages of dialogue not remarkable for dramatic force, had predicted that Millicent would inevitably lose ground as the evening advanced. They were, however, deceived. Her delivery of the phrase 'I am miserable beyond description' brought the house down by its coquettish artificiality; and the renowned ballad, 'Love is a plaintive song, ' established her unforgettably in the affections of the audience. Her 'exit weeping' was a tremendous stroke, though all knew that she meant them to see that these tears were simply a delightful pretence. The opera came to a standstill while she responded to an imperative call. She bowed, laughing, and then, suddenly affecting to cry again, ran off, with the result that she had to return.

'D——n it! She hasn't got much to learn, has she? ' the conductor murmured to the first violin, a professional from Manchester.

But her greatest efforts she reserved for the difficult and critical prose conversations which now alone remained to her, those dialogues which seem merely to exist for the purpose of separating the numbers allotted to all the other principals. It was as though, during the entr'acte, surrounded by the paint-pots, the intrigues, and the wild confusion of the dressing-room, Millicent had been able to commune with herself, and to foresee and take arms against the peril of an anti-climax. By sheer force, ingenuity, vivacity, flippancy, and sauciness, she lifted her lines to the level, and above the level, of the rest of the piece. She carried the audience with her; she knew it; all her colleagues knew it, and if they chafed they chafed in secret. The performance went better and better as the end approached. The audience had long since ceased to notice defects; only the conductor, the leader, and a few discerning members of the troupe were aware that a catastrophe had been escaped by pure luck two minutes before the descent of the curtains.

And at that descent the walls of the Town Hall, which had echoed to political tirades, the solemn recitatives of oratorios, the mercantile uproar of bazaars, the banal compliments of prize-givings, the arid utterances of lecturers on science and art, and the moans of sinners stricken with a sense of guilt at religious revivals—those walls resounded to a gay and frenzied ovation which is memorable in the town for its ungoverned transports of approval. The Operatic Society as a whole was first acclaimed, all the performers posing in rank on the stage. Then, as the deafening applause showed no sign of diminution, the curtains were drawn back instead of being raised again, and the principals, beginning with the humblest, paraded in pairs in front of the footlights. Milly and her fortunate cavalier came last. The cavalier advanced two paces, took Milly's hand, signed to her to cross over, and retired. The child was left solitary on the stage—solitary, but unabashed, glowing with delight, and smiling as pertly as ever. The leader of the orchestra stood up and handed her a wreath, which she accepted like an oath of fealty; and the wreath, hurriedly manufactured by the barmaid of the Tiger out of some cut flowers and the old laurel tree in the Tiger yard, became, when Milly grasped it, a mysterious and impressive symbol. Many persons in the audience wanted to cry as they beheld this vision of the proud, confident, triumphant child holding the wreath, while the fierce upward ray of the footlights illuminated her small chin and her quivering nostrils. She tripped off backwards, with a gesture of farewell. The applause continued. Would she return? Not if the ferocious jealousies behind could have paralysed her as she hesitated in the wings. But the world was on her side that night; she responded again, she kissed her hands to her world, and disappeared still kissing them; and the evening was finished.

* * * * *

'Well, ' said Twemlow calmly, 'I guess you've got an actress in the family. '

Leonora and he remained in their seats, waiting till the press of people in the aisles should have thinned, and also, so far as Leonora was concerned, to avoid the necessity of replying to remarks about Milly. The atmosphere was still charged with excitement, but Leonora observed that Arthur Twemlow did not share it. Though he had applauded vigorously, there had been no trace of emotional transport in his demeanour. He spoke at once, immediately the lights were turned up, giving her no chance to collect herself.

'But do you think so? ' she said. She remembered she had made the same foolish reply to Mrs. Burgess. With Twemlow she wished to be unconventional and sincere, but she could not succeed.

'Don't you? ' He seemed to regard the situation as rather amusing.

'You surely can't mean that she would *do* for the stage? '

'Ask any one here whether she isn't born for it, ' he answered.

'This is only an amateurs' affair, ' Leonora argued.

'And she's only an amateur. But she won't be an amateur long. '

'But a girl like Milly can't be clever enough— —'

'It depends on what you call clever. She's got the gift of making the audience hug itself. You'll see. '

'See Milly on the stage? ' Leonora asked uneasily. 'I hope not. '

'Why, my dear lady? Isn't she built for it? Doesn't she enjoy it? Isn't she at home there? What's the matter with the stage anyhow? '

'Her father would never hear of such a thing, ' said Leonora. Towards the close of the opera she had seen John, in morning attire, propped against a side-wall and peering at the stage and his daughter with a bewildered, bored, unsympathetic air.

'Ah! ' Twemlow ejaculated grimly.

A moment later, as he was putting her cloak over her shoulders, he said in a different, kinder, more soothing tone: 'I guess I know just how you feel. '

She looked at him, raising her eyebrows, and smiling with melancholy amusement.

In the corridor, Stanway came hurrying up to them, obviously excited.

'Oh, you're here, Nora! ' he burst out. 'I've been hunting for you everywhere. I've just been told that a messenger came for Uncle Meshach a the interval to say that Aunt Hannah was ill. Do you know anything about it? '

'No, ' she said. 'Uncle only told me that aunt wasn't equal to coming. I wondered where uncle had got to. '

'Well, ' Stanway continued, 'you'd better go to Church Street at once, and see after things. '

Leonora seemed to hesitate.

'As quick as you can, ' he said with irritation and increasing excitement. 'Don't waste a moment. It may be serious. I'll drive the girls home, and then I'll come and fetch you. '

'If Mrs. Stanway cares, I will walk down with her, ' said Arthur Twemlow.

'Yes, do, Twemlow, there's a good chap, ' he welcomed the idea. And with that he wafted them impulsively into the street.

Then Stanway stood waiting by his equipage for Ethel and Milly. He spoke to no one, but examined the harness critically, and put some curt question to Carpenter about the breeching. It was a chilly night, and the glare of the lamps showed that Prince steamed a little under his rug. Ten minutes elapsed before Ethel came.

'Here we are, father, ' she said with pleasant satisfaction. 'Where's mother? '

'I should think so! ' he returned. 'The horse taking cold, and me waiting and waiting. Your mother's had to go to Aunt Hannah's. What's become of Milly? ' He was losing his temper.

Milly had to traverse the whole length of the corridor. The Mayor heartily congratulated her. The middle-aged violinist from Manchester spoke to her amiably as one public artist to another, and the conductor, who was with him, told her, in an unusual and indiscreet mood of candour, that she had simply made the show. Others expressed the same thought in more words. Near the entrance stood Harry Burgess, patently expectant. He was flushed, and looked handsomely dandiacal and rakish as he rolled a cigarette in those quick fingers of his. He meant to explain to her that the happy idea of the wreath was his own.

He accosted her unceremoniously, confidently, but she drew away, with a magnificent touch of haughtiness.

'Good-night, Harry, ' she said coldly, and passed on.

The rash and conceited boy had not divined, as he should have done, that a prima donna is a prima donna, whether on the stage in a brilliant costume, or traversing a dingy corridor in the plain blue serge and simple hat of a manufacturer's daughter aged eighteen. Offering no reply to her formal salutation, he remained quite still for a moment, and then swaggered off to the Tiger.

'Look here, my girl, ' said Stanway furiously to his youngest. 'Do you suppose we're going to wait for you all night? Jump in. '

Milly's lips did not move, but she faced the rude blusterer with a frigid, angry, insolent gaze. And her girlish eyes said: 'You've got me under your thumb now, you horrid beast! But never mind! Long after you are dead and buried and rotten, I shall be famous and pretty and rich, and if you are remembered it will only be because you were my father. Do your worst, odious man; you can't kill me! '

And all the way home the cruel, just, unmerciful thoughts of insulted youth mingled with the generous and beautiful sensations of her triumph.

* * * * *

'Nay, it's all over, ' said Meshach when Twemlow and Leonora entered.

'What! ' Leonora exclaimed, glancing quickly at Arthur Twemlow as if for support in a crisis.

'Doctor's gone but just this minute. Her's gotten over it. '

For a moment she had thought that Aunt Hannah was dead. John's anxious excitement had communicated itself to her; she had imagined the worst possibilities. Now the sensation of relief took her unawares, and she was obliged to sit down suddenly.

In the little parlour wizened Meshach sat by the hob as he always sat, warming one hand at the fire, and looking round sideways at the tall visitors in their rich evening attire. Leonora heard Twemlow say something about a heart attack, and the thick hard veins on Aunt Hannah's wrist.

'Ay! ' Meshach went on, employing the old dialect, a sign with him of unusual agitation. 'I brought Dr. Hawley with me, he was at yon show. And when us got here Hannah was lying on th' floor, just there, with her head on this 'ere hearthrug. Susan, th' woman, told us as th' missis said she felt as if she were falling down, and then down her falls. She was staring hard at th' ceiling, with eyes fit to burst, and her face as white as a sheet. Doctor lifts her up and puts her in a chair. Bless us! How her did gasp! And her lips were blue. "Hannah! " I says. Her heard but her couldna' answer. Her limbs were all of a tremble. Then her sighed, and fetched up a long breath or two. "Where am I, Meshach? " her says, "what's amiss? " Doctor told her for stick her tongue out, and her could do that, and he put a candle to her eyes. Her's in bed now. Susan's sitting with her. '

'I'll go up and see if I can do anything, ' said Leonora, rising.

'No, ' Meshach stopped her. 'You'll happen excite her. Doctor said her was to go to sleep, and he's to send in a soothing draught. There's no danger—not now—not till next time. Her mun take care, mun Hannah. '

'Then it is the heart? ' Leonora asked.

'Ay! It's the heart. '

Leonora

Twemlow and Leonora sat silent, embarrassed in the little parlour with its antimacassars, its stiff chairs, its high mantelpiece, and the glass partition which seemed to swallow up like a pit the rays from the hissing gas-jet over the table. The image of the diminutive frail creature concealed upstairs obsessed them, and Leonora felt guilty because she had been unwittingly absorbed in the gaiety of the opera while Aunt Hannah was in such danger.

'I doubt I munna' tap that again, ' Meshach remarked with a short dry plaintive laugh, pointing to the pewter platter on the mantelpiece by means of which he was accustomed to summon his sister when he wanted her.

The visitors looked at each other; Leonora's eyes were moist.

'But isn't there anything I can do, uncle? ' she demanded.

'I'll see if her's asleep. Sit thee still, ' said Meshach, and he crept out of the room, and up the creaking stair.

'Poor old fellow! ' Twemlow murmured, glancing at his watch.

'What time is it? ' she asked, for the sake of saying something. 'It's no use me staying. '

'Five to eleven. If I run off at once I can catch the last train. Good-night. Tell Mr. Myatt, will you? '

She took his hand with a feeling of intimacy.

It seemed to her that they had shared many emotions that night.

'I'll let you out, ' she suggested, and in the obscurity of the narrow lobby they came into contact and shook hands again; she could not at first find the upper latch of the door.

'I shall be seeing you all soon, ' he said in a low voice, on the step. She nodded and closed the door softly.

She thought how simple, agreeable, reliable, honest, good-natured, and sympathetic he was.

'Her's sleeping like a babby, ' Meshach stated, returning to the parlour. He lighted his pipe, and through the smoke looked at Leonora in her dark magnificent dress.

Then John arrived, pompous and elaborately calm; but he had driven Prince to Hillport and back in twenty-five minutes. John listened to the recital of events.

'You're sure there's no danger now? ' He could disguise neither his present relief nor his fear for the future.

'Thou'rt all right yet, nephew, ' said Meshach with an ironic inflection, as he gazed into the dying fire. 'Her may live another ten year. And I might flit to-morrow. Thou'rt too anxious, my lad. Keep it down. '

John, deeply offended, made no reply.

'Why shouldn't I be anxious? ' he exclaimed angrily as they drove home. 'Whose fault is it if I am? Does he expect me not to be? '

CHAPTER VII

THE DEPARTURE

As I approach the crisis in Leonora's life, I hesitate, fearing lest by an unfit phrase I should deprive her of your sympathies, and fearing also that this fear may incline me to set down less than the truth about her.

She was possessed by a mysterious sensation of content. She wished to lie supine—except in her domestic affairs—and to dream that all was well or would be well. It was as though she had determined that nothing could extinguish or even disturb the mild flame of happiness which burned placidly within her. And yet the anxieties of her existence were certainly increasing again. On the morning after the opera, John had departed on one of his sudden flying visits to London; these journeys, formerly frequent, had been in abeyance for a time, and their resumption seemed to point to some renewal of his difficulties. He had called at Church Street on his way to Knype, and Carpenter had brought back word that Miss Myatt was wonderfully better; but when Leonora herself called at Church Street later in the morning and at last saw Aunt Hannah, she was impressed by the change in the old creature, whose nervous system had the appearance of being utterly disorganised. Then there was the difficult case of Ethel and Fred Ryley, in which Leonora had done nothing whatever; and there was the case of Rose, whose alienation from the rest of the household became daily more marked. Finally there was the new and portentous case of Millicent, probably the most disconcerting of the three. Nevertheless, amid all these solicitudes, Leonora remained equable, optimistic, and quietly joyous. Her state of mind, so miraculously altered in a few hours, gave her no surprise. It seemed natural; everything seemed natural; she ceased for a period to waste emotion in the futile desire for her lost youth.

On the second day after the opera she was sitting at her Sheraton desk in the small nondescript room which opened off the dining-room. In front of her lay a large tablet with innumerable names of things printed on it in three columns; opposite each name a little hole had been drilled, and in many of the holes little sticks of wood stood upright. Leonora uprooted a stick, exiling it to a long horizontal row of holes at the top of the tablet, and then wrote in a pocket-book; she uprooted another stick and wrote again, so continuing till only a few sticks were left in the columns; these she spared. Then she rang the bell for the parlourmaid and relinquished to her the tablet; the peculiar rite was over.

'Is dinner ready? ' she asked, looking at the small clock which she usually carried about with her from room to room.

'Yes 'm. '

'Then ring the gong. And tell Carpenter I shall want the trap at a quarter past two, for two. I'm going to shop in Hanbridge and then to meet Mr. Stanway at Knype. We shall be in before four. Have some tea ready. And don't forget the eclairs to-day, Bessie. ' She smiled.

'No 'm. Did you think on to write about them new dog-biscuits, ma'am? '

'I'll write now, ' said Leonora, and she turned to the desk.

The gong sounded; the dinner was brought in. Through the doorway between the two rooms—there was no door, only a portière— Leonora heard Ethel's rather heavy footsteps. 'I don't think mother will want you to wait to-day, Bessie, ' Ethel's voice said. Then followed, after the maid's exit, the noise of a dish-cover being lifted and dropped, and Ethel's exclamation: 'Um! ' And then the voices of Rose and Millicent approached, in altercation.

'Come along, mother, ' Ethel called out.

'Coming, ' answered Leonora, putting the note in an envelope.

'The idea! ' said Rose's voice scornfully.

'Yes, ' retorted Milly's voice. 'The idea. '

Leonora listened as she wrote the address.

'You always were a conceited thing, Milly, and since this wonderful opera you're positively ridiculous. I almost wish I'd gone to it now, just to see what you *were* like. '

'Ah well! You just didn't, and so you don't know. '

'No indeed! I'd got something better to do than watch a pack of amateurs— —' There was a pause for silent contempt.

'Well? Keep it up, keep it up. '

'Anyhow I'm perfectly certain father won't let you go. '

'I shall go. '

'And besides, *I* want to go to London, and you may be absolutely certain, my child, that he won't let two of us go. '

'I shall speak to him first. '

'Oh no, you won't. '

'Shan't I? You'll see. '

'No, you won't. Because it just happens that I spoke to him the night before last. And he's making inquiries and he'll tell me to-night. So what do you think of that? '

Leonora drew aside the portière.

'My dear girls! ' she protested benevolently, standing there.

The feud, always apt thus to leap into a perfectly Corsican fury of bitterness, sank back at once to its ordinary level of passive mutual repudiation. Rose and Millicent were not bereft of the finer feelings which distinguish humanity from the beasts of the jungle; sometimes they could be almost affectionate. There were, however, moments when to all appearance they hated each other with a tigerish and crouching hatred such as may be found only between two opposing feminine temperaments linked together by the family tie.

'What's this about your going to London, Rosie? ' Leonora asked in a voice soothing but surprised, when the meal had begun.

'You know, mamma. I mentioned it to you the other day. ' The girl's tone implied that what she had said to Leonora perhaps went in at one ear and out at the other.

Leonora remembered. Rose had in fact casually told her that a school friend in Oldcastle who was studying for the same examination as herself had gone to London for six weeks' final coaching under what Rose called a 'lady-crammer. '

'But you didn't tell me that you wanted to go as well, ' Leonora said.

'Yes, mother, I did, ' Rose affirmed with calm. 'You forget. I'm sure I shan't pass if I don't go. So I asked father while you were all at this opera affair. '

'And what did he say? ' Ethel demanded.

'He said he would make inquiries this morning and see. '

Ethel gave a laugh of good-natured derision. 'Yes, ' she exclaimed, 'and you'll see, too! '

In response to this oracular utterance, Rose merely bent lower over her plate.

Millicent, conscious of a brilliant vocation and of an impassioned resolve, refrained from the discussion, and the sense of her ineffable superiority bore hard on that lithe, mercurial youthfulness. The 'Signal, ' in praising Millicent's performance at the opera, had predicted for her a career, and had thoughtfully quoted instances of well-born amateurs who had become professionals and made great names on the stage. Millicent knew that all Bursley was talking about her. And yet the family life was unaltered; no one at home seemed to be much impressed, not even Ethel, though Ethel's sympathy could be depended upon; Milly was still Milly, the youngest, the least important, the chit of a thing. At times it appeared to her as though the triumph of that ecstatic and glorious night was after all nothing but an illusion, and that only the interminable dailiness of family life was real. Then the ruthless and calculating minx in her shut tight those pretty lips and coldly determined that nothing should stand against ambition.

'I do hope you will pass, ' said Leonora cordially to Rose. 'You certainly deserve to. '

'I know I shan't, unless I get some outside help. My brain isn't that sort of brain. It's another sort. Only one has to knuckle down to these wretched exams first. '

Leonora did not understand her daughter. She knew, however, that there was not the slightest chance of Rose being allowed to go to London alone for any lengthened period, and she wondered that Rose could be so blind as not to perceive this. As for Millicent's vague notions, which the child had furtively broached during her father's absence, the more Leonora thought upon them, the more fantastically impossible they seemed. She changed the subject.

The repast, which had commenced with due ceremony, degenerated into a feminine mess, hasty, informal, counterfeit. That elaborate and irksome pretence that a man is present, with which women when they are alone always begin to eat, was gradually dropped, and the meal ended abruptly, inconclusively, like a bad play.

'Let's go for a walk, ' said Ethel.

'Yes, ' said Milly, 'let's. '

* * * * *

'Mamma! ' Milly called from the drawing-room window.

Leonora was walking about the misty garden, where little now remained that was green, save the yews, the cypresses, and the rhododendrons; Bran, his white-and-fawn coat glittering with minute drops of water, plodded heavily and content by her side along the narrow damp paths. She was dressed for driving, and awaited Carpenter with the trap.

In reply to Leonora's gesture of attention, Milly, instead of speaking from the window, ran quickly to her across the sodden lawn. And Milly's running was so girlish, simple, and unaffected, that Leonora seemed by means of it to have found her daughter again, the daughter who had disappeared in the adroit and impudent creature of the footlights. She was glad of the reassurance.

'Here's Mr. Twemlow, mamma, ' said Milly, with a rather embarrassed air; and they looked at each other, while Bran frowned in glancing upwards.

At the same moment, Arthur Twemlow and Ethel entered the garden together. The social atmosphere was rendered bracing by this invasion of the masculine; every personality awoke and became vigilantly itself.

'We met Mr. Twemlow on the marsh, mother, walking from Oldcastle to Bursley, ' said Ethel, after the ritual of greeting, 'and so we brought him in. '

As Leonora was on the point of leaving the house, the situation was somewhat awkward, and a slight hesitation on her part showed this.

'You're going out? ' he said.

'Oh, mamma, ' Milly cried quickly, 'do let me go and meet father instead of you. I want to. '

'What, alone? ' Leonora exclaimed in a kind of dream.

'I'll go too, ' said Ethel.

'And suppose you have the horse down? '

'Well then, we'll take Carpenter, ' Milly suggested. 'I'll run and tell him to put his overcoat on and put the back-seat in. ' And she scampered off.

Twemlow was fondling the dog with an air of detachment.

In the fraction of an instant, a thousand wild and disturbing thoughts swept through Leonora's brain. Was it possible that Arthur Twemlow had suggested this change of plan to the girls? Or had the girls already noticed with the keen eyes of youth that she and Arthur Twemlow enjoyed each other's society, and naïvely wished to give her pleasure? Would Arthur Twemlow, but for the accidental encounter on the Marsh, have passed by her home without calling? If she remained, what conclusion could not be drawn? If she persisted in going, might not he want to come with her? She was ashamed of the preposterous inward turmoil.

'And my shopping? ' she smiled, blushing.

'Give me the list, mater, ' said Ethel, and took the morocco book out of her hand.

Never before had Leonora felt so helpless in the sudden clutch of fate. She knew she was a willing prey. She wished to remain, and politeness to Arthur Twemlow demanded that this wish should not be disguised. Yet what would she not have given even to have felt herself able to disguise it?

'How incredibly stupid I am! ' she thought.

No sooner had the two girls departed than Twemlow began to laugh.

'I must tell you, ' he said, with candid amusement, 'that this is a plant. Those two daughters of yours calculated to leave you and me here alone together. '

'Yes? ' she murmured, still constrained.

'Miss Milly wants me to talk you round about her going in for the stage. When I met them on the Marsh, of course I began to pay her compliments, and I just happened to say I thought she was a born *comédienne*, and before I knew it T was blindfolded, handcuffed, and carried off, so to speak. '

This was the simple, innocent explanation! 'Oh, how incredibly stupid, stupid, stupid, I was! ' she thought again, and a feeling of exquisite relief surged into her being. Mingled with that relief was the deep joy of realising that Ethel and Milly fully shared her instinctive predilection for Arthur Twemlow. Here indeed was the supreme security.

'I must say my daughters get more and more surprising every day, ' she remarked, impelled to offer some sort of conventional apology for her children's unconventional behaviour.

'They are charming girls, ' he said briefly.

On the surface of her profound relief and joy there played like a flying fish the thought: 'Was he meaning to call in any case? Was he on his way here? '

They talked about Aunt Hannah, whom Twemlow had seen that morning and who was improving rapidly. But he agreed with Leonora that the old lady's vitality had been irretrievably shattered. Then there was a pause, followed by some remarks on the weather, and then another pause. Bran, after watching them attentively for a few moments as they stood side by side near the French window, rose up from off his haunches, and walked gloomily away.

'Bran, Bran! ' Twemlow cried.

'It's no use, ' she laughed. 'He's vexed. He thinks he's being neglected. He'll go to his kennel and nothing will bring him out of it, except food. Come into the house. It's going to rain again. '

* * * * *

'Well, ' the visitor exclaimed familiarly.

They were seated by the fire in the drawing-room. Leonora was removing her gloves.

'Well? ' she repeated. 'And so you still think Milly ought to be allowed to go on the stage? '

'I think she *will* go on the stage, ' he said.

'You can't imagine how it upsets me even to think of it. ' Leonora seemed to appeal for his sympathy.

'Oh, yes, I can, ' he replied. 'Didn't I tell you the other night that I knew exactly how you felt? But you've got to get over that, I guess. You've got to get on to yourself. Mr. Myatt told me what he said to you——'

'So Uncle Meshach has been talking about it too? ' she interrupted.

'Why, yes, certainly. Of course he's quite right. Milly's bound to go her own way. Why not make up your mind to it, and help her, and straighten things out for her? '

'But——'

'Look here, Mrs. Stanway, ' he leaned forward; 'will you tell me just why it upsets you to think of your daughter going on the stage? '

'I don't know. I can't explain. But it does. '

She smiled at him, smoothing out her gloves one after the other on her lap.

'It's nothing but superstition, you know, ' he said gently, returning her smile.

'Yes, ' she admitted. 'I suppose it is. '

He was silent for a moment, as if undecided what to say next. She glanced at him surreptitiously, and took in all the details of his attire—the high white collar, the dark tweed suit obviously of American origin, the thin silver chain that emerged from beneath his waistcoat and disappeared on a curve into the hip pocket of his trousers, the boots with their long pointed toes. His heavy moustache, and the smooth bluish chin, struck her as ideally masculine.

'No parents, ' he burst out, 'no parents can see things from their children's point of view. '

'Oh! ' she protested. 'There are times when I feel so like my daughters that I *am* them. '

He nodded. 'Yes, ' he said, abandoning his position at once, 'I can believe that. You're an exception. If I hadn't sort of known all the time that you were, I wouldn't be here now talking like this. '

'It's so accidental, the whole business, ' she remarked, branching off to another aspect of the case in order to mask the confusion caused by the sincere flattery in his voice. 'It was only by chance that Milly had that particular part at all. Suppose she hadn't had it. What then?'

'Everything's accidental, ' he replied. 'Everything that ever happened is accidental, in a way—in another it isn't. If you look at your own life, for instance, you'll find it's been simply a series of coincidences. I'm sure mine has been. Sheer chance from beginning to end. '

'Yes, ' she said thoughtfully, and put her chin in the palm of her left hand.

'And as for the stage, why, nearly every one goes on the stage by chance. It just occurs, that's all. And moreover I guarantee that the parents of fifty per cent. of all the actresses now on the boards began by thinking what a terrible blow it was to them that *their* daughters should want to do *that*. Can't you see what I mean? ' He emphasised his words more and more. 'I'm certain you can. '

She signified assent. It seemed to her, as he continued to talk, that for the first time she was listening to natural convincing common sense in that home of hers, where existence was governed by precedent and by conventional ideas and by the profound parental instinct which meets all requests with a refusal. It seemed to her that her children, though to outward semblance they had much freedom, had never listened to anything but 'No, ' 'No, dear, ' 'Of course you can't, ' 'I think you had better not, ' and 'Once for all, I forbid it. ' She wondered why this should have been so, and why its strangeness had not impressed her before. She had a distant fleeting vision of a household in which parents and children behaved like free and sensible human beings, instead of like the virtuous and the martyrised puppets of a terrible system called 'acting for the best. ' And she thought again what an extraordinary man Arthur Twemlow was, strong-minded, clear-headed, sympathetic, and delightful. She enjoyed intensely the sensation of their intimacy.

'Jack will never agree, ' she said, when she could say nothing else.

'Ah! "Jack! "' He slightly imitated her tone. 'Well, that remains to be seen. '

'Why do you take all this trouble for Milly? ' she asked him. 'It's very good of you. '

'Because I'm a fool, a meddling ass, ' he replied lightly, standing up and stroking his clothes.

'You aren't, ' her eyes said, 'you are a dear. '

'No, ' he went on, in a serious tone, 'Milly just wanted me to speak to you, and after all I didn't see why I shouldn't. It's no earthly business of mine, but—oh, well! Good-bye, I must be getting along. '

'Have you got an appointment to keep? ' she questioned him.

'No—not an appointment. '

'Well then, you will stay a little longer. The trap will be back quite soon. ' Her voice seemed playfully to indicate that, as she had submitted to his domination, so he must submit now to hers. 'And if you will excuse me one moment, I will go and take off this thick jacket. '

Up in the bedroom, as she removed her coat in front of the pier-glass, she smiled at her image timorously, yet in full content. Milly's prospects did not appear to her to have been practically improved, nor could she piece out of Arthur Twemlow's conversation a definite argument; nevertheless she felt that he had made her see something more clearly than heretofore, that he had induced in her, not by logic but by persuasiveness, a mood towards her children which was brighter, more sanguine, and even more loving, than any in her previous experience. She was glad that she had left him alone for a minute, because such familiar treatment of him somehow established definitely his status as a friend of the house.

'Listen, Twemlow, ' said Stanway loudly, 'I meant to run down to the office for an hour this afternoon, but if you'll stay, I'll stay. That's a bargain, eh? '

* * * * *

John had returned from London blusterously cheerful, and Twemlow stood in the centre of his vehement noisy hospitality as in the centre of a typhoon. He consented to stay, because the two girls, with hair blown and still in their wet macintoshes, took him by the arm and said he must. He was not the first guest in that house whom the apparent heartiness of the host had failed to convince. Always there was something sinister, insincere, and bullying in the invitations which John gave, and in his reception of visitors. Hence it was, perhaps, that visitors did not abound under his roof, despite the richness of the table and the ordered elegance of every appointment. Women paid calls; the girls, unlike Leonora, had their intimates, including Harry; but men seldom came; and it was not often that the principal meals of the day were shared by an outsider of either sex.

Arthur's presence on a second occasion was therefore the more stimulating. It affected the whole house, even to the kitchen, which, indeed, usually vibrates in sympathy with the drawing-room. In Bessie's vivacious demeanour as she served the high-tea at six o'clock might be observed the symptoms of the agreeable excitation which all felt. Even Rose unbent, and Leonora thought how attractive the girl could be when she chose. But towards the end of the meal, it became evident that Rose was preoccupied. Leonora, Ethel, and Millicent passed into the drawing-room. John pulled out his immense cigar-case, and the two men began to smoke.

'Come along, ' said Stanway, speaking thickly with the cigar in his mouth.

'Papa, ' said Rose ominously, just as he was following Twemlow out of the door. She spoke with quiet, cold distinctness.

'What is it? '

'Did you inquire about that? '

He paused. 'Oh yes, Rose, ' he answered rapidly. ' I inquired. She seemed a very clever woman, I must say. But I've been thinking it over, and I've come to the conclusion that it won't do for you to go. I don't like the idea of it—you in London for six weeks or more alone. You must do what you can here. And if you fail this time you must try again. '

'But I can stay in the same lodgings as Sarah Fuge. The house is kept by her cousin or some relation. '

'And then there's the expense, ' he proceeded.

'Father, I told you the other night I didn't want to put you to any expense. I've got thirty-seven pounds of my own, and I will pay; I prefer to pay. '

'Oh, no, no! ' he exclaimed.

'Well, why can't I go? ' she demanded bluntly.

'I'll think it over again—but I don't like it, Rose, I don't like it. '

'But there isn't a day to waste, father! ' she complained.

Bessie entered to clear the table.

'Hum! Well! I'll think it over again. ' He breathed out smoke, and departed. Rose set her lips hard. She was seen no more that evening.

In the drawing-room, Stanway found Twemlow and Millicent talking in low voices on the hearthrug. Ethel lounged on the sofa. Leonora was not present, but she came in immediately.

'Let's have a game at solo, ' John suggested. And because five was a convenient number they all played. Twemlow and Milly were the best performers; Milly's gift for card-playing was notorious in the family.

'Do you ever play poker? ' Twemlow asked, when the other three had been beggared of counters.

'No, ' said John, cautiously. 'Not here. '

'It's lots of fun, ' Twemlow went on, looking at the girls.

'Oh, Mr. Twemlow, ' Milly cried. 'It's awfully gambly, isn't it? Do teach us. '

In a quarter of an hour Milly was bluffing her father with success. She said that in future she should never want to play at any other game. As for Leonora, though she lost and gained counters with happy equanimity, she did not like the game; it frightened her. When Milly had shown a straight flush and scooped the kitty she sent the child out of the room with a message to the kitchen concerning coffee and sandwiches.

'Won't Milly sing? ' Twemlow asked.

'Certainly, if you wish, ' Leonora responded.

'Ay! Let's have something, ' said Stanway, lazily.

And when Millicent returned, she was told that she must sing before eating. She sang 'Love is a Plaintive Song, ' to Ethel's inert accompaniment, and she gave it exactly as though she had been on the stage, with all the dramatic action, all the freedom, all the allurements, which she had lavished on the audience in the Town Hall.

'Very good, ' said her father. 'I like that. It's very pretty. I didn't hear it the other night. ' Twemlow merely thanked the artist. Leonora was silently uncomfortable.

After coffee both the girls disappeared. Twemlow looked round, and then spoke to Stanway.

'I've been very much impressed by your daughter's talent, ' he said. His tone was extremely serious. It implied that, now the children were gone, the adults could talk with freedom.

Stanway was a little startled, and more than a little flattered.

'Really? ' he questioned.

'Really, ' said Twemlow, emphasising still further his seriousness. 'Has she ever been taught? '

'Only by a local teacher up here at Hillport, ' Leonora told him.

'She ought to have lessons from a first-class master. '

'Why? ' asked Stanway abruptly.

'Well, ' Twemlow said, 'you never know——'

'You honestly think her voice is worth cultivating? ' John demanded, impelled to participate in Twemlow's gravity.

'I do. And not only her voice——'

'Ah, ' Stanway mused, 'there's no first-class masters in this district. '

'Why, I met a man from Manchester at the Five Towns Hotel last night, ' said Twemlow, 'who comes down to Knype once a week to give lessons. He used to sing in opera. They say he's the best man about, and that he's taught a lot of good people. I forget his name. '

'I expect you mean Cecil Corfe, ' Leonora said cheerfully. She had been amazed at the compliance of John's attitude.

'Yes, that's it. '

At the same moment there was a faint noise at the French window. John went to investigate. As soon as his back was turned, Twemlow glanced at Leonora with eyes full of a private amusement which he invited her to share. 'Can't I just handle him? ' he seemed to say. She smiled, but cautiously, less she should disclose too fully her intense appreciation of his personality.

'Why, it's the dog! ' Stanway proclaimed, 'and wet through! What's he doing loose? It's raining like the devil. '

'I'm afraid I didn't fasten him up this afternoon. I forgot, ' said Leonora. 'Oh! my new rug! '

Bran plunged into the room with a glad deafening bark, his tail thwacking the furniture like the flat of a sword.

'Get out, you great brute! ' Stanway ordered, and then, on the step, he shouted into the darkness for Carpenter.

Twemlow rose to look on.

'I can't let you walk to the station to-night, Twemlow, ' said Stanway, still outside the room. 'Carpenter shall drive you. Yes, he shall, so don't argue. And while he's about it he may as well take you straight to Knype. You can go in the buggy—there's a hood to it. '

When the time came for departure, John insisted on lending to Twemlow a large driving overcoat. They stood in the hall together, while Twemlow fumbled with the complicated apparatus of buttons. Stanway whistled.

'By the way, ' he said, 'when are you coming in to look through those old accounts? '

'Oh, I don't know, ' Twemlow answered, somewhat taken by surprise.

'I tell you what I'll do—I'll send you copies of them, eh? '

'I think you needn't trouble, ' said Twemlow, carelessly. 'I guess I shall write to my sister, and tell her I can't see any use in trying to worry out the old man's finances at this time of day. '

'However, ' Stanway repeated, 'I'll send you the copies all the same. And when you write to your sister, will you give her my kindest regards? '

The whole family, except Rose, came into the porch to bid him good-night. In the darkness and the heavy rain could dimly be seen the rounded form of the buggy; the cob's flanks shone in the glittering ray of the lamps; Carpenter was hidden under the hood; his mysterious hand raised the apron, and Twemlow stepped quickly in.

'Good-night, ' said Ethel.

'Good-night, Mr. Twemlow, ' said Milly. 'Be good. '

'You'll see us again before you leave, Twemlow? ' said John's imperious voice.

'You aren't going back to America just yet, are you? ' Leonora asked, from the back.

No reply came from within the hood.

'Mother says you aren't going back to America just yet, are you, Mr. Twemlow? ' Milly screamed in her treble.

Arthur Twemlow showed his face. 'No, not yet, I think, ' he called. 'See you again, certainly.... And thanks once more. '

'Tchick! ' said Carpenter.

* * * * *

The next evening, after tea, John, Leonora, and Rose were in the drawing-room. Milly had run down to see her friend Cissie Burgess, having with fine cruelty chosen that particular night because she happened to know that Harry would be out. Ethel was invisible. Rose had returned with bitter persistence to the siege of her father's obstinacy.

'I should have six weeks clear, ' she was saying.

John consulted his pocket-calendar.

'No, ' he corrected her, 'you would only have a month. It isn't worth while. '

'I should have six weeks, ' she repeated. 'The exam isn't till January the seventh. '

'But Christmas, what about Christmas? You must be here for Christmas. '

'Why? ' demanded Rose.

'Oh, Rosie! ' Leonora protested. ' You can't be away for Christmas! '

'Why not? ' the girl demanded again, coldly.

Both parents paused.

'Because you can't, ' said John angrily. 'The idea's absurd. '

'I don't see it, ' Rose persevered.

'Well, I do, ' John delivered himself. 'And let that suffice. '

Rose's face indicated the near approach of tears.

It was at this juncture that Bessie opened the door and announced Mr. Twemlow.

'I just called to bring back that magnificent great-coat, ' he said. 'It's hanging up on its proper hook in the hall. '

Then he turned specially to Leonora, who sat isolated near the fire. She was not surprised to see him, because she had felt sure that he would at once return the overcoat in person; she had counted on him doing so. As he came towards her she languorously lifted her arm, without rising, and the two bangles which she wore slipped tinkling down the wide sleeve. They shook hands in silence, smiling.

'I hope you didn't take cold last night? ' she said at length.

'Not I, ' he replied, sitting down by her side.

He was quick to detect the disturbance in the social atmosphere, and though he tried to appear unconscious of it, he did not succeed in the impossible. Moreover, Rose had evidently decided that despite his presence she would finish what she had begun.

'Very well, father, ' she said. 'If you'll let me go at once I'll come down for two days at Christmas. '

'Yes, ' John grumbled, 'that's all very well. But who's to take you? You can't go alone. And you know perfectly well that I only came back yesterday. ' He recited this fact precisely as though it constituted a grievance against Rose.

'As if I couldn't go alone! ' Rose exclaimed.

'If it's London you're talking about, ' Twemlow said, 'I will be going up to-morrow by the midday flyer, and could look after any lady that happened to be on that train and would accept my services. ' He glanced pleasantly at Rose.

'Oh, Mr. Twemlow! ' the girl murmured. It was a ludicrously inadequate expression of her profound passionate gratitude to this knight; but she could say no more.

'But can you be ready, my dear? ' Leonora inquired.

'I am ready, ' said Rose.

'It's understood then, ' Twemlow said later. 'We shall meet at the dep't. I can't stop another moment now. I've got a cab waiting outside. '

Leonora wished to ask him whether, notwithstanding his partial assurance of the previous evening, his journey would really end at Euston, or whether he was not taking London *en route* for New York. But she could not bring herself to put the question. She hoped that John might put it; John, however, was taciturn.

'We shall see Rose off to-morrow, of course, ' was her last utterance to Twemlow.

* * * * *

Leonora and her three daughters stood in the crowd on the platform of Knype railway station, waiting for Arthur Twemlow and for the London express. John had brought them to the station in the waggonette, had kissed Rose and purchased her ticket, and had then driven off to a creditors' meeting at Hanbridge. All the women felt rather mournful amid that bustle and confusion. Leonora had said to herself again and again that it was absurd to regard this absence of Rose for a few weeks as a break in the family existence. Yet the phrase, 'the first break, the first break, ' ran continually in her mind. The gentle sadness of her mood noticeably affected the girls. It was as though they had all suddenly discovered a mutual unsuspected tenderness. Milly put her hand on Rose's shoulder, and Rose did not resent the artless gesture.

'I hope Mr. Twemlow isn't going to miss it, ' said Ethel, voicing the secret apprehension of all.

'I shan't miss it, anyhow, ' Rose remarked defiantly.

Scarcely a minute before the train was due, Milly descried Twemlow coming out of the booking office. They pressed through the crowd towards him.

'Ah! ' he exclaimed genially. 'Here you are! Baggage labelled? '

'We thought you weren't coming, Mr. Twemlow, ' Milly said.

'You did? I was kept quite a few minutes at the hotel. You see I only had to walk across the road. '

'We didn't really think any such thing, ' said Leonora.

The conversation fell to pieces.

Then the express, with its two engines, its gilded luncheon-cars, and its post-office van, thundered in, shaking the platform, and seeming to occupy the entire station. It had the air of pausing nonchalantly, disdainfully, in its mighty rush from one distant land of romance to another, in order to suffer for a brief moment the assault of a puny and needlessly excited multitude.

'First stop Willesden, ' yelled the porters.

'Say, conductor, ' said Twemlow sharply, catching the luncheon-car attendant by the sleeve, 'you've got two seats reserved for me— Twemlow? '

'Twemlow? Yes, sir. '

'Come along, ' he said, 'come along. '

The girls kissed at the steps of the car: 'Good-bye. '

'Well, good-bye all! ' said Twemlow. 'I hope to see you again some time. Say next fall. '

'You surely aren't— —' Leonora began.

'Yes, ' he resumed quickly, 'I sail Saturday. Must get back. '

'Oh, Mr. Twemlow! ' Ethel and Milly complained together.

Rose was standing on the steps. Leonora leaned and kissed the pale girl madly, pressing her lips into Rose's cheek. Then she shook hands with Arthur Twemlow.

'Good-bye! ' she murmured.

'I guess I shall write to you, ' he said jauntily, addressing all three of them; and Ethel and Milly enthusiastically replied: 'Oh, do! '

The travellers penetrated into the car, and reappeared at a window, one on either side of a table covered with a white cloth and laid for two persons.

'Oh, don't I wish I was going! ' Milly exclaimed, perceiving them.

Rose was now flushed with triumph. She looked at Twemlow, her lips moved, she smiled. She was a woman in the world. Then they nodded and waved hands.

The guard unfurled his green flag, the engine gave a curt, scornful whistle, and lo! the luncheon-car was gliding away from Leonora, Ethel, and Milly! Lo! the station was empty!

'I wonder what he will talk to her about, ' thought Leonora.

They had to cross the station by the under-ground passage and wait twenty minutes for a squalid, shambling local train which took them to Shawport, at the foot of the rise to Hillport.

CHAPTER VIII

THE DANCE

About three months after its rendering of *Patience*, the Bursley Amateur Operatic Society arranged to give a commemorative dance in the very scene of that histrionic triumph. The fête was to surpass in splendour all previous entertainments of the kind recorded in the annals of the town. It was talked about for weeks in advance; several dressmakers nearly died of it; and as the day approached the difficulty of getting one's self invited became extreme.

'You know, Mrs. Stanway, ' said Harry Burgess when he met Leonora one afternoon in the street, 'we are relying on you to be the best-dressed woman in the place. '

She smiled with a calmness which had in it a touch of gentle cynicism. 'You shouldn't, ' she answered.

'But you're coming, aren't you? ' he inquired with eager concern. Of late, owing to the capricious frigidity of Millicent's attitude towards him, he had been much less a frequenter of Leonora's house, and he was no longer privy to all its doings.

'Oh, yes, ' she said, 'I suppose I shall come. '

'That's all right, ' he exclaimed. 'If you come you conquer. ' They passed on their ways.

Leonora's existence had slipped back into its old groove since the departure of Twemlow, and the groove had deepened. She lived by the force of habit, hoping nothing from the future, but fearing more than a little. She seemed to be encompassed by vague and sinister portents. After another brief interlude of apparent security, John's situation was again disquieting. Trade was good in the Five Towns; at least the manufacturers had temporarily forgotten to complain that it was very bad, and the Monday afternoon football-matches were magnificently attended. Moreover, John had attracted favourable attention to himself by his shrewd proposals to the Manufacturers' Association for reform in the method of paying firemen and placers; his ability was everywhere recognised. At the same time, however, the Five Towns looked askance at him. Rumour revived, and said that he could not keep up his juggling performance for ever. He was known to have speculated heavily for a rise in the shares of a great brewery which had falsified the prophecies of its founders when they benevolently sold it to the investing public. Some people wondered how long John could hold those shares in a falling market. Leonora had no definite knowledge of her husband's affairs, since neither John nor any other person breathed a word to her about them. And yet she knew, by certain vibrations in the social atmosphere as mysterious and disconcerting as those discovered by Röntgen in the physical, that disaster, after having been repelled, was returning from afar. Money flowed through the house as usual; nevertheless often, as she drove about Bursley, consciously exciting the envy and admiration which a handsome woman behind a fast cob is bound to excite, her shamed fancy pictured the day when Prince should belong to another and she should walk perforce on the pavement in attire genteelly preserved from past affluence. Only women know the keenest pang of these secret misgivings, at once desperate and helpless.

Nor did she find solace in her girls. One Saturday afternoon Ethel came back from the duty-visit to Aunt Hannah and said as it were confidentially to Leonora: 'Fred called in while I was there, mother, and stayed for tea. ' What could Leonora answer? Who could deny Fred the right to visit his great-aunt and his great-uncle, both rapidly ageing? And of what use to tell John? She desired Ethel's happiness, but from that moment she felt like an accomplice in the furtive wooing, and it seemed to her that she had forfeited both the confidence of her husband and the respect of her daughter. Months ago she had meant by force of some initiative to regularise this idyll which by its stealthiness wounded the self-respect of all concerned. Vain aspiration! And now the fact that Fred Ryley had begun to call at Church Street appeared to indicate between him and Uncle Meshach a closer understanding which could only be detrimental to the interests of John.

As for Rose, that child of misfortune did well during the first four days of the examination, but on the fifth day one of her chronic sick-headaches had in two hours nullified all the intense and ceaseless effort of two years. It was precisely in chemistry that she had failed. She arrived from London in tears, and the tears were renewed when the formal announcement of defeat came three weeks later by telegraph and John added gaiety to the occasion by remarking: 'What did I tell you? ' The girl's proud and tenacious spirit, weakened by the long strain, was daunted at last. She lounged in the house and garden, listless, supine, torpid, instinctively waiting for Nature's recovery.

Millicent alone in the house was unreservedly cheerful and light-hearted. She had the advantage of Mr. Corfe's instruction for two hours every Wednesday, and expressed herself as well satisfied with his methods. Her own intimate friends knew that she quite intended to go on the stage, but they were enjoined to say nothing. Consequently John Stanway was one of the few people in Bursley unaware of the definiteness of Milly's private plans; Leonora was another. Leonora sometimes felt that Milly's assertive and indestructible vivacity must be due to some specific cause, but Mr. Cecil Corfe's reputation for seriousness and discretion precluded the idea that he was encouraging the girl to dream dreams without the consent of her parents.

Leonora might have questioned Milly, but she perceived the futility of doing so. It became more and more clear to her that she did not possess the confidence of her daughters. They loved her and they admired her; and she for her part made a point of trusting them; but their confidence was withheld. Under the influence of Arthur Twemlow she had tried to assuage the customary asperities of home life, so far as possible, by a demeanour of generous quick acquiescence, and she had not entirely failed. Yet the girls, with all the obtuseness and insensibility of adolescence, never thought of giving her the one reward which she desired. She sought tremulously to win their intimacy, but she sought too late. Rose and Milly simply ignored her diffident advances, and even Ethel was not responsive. Leonora had trained up her children as she herself had been trained. She saw her error only when it could not be retrieved. The dear but transient vision of four women who had no secrets from each other, who understood each other, was finally dissolved.

Amid the secret desolation of a life which however was not without love, amid her vain regrets for an irrecoverable youth and her horror of the approach of age, amid the empty lassitudes which apparently were all that remained of the excitement caused by Arthur Twemlow's presence, Leonora found a mournful and sweet pleasure in imagining that she had a son. This son combined the best qualities of Harry Burgess and Fred Ryley. She made him tall as herself, handsome as herself, and like herself elegant. Shrewd, clever, and passably virtuous, he was nevertheless distinctly capable of follies;

but he told her everything, even the worst, and though sometimes she frowned he smiled away the frown. He adored her; he appreciated all the feminine in her; he yielded to her whims; he kissed her chin and her wrist, held her sunshade, opened doors for her, allowed her to beat him at tennis, and deliciously frightened her by driving her very fast round corners in a very high dog-cart. And if occasionally she said, 'I am not as young as I was, Gerald, ' he always replied: 'Oh rot, mater! '

When Ethel or Milly remarked at breakfast, as they did now and then, that Mr. Twemlow had not fulfilled his promise of writing, Leonora would answer evenly, 'No, I expect he's forgotten us. ' And she would go and live with her son for a little.

* * * * *

She summoned this Gerald—and it was for the last time—as she stood irresolutely waiting for her husband at the door of the ladies' cloak-room in the Town Hall. She was dressed in black mousseline de soie. The corsage, which fitted loosely except at the waist and the shoulders, where it was closely confined, was not too low, but it disclosed the beautiful diminutive rondures above the armpits, and, behind, the fine hollow of her back. The sleeves were long and full with tight wrists, ending in black lace. A band of pale pink silk, covered with white lace, wandered up one sleeve, crossed her breast in strict conformity with the top of the corsage, and wandered down the other sleeve; at the armpits, below the rondures, this band was punctuated with a pink rose. An extremely narrow black velvet ribbon clasped her neck. From the belt, which was pink, the full skirt ran down in a thousand perpendicular pleats. The effect of the loose corsage and of the belt on Leonora's perfect figure was to make her look girlish, ingenuous, immaculate, and with a woman's instinct she heightened the effect by swinging her programme restlessly on its ivory-tinted cord.

They had arrived somewhat late, owing partly to John's indecision and partly to an accident with Rose's costume. On reaching the Town Hall, not only Ethel and Milly, but Rose also, had deserted Leonora eagerly, impatiently, as ducklings scurry into a pond; they passed through the cloak-room in a moment, Rose first; Rose was human that evening. Leonora did not mind; she anticipated the dance with neither joy nor melancholy, hoping nothing from it in her mood of neutral calm. John was talking with David Dain at the entrance to the gentlemen's cloak-room, further down the corridor. Presently, old Mr. Hawley, the doctor at Hillport, joined the other two, and then Dain moved away, leaving John and the doctor in conversation. Dain approached and saluted his client's wife with characteristic sheepishness.

'Large company, I believe, ' he said awkwardly. In evening dress he was always particularly awkward.

She smiled kindly on him, thinking the while what a clumsy and objectionable fat little man he was. She knew he admired her, and would have given much to dance with her; but she did not care for his heavy eyes, and she despised him because he could not screw himself up to demand a place on her programme.

'Yes, very large company, I believe, ' he said again, moving about nervously on his toes.

'Do you know how many invitations? ' she asked.

'No, I don't. '

'Dain! ' John called out, 'come and listen to this. ' And the lawyer escaped from her presence like a schoolboy running out of school.

'What men! ' she thought bitterly, standing neglected with all her charm and all her distinction. 'What chivalry! What courtliness! What style! ' Her son belonged to a different race of beings.

Down the corridor came Harry Burgess deep in converse with a male friend; the two were walking quickly. She did not choose to greet them waiting there alone, and so she deliberately turned and put her head within the curtains of the cloak-room as if to speak to some one inside.

'Twemlow was saying ——'

It seemed to her that Harry in passing had uttered that phrase to his companion. She flushed, and shook from head to foot. Then she reflected that Twemlow was a name common to dozens of people in the Five Towns. She bit her lip, surprised and angered at her own agitation. At the same time she remembered—and why should she remember? —some gossip of John's to the effect that Harry Burgess was under a cloud at the Bank because he had gone to London by a day-trip on the previous Thursday without leave. London... perhaps....

'Am I forty—or fourteen? ' she contemptuously asked herself.

She heard John and Dain laugh loudly, and the jolly voice of the old doctor: 'Come along into the refreshment-room for a minute. ' Determined not to linger another moment for these boors, she moved into the corridor.

At the end of the vista of red carpet and gas-jets rose the grand staircase, and on the lowest stair stood Arthur Twemlow. She had begun to traverse the corridor and she could not stop now, and fifty feet lay between them.

'Oh! ' her heart cried in the intolerable spasm of a swift and mysterious convulsion. 'Why do you thus torture me? ' Every step was an agony.

He moved towards her, and she noticed that he was extremely pale. They met. His hand found hers. Then it was that she perceived, with a passionate gratitude, how heaven had been watching over her. If John had not hesitated about coming, if her daughters had not deserted her in the cloak-room, if the old doctor had not provided himself with a new supply of naughty stories, if indeed everything had not occurred exactly as it had occurred—she would have been forced to undergo in the presence of witnesses the shock which she had just experienced; and she would have died. She felt that in those seconds she had endured emotion to the last limit of her capacity. She traced a providence even in Harry's chance phrase, which had warned her and so broken the force of the stroke.

'Why, cruel one, did you play this trick on me? Can you not see what I suffer! ' It was her sad glittering eyes that reproachfully appealed to him.

'Did I know what would happen? ' his answered. 'Am I not equally a victim? '

She smiled pensively, and her lips murmured: 'Well, wonders will never cease. '

Such were the first words.

'I found I had to come back to London, ' he was soon explaining. 'And I met young Burgess at the Empire on Thursday night, and he told me about this affair and gave me a ticket, and so I thought as I had been at the opera I might as well——' He hesitated.

'Have you seen the girls? ' she inquired.

He had not.

On the flower-bordered staircase her foot slipped; she felt like a convalescent trying to walk after a long illness. Arthur with a silent questioning gesture offered his arm.

'Yes, please, ' she said, gladly. She wished not to say it, but she said it, and the next instant he was supporting her up the steps. Anything might happen now, she thought; the most impossible things might come to pass.

At the top of the staircase they paused. They could hear the music faintly through closed doors. They had the precious illusion of being aloof, apart, separated from the world, sufficient to themselves and gloriously sufficient. Then some one opened the doors from within; the sound of the music, suddenly freed, rushed out and smote them; and they entered the ball-room. She was acutely conscious of her beauty, and of the distinction of his blanched, stern face.

* * * * *

The floor was thronged by entwined couples who, under the rhythmic domination of the music, glided and revolved in the elaborate pattern of a mazurka. With their rapt gaze, and their rigid bodies floating smoothly over a hidden mechanism of flying feet, they seemed to be the victims of some enchantment, of which the music was only a mode, and which led them enthralled through endless curves of infallible beauty and grace. Form, colour, movement, melody, and the voluptuous galvanism of delicate contacts were all combined in this unique ritual of the dance, this strange convention whose significance emerged from one mystery deeper than the fundamental notes of the bass-fiddle, and lost itself in another more light than the sudden flash of a shirt-front or the tremor of a lock of hair. The goddess reigned. And round about the hall, the guardians of decorum, the enemies of Aphrodite, enchanted too, watched with the simplicity of doves the great Aphrodisian festival, blind to the eternal verities of a satin slipper, a drooping eyelash, a parted lip.

The music ceased, the spell was lifted for a time. And while old alliances were being dissolved and new ones formed in the eager promiscuity of this interval, all remarked proudly on the success of the evening; in the gleam of every eye the sway of the goddess was acknowledged. Romance was justified. Life itself was justified. The shop-girl who had put ten thousand stitches into the ruching of her crimson skirt well symbolised the human attitude that night. As leaning heavily on a man's arm she crossed the floor under the blazing chandelier, she secretly exulted in each stitch of her incredible labour. Two hours, and she would be back in the cold, celibate bedroom, littered with the shabby realities of existence; and the spotted glass would mirror her lugubrious yawn! Eight hours, and she would be in the dreadful shop, tying on the black apron! The crimson skirt would never look the same again; such rare blossoms fade too soon! And in exchange for the toil, the fatigue, and the distressing reaction, what had she won? She could not have said what she had won, but she knew that it was worth the ruinous cost—this bright fallacy, this fleeting chimera, this delusive ecstasy, this shadow and counterfeit of bliss which the goddess vouchsafed to her communicants.

* * * * *

So thick and confused was the crowd that Leonora and Arthur, having inserted themselves into a corner near the west door, escaped the notice of any of their friends. They were as solitary there as on the landing outside. But Leonora saw quite near, in another corner, Ethel talking to Fred Ryley; she noticed how awkward Fred looked in his new dress-suit, and she liked him for his awkwardness; it seemed to her that Ethel was very beautiful. Arthur pointed out Rose, who was standing up with the lady member of the School Board. Then Leonora caught sight of Millicent in the distance, handing her programme to the conductor of the opera; she recalled the notorious boast of the conductor that he never knowingly danced with a bad dancer, whatever her fascinations. Always when they met at a ball the conductor would ask Leonora for a couple of waltzes, and would lead her out with an air of saying to the company: 'Now see what fine dancing is! ' Like herself, he danced with the frigidity of a professor. She wondered whether Arthur could dance really well.

The placard by the orchestra said, 'Extra. '

'Shall we? ' Arthur whispered.

He made a way for her through the outer fringe of people to the middle space where the couples were forming. Her last thoughts as she gave him her hand were thoughts half-pitiful and half-scornful of John, David Dain, and the doctor, brutishly content in the refreshment-room.

There stole out, troubling the expectant air, softly, alluringly, invocatively, the first warning notes of that unique classic of the ball-room, that extraordinary composition which more than any other work of art unites all western nations in a common delight, which is adored equally by profound musicians and by the lightest cocottes, and which, unscathed and splendid, still miraculously survives the deadly ordeal of eternal perfunctory reiterance: the masterpiece of Johann Strauss.

'Why, ' Leonora exclaimed, her excitement straining impatiently in the leash, 'The Blue Danube! '

He laughed, quietly gay.

While the chords, with tantalising pauses and deliberation, approached the magic moment of the waltz itself, she was conscious that his hold of her became firmer and more assertive, and she surrendered to an overmastering influence as one surrenders to chloroform, desperately, but luxuriously.

And when at the invitation of the melody the whole company in the centre of the floor broke into movement, and the spell was resumed, she lost all remembrance of that which had passed, and all apprehension of that which was to come. She lived, passionately and yet languorously, in the vivid present. Her eyes were level with his shoulder, and they looked with an entranced gaze along his arm, seeing automatically the faces, the lights, and the colours which swam in a rapid confused procession across their field of vision. She did not reason nor recognise. These fleeting images, appearing and disappearing on the horizon of Arthur's elbow, produced no effect on her. She had no thoughts. Her entire being was absorbed in a transport of obedience to the beat of the music, and to Arthur's directing pressures. She was happy, but her bliss had in it that element of stinging pain, of intolerable anticipation, which is seldom absent from a felicity too intense. 'Surely I shall sink down and die! ' said her heart, seeming to faint at the joyous crises of the music, which rose and fell in tides of varying rapture. Nevertheless she was determined to drink the cup slowly, to taste every drop of that sweet and excruciating happiness. She would not utterly abandon herself. The fear of inanition was only a wayward pretence, after all, and her strong nature cried out for further tests to prove its fortitude and its power of dissimulation. As the band slipped into the final section of the waltz, she wilfully dragged the time, deepening a little the curious superficial languor which concealed her secrets, and at the same time increasing her consciousness of Arthur's control. She dreaded now that what had been intolerable should cease; she wished ardently to avert the end. The glare of lights, the separate sounds of the instruments, the slurring of feet on the smooth floor, the lineaments of familiar faces, all the multitudinous and picturesque detail of gyrating humanity around her—these phenomena forced themselves on her unwilling perception; and she tried to push them back, and to spend every faculty in savouring the ecstasy of that one physical presence which was so close, so enveloping, and so inexplicably dear. But in vain, in vain! The band rioted through the last bars of the waltz, a strange, disconcerting silence and inertia supervened, and Arthur loosed her.

* * * * *

As she sat down on the cane chair which Arthur had found, Leonora's characteristic ease of manner deserted her. She felt conspicuous and embarrassed, and she could neither maintain her usual cold nonchalant glance in examining the room, nor look at Arthur in a natural way. She had the illusion that every one must be staring at her with amazed curiosity. Yet her furtive searching eye could not discover a single person except Arthur who seemed to notice her existence. All were preoccupied that night with immediate neighbours.

'Will you come down into the refreshment-room? ' Arthur asked. She observed with annoyance that he too was confused, nervous, and still very pale.

She shook her head, without meeting his gaze. She wished above all things to behave simply and sincerely, to speak in her ordinary voice, and to use familiar phrases. But she could not. On the contrary she was seized with a strong impulse to say to him entreatingly: 'Leave me, ' as though she were a person on the stage. She thought of other phrases, such as 'Please go away, ' and 'Do you mind leaving me for a while? ' but her tongue, somehow insisting on the melodramatic, would not utter these.

'Leave me! ' She was frightened by her own words, and added hastily, with the most seductive smile that her lips had ever-framed: 'Do you mind? '

'I shall call to-morrow, ' he said anxiously, almost gruffly. 'Shall you be in? '

She nodded, and he left her; she did not watch him depart.

'May I have the honour, gracious lady? '

It was the conductor of the opera who addressed her in his even, apparently sarcastic tones.

'I'm afraid I must rest a bit, ' she said, smiling quite naturally. 'I've hurt my foot a little—Oh, it's nothing, it's nothing. But I must sit still for a bit. '

She could not comprehend why, unintentionally and without design, she should have told this stupid lie, and told it so persuasively. She foresaw how the tedious consequences of the fiction might continue throughout the evening. For a moment she had the idea of announcing a sprained ankle and of returning home at once. But the thought of old Dr. Hawley's presence in the building deterred her. She perceived that her foot must get gradually better, and that she must be resigned.

'Oh, mamma! ' cried Rose, coming up to her. 'Just fancy Mr. Twemlow being back again! But why did you let him leave? '

'Has he gone? '

'Yes. He just saw me on the stairs, and told me he must catch the last car to Knype. '

'Our dance, I think, Miss Rose, ' said a young man with a gardenia, and Rose, flushed and sparkling, was carried off. The ball proceeded.

* * * * *

John Stanway had a singular capacity for not enjoying himself on those social occasions when to enjoy one's self is a duty to the company. But this evening, as the hour advanced, he showed the symptoms of a sharp attack of gaiety such as visited him from time to time. He and Dr. Hawley and Dain formed an ebullient centre of high spirits, and they upheld the ancient traditions; they professed a liking for old-fashioned dances, and for old-fashioned ways of dancing the steps which modern enthusiasm for the waltz had not extinguished. And they found an appreciable number of followers. The organisers of the ball, the upholders of correctness, punctilio, and the mode, fretted and fought against the antagonistic influence. 'Ass! ' said the conductor of the opera bitterly when Harry Burgess told him that Stanway had suggested Sir Roger de Coverley for an extra, 'I wonder what his wife thinks of him! ' Sir Roger de Coverley was not danced, but twenty or thirty late stayers, with Stanway and Dain in charge, crossed hands in a circle and sang 'Auld Lang Syne' at the close. It was one of those incredible things that can only occur between midnight and cock-crow. During this revolting rite, the conductor and his friends sought sanctuary in the refreshment-room. Leonora, Ethel, and Milly were also there, but Rose and the lady-member of the School Board had remained upstairs to sing 'Auld Lang Syne. '

'Now, girls, ' said Stanway with loud good humour, invading the select apartment with his followers, 'time to go. Carpenter's been waiting half-an-hour. Your foot all right again, Nora? '

'Quite, ' she replied. 'Are you really ready? '

She had so interminably waited that she could not believe the evening to be at length actually finished.

They all exchanged adieux, Stanway and his cronies effusively, the opposing and outraged faction with a certain fine acrimony. 'Good-night, Fred, ' said John, throwing a backward patronising glance at Ryley, who had strolled uneasily into the room. The young man paused before replying. 'Good-night, ' he said stiffly, and his demeanour indicated: 'Do not patronise me too much. ' Fred could not dance, but he had audaciously sat out four dances with Ethel, at this his first ball, and the serious young man had the strange agreeable sensation of feeling a dog. He dared not, however, accompany Ethel to the carriage, as Harry Burgess accompanied Millicent. Harry had been partially restored to favour again during the latter half of the entertainment, just in time to prevent him from getting tipsy. The fact was that Millicent had vaguely expected, in view of her position as prima donna, to be 'the belle of the ball'; but there had been no belle, and Millicent was put to the inconvenience of discovering that she could do nothing without footlights.

'I asked Twemlow to come up to-morrow night, Nora, ' said John, still elated, turning on the box-seat as the waggonette rattled briskly over the paved crossing at the top of Oldcastle Street.

She mumbled something through her furs.

'And is he coming? ' asked Rose.

'He said he'd try to. ' John lighted a cigar.

'He's very queer, ' said Millicent.

'How? ' Rose aggressively demanded.

'Well, imagine him going off like that. He's always going off suddenly. ' Millicent stopped and then added: 'He only danced with mother. But he's a good dancer. '

'I should think he was! ' Ethel murmured, roused from lethargy. 'Isn't he just, mother? '

Leonora mumbled again.

'Your mother's knocked up, ' said John drily. 'These late nights don't suit her. So you reckon Mr. Twemlow's a good dancer, eh? '

No one spoke further. John threw his cigar into the road.

Under the rug Leonora could feel the knees of all her daughters as they sat huddled and limp with fatigue in the small body of the waggonette. Her shoulders touched Ethel's, and every one of Milly's fidgety movements communicated itself to her. Mother and children were so close that they could not have been closer had they lain in the same grave. And yet the girls, and John too, had no slightest suspicion how far away the mother was from them, how blind they were, how amazingly they had been deceived. They deemed Leonora to be like themselves, the victim of reaction and weariness; so drowsy that even the joltings of the carriage could not prevent a doze. She marvelled, she could not help marvelling, that her spiritual detachment should remain unnoticed; the phenomenon frightened her as something full of strange risks. Was it possible that none had caught a glimpse of the intense illumination and activity of her brain, burning and labouring there so conspicuously amid the other brains sombre and dormant? And was it possible that the girls had observed the qualities of Arthur's dancing and had observed nothing else? Common sense tried to reassure her, and did not quite succeed. Her attitude resembled that of a person who leans against a firm rail over the edge of a precipice: there is no danger, but the precipice is so deep that he fears; and though the fear is a torture the sinister magnetism of the abyss forbids him to withdraw. She lived again in the waltz; in the gliding motions of it, the delicious fluctuations of the reverse, the long trance-like union, the instinctive avoidances of other contact. She whispered the music, endlessly repeating those poignant and voluptuous phrases which linger in the memory of all the world. And she recalled and reconstituted Arthur's physical presence, and the emanating charm of his disposition, and dwelt on them long and long. Instead of lessening, the secret commotion within her increased and continued to increase. While brooding with feverish joy over the immediate past, her mind reached forward and existed in the appalling and fatal moment, for whose reality however her eagerness could scarcely wait, when she should see him once more. And it asked unanswerable questions about his surprising return from New York, and his pallor, and the tremor in his voice, and his swift departure. Suddenly she knew that she was planning to have the girls out of the house to-morrow afternoon between four and five o'clock.... Her spine shivered, she grew painfully hot, and tears rushed to her eyes. She pitied herself profoundly. She said that she did not know what was the matter with her, or what was going to happen. She could not give names to things. She only felt that she was too violently alive.

'Now, missis, ' John roused her. The carriage had stopped and he had already descended. She got out last, and Carpenter drove away while John was still fumbling in his hip-pocket for the latchkey. The night was humid and very dark. Leonora and the girls stood waiting on the gravel, and John groped his way into the blackness of the portico to unfasten the door. A faint gleam from the hall-gas came through the leaded fanlight. This scarcely perceptible glow and the murmur of John's expletives were all that came to the women from the mystery of the house. The key grated in the lock, and the door opened.

'G——d d——n! ' Stanway exclaimed distinctly, with fierce annoyance. He had fallen headlong into the hall, and his silk hat could be heard hopping towards the staircase.

'Pa! 'Milly protested, shocked.

John sprang up, fuming, turned the gas on to the full, and rushed back to the doorway.

'Ah! ' he shouted. 'I knew it was a tramp lying there. Get up. Is the beggar asleep? '

They all bent down, startled into gravity, to examine a form which lay in the portico, nearly parallel with the step and below it.

'It's Uncle Meshach, ' said Ethel. 'Oh! mother! '

'Then my aunt's had another attack, ' cried John, 'and he's come up to tell us, and—Milly, run for Carpenter. '

It seemed to Leonora, as with sudden awe she vaguely figured an august and capricious power which conferred experience on mortals like a wonderful gift, that that bestowing hand was never more full than when it had given most.

CHAPTER IX

A DEATH IN THE FAMILY

While Prince, tethered summarily outside the stable-door with all his harness on, was trying in vain to understand this singular caprice on the part of Carpenter, Carpenter and the head of the house lifted Uncle Meshach's form and carried it into the hall. The women watched, ceasing their wild useless questions.

'Into the breakfast-room, on the sofa, ' said John, breathing hard, to the man.

'No, no, ' Leonora intervened, 'you had better take him upstairs at once, to Ethel and Milly's bedroom. '

The procession, undignified and yet impressive, came to a halt, and Carpenter, who was holding Meshach's feet, glanced with canine anxiety from his master to his mistress.

'But look here, Nora, ' John began.

'Yes, father, upstairs, ' said Rose, cutting him short.

Preoccupied with the cumbrous weight of Meshach's shoulders, John could not maintain the discussion; he hesitated, and then Carpenter moved towards the stairs. The small dangling body seemed to say: 'I am indifferent, but it is perhaps as well that you have done arguing. '

'Run over to Dr. Hawley's, and ask him to come across at *once*, John instructed Carpenter, when they had steered Uncle Meshach round the twist of the staircase, and insinuated him through a doorway, and laid him at length, in his overcoat and his muffler and his quaint boots, on Ethel's virginal bed.

'But has the doctor come home, Jack? ' Leonora inquired.

'Of course he has, ' said John. 'He drove up with Dain, and they passed us at Shawport. Didn't you hear me call out to them? '

'Oh yes, ' she agreed.

Then John, hatless but in his ulster, and the women, hooded and shawled, drew round the bed; but Ethel and Milly stood at the foot. The inanimate form embarrassed them all, made them feel self-conscious and afraid to meet one another's eyes.

'Better loosen his things, ' said Leonora, and Rose's fingers were instantly at work to help her.

Uncle Meshach was white, rigid, and stonecold; the stiff 'Myatt' jaw was set; the eyes, wide open, looked upwards, and strangely outwards, in a fixed stare. And his audience thought, as they gazed in a sort of foolish astonishment at the puny, grotesque, and unfamiliar thing, 'Is this really Uncle Meshach? ' John lifted the wrist and felt for the pulse, but he could distinguish no beat, and he shook his head accordingly. 'Try the heart, mother, ' Rose suggested, and Leonora, after penetrating beneath garment after garment, placed her hand on Meshach's icy and tranquil breast. And she too shook her head. Then John, with an air of finality, took out his gold repeater and when he had polished the glass he held it to Uncle Meshach's parted lips. 'Can you see any moisture on it? ' he asked, taking it to the light, but none of them could detect the slightest dimness.

'I do wish the doctor would be quick, ' said Milly.

'Doctor'll be no use, ' John remarked gruffly, returning to gaze again at the immovable face. 'Except for an inquest, ' he added.

'I think some one had better walk down to Church Street at once, and tell Aunt Hannah that uncle is here, ' said Leonora. 'Perhaps she is ill. Anyhow, she'll be very anxious. ' But she faltered before the complicated problem. 'Rose, go and wake Bessie, and ask her if uncle called here during the evening, and tell her to get up at once and light the gas-stove and put some water on to boil, and then to light a fire here. '

'And who's to go to Church Street? ' John asked quickly.

Leonora looked for an instant at Rose, as the girl left the room. She felt that on such an occasion she could more easily spare Ethel's sweet eagerness to help than Rose's almost sinister self-possession. 'Ethel and Milly, ' she said promptly. 'At least they can run on first. And be very careful what you say to Aunt Hannah, my dears. And one of you must hurry back at once in any case, by the road, not by the fields, and tell us what has happened. '

Rose came in to say that Bessie and the other servants had seen nothing of Uncle Meshach, and that they were all three getting up, and then she disappeared into the kitchen. Ethel and Milly departed, a little scared, a little regretful, but inspirited by the dreadful charm and fascination of the whole inexplicable adventure.

'Aunt Hannah's had another attack, depend on it, ' said John, 'that's it. '

'I hope not, ' Leonora murmured perfunctorily. Now that she had broken the spell of futile inactivity which the discovery of Uncle Meshach's body seemed for a few dire moments to have laid upon them, she was more at ease.

'I fancy you'd better go down there yourself as soon as the doctor's been, ' John continued. 'You're perhaps more likely to be useful there than here. What do you think? '

She looked at him under her eyelids, saying nothing, and reading all his mind. He had obstinately determined that Uncle Meshach was dead, and he was striving to conceal both his satisfaction on that account and his rapidly growing anxiety as to the condition of Aunt Hannah. His terrible lack of frankness, that instinct for the devious and the underhand which governed his entire existence, struck her afresh and seemed to devastate her heart. She felt that she could have tolerated in her husband any vice with less effort than that one vice which was specially his, that vice so contemptible and odious, so destructive of every noble and generous sentiment. Her silent, measured indignation fed itself on almost nothing—on a mere word, a mere inflection of his voice, a single transient gleam of his guilty eye. And though she was right by unerring intuition, John, could he have seen into her soul, might have been excused for demanding, 'What have I said, what have I done, to deserve this scorn? '

Rose returned, bearing materials for a fire; she had changed her Liberty dress for the dark severe frock of her studious hours, and she had an irritating air of being perfectly equal to the occasion. John, having thrown off his ulster, endeavoured to assist her in lighting the fire, but she at once proved to him that his incapacity was a hindrance to her; whereupon he wondered what in the name of goodness Carpenter and the doctor were doing to be so long. Leonora began to tidy the room, which bore witness to the regardless frenzy of anticipation with which its occupants had cast aside the soiled commonplaces of life six hours before.

'But look! ' Rose cried suddenly, examining Uncle Meshach anew, after the fire was lighted.

'What? ' John and Leonora demanded together, rushing to the bed.

'His lips weren't like that! ' the girl asserted with eagerness.

All three gazed long at the impassive face.

'Of course they were, ' said John, coldly discouraging. Leonora made no remark.

The unblinking eyes of Uncle Meshach continued to stare upwards and outwards, indifferently, interested in the ceiling. Outside could be heard the creaking of stairs, and the affrighted whisper of the maids as they descended in deshabillé from their attics at the bidding of this unconscious, cynical, and sardonic enigma on the bed.

* * * * *

'His heart is beating faintly. '

Old Dr. Hawley dropped the antique stethoscope back into the pocket of his tight dress coat, and, still bending over Uncle Meshach, but turning slightly towards John and Leonora, smiled with all his invincible jollity.

'Is it, by Jove? ' John exclaimed.

'You thought he was dead? ' said the doctor, beaming.

Leonora nodded.

'Well, he isn't, ' the doctor announced with curt cheerfulness.

'That's good, ' said John.

'But I don't think he can get over it, ' the doctor concluded, with undiminished brightness, his eyes twinkling.

While he spoke he was busy with the hot water and the cloths which Leonora and Rose had produced immediately upon demand. In a few minutes Uncle Meshach was covered almost from head to foot with cloths drenched in hot mustard-and-water; he had hot-water bags under his arms, and he was swathed in a huge blanket.

'There! ' said the rotund doctor. 'You must keep that up, and I'll send a stimulant at once. I can't stop now; not another minute. I was called to an obstetric case just as I started out. I'll come back the moment I'm free. '

'What is it—this thing? ' John inquired.

'What is it! ' the doctor repeated genially. 'I'll tell you what it is. Put your nose there. ' He indicated Uncle Meshach's mouth. 'Do you notice that ammoniacal smell? That's due to uraemia, a sequel of Bright's disease. '

'Bright's disease? ' John muttered.

'Bright's disease, ' affirmed the doctor, dwelling on the famous and striking syllables. 'Your uncle is the typical instance of the man who has never been ill in his life. He walks up a little slope or up some steps to a friend's house, and just as he is lifting his hand to the knocker, he has a convulsion and falls down unconscious. That's Bright's disease. Never been ill in his life! Not so far as *he* knew! Not so far as *he* knew! Nearly all you Myatts had weak kidneys. Do you remember your great-uncle Ebenezer? You've sent down to Miss Myatt, you say? Good.... Perhaps he was lying on your steps for two or three hours. He may pull round. He may. We must hope so. '

The doctor put on his overcoat, and his cap with the ear-flaps, and after a final glance at the patient and a friendly, reassuring smile at Leonora, he went slowly to the door. Girth and good humour and funny stories had something to do with his great reputation in Bursley and Hillport. But he possessed shrewdness and sagacity; he belonged to a dynasty of doctors; and he was deeply versed in the social traditions of the district. Men consulted him because their grandfathers had consulted his father, and because there had always been a Dr. Hawley in Bursley, and because he was acquainted with the pathological details of their ancestral history on both sides of the hearth. His patients, indeed, were not individuals, but families. There were cleverer doctors in the place, doctors of more refined appearance and manners, doctors less monotonously and loudly gay; but old Hawley, with his knowledge of pedigrees and his unique instinctive sympathy with the idiosyncrasies of local character, could hold his own against the most assertive young M. D. that ever came out of Edinburgh to monopolise the Five Towns.

'Can you send some one round with me for the medicine? ' he asked in the doorway. 'Happen you'll come yourself, John? '

There was a momentary hesitation.

'I'll come, doctor, ' said Rose. 'And then you can give me all your instructions. Mother must stay here. ' She completely ignored her father.

'Do, my dear; come by all means. ' And the doctor beamed again suddenly with the maximum of cheerfulness.

* * * * *

Meshach had given no sign of life; his eyes, staring upwards and outwards, were still unchangeably fixed on the same portion of the ceiling. He ignored equally the nonchalant and expert attentions of the doctor, the false solicitude of John, Leonora's passionate anxiety, and Rose's calm self-confidence. He treated the fomentations with the apathy which might have been expected from a man who for fifty years had been accustomed to receive the meek skilled service of women in august silence. One could almost have detected in those eyes a glassy and profound secret amusement at the disturbance which he had caused—a humorous appreciation of all the fuss: the maids with their hair down their backs bending and whispering over a stove; Ethel and Milly trudging scared through the nocturnal streets; Rose talking with demure excitement to old Hawley in his aromatic surgery; John officiously carrying kettles to and fro, and issuing orders to Bessie in the passage; Leonora cast violently out of one whirlpool into another; and some unknown expectant terrified pair wondering why the doctor, who had been warned months before, should thus culpably neglect their urgent summons. As he lay there so grim and derisive and solitary, so fatigued with days and nights, so used up, so steeped in experience, and so

144

contemptuously unconcerned, he somehow baffled all the efforts of blankets, cloths, and bags to make his miserable frame look ridiculous. He had a majesty which subdued his surroundings. And in this room hitherto sacred to the charming mysteries of girlhood his cadaverous presence forced the skirts and petticoats on Milly's bed, and the disordered apparatus on the dressing-table, and the scented soaps on the washstand, and the row of tiny boots and shoes which Leonora had arranged near the wardrobe, to apologise pathetically and wistfully for their very existence.

'Is that enough mustard? ' John inquired idly.

'Yes, ' said Leonora.

She realised—but not in the least because he had asked a banal question about mustard—that he was perfectly insensible to all spiritual significances. She had been aware of it for many years, yet the fact touched her now more sharply than ever. It seemed to her that she must cry out in a long mournful cry: 'Can't you see, can't you feel! ' And once again her husband might justifiably have demanded: 'What have I done this time? '

'I wish one of those girls would come back from Church Street, ' he burst out, frowning. 'They're here! ' He became excited as he listened to light rapid footsteps on the stair. But it was Rose who entered.

'Here's the medicine, mother, ' said Rose eagerly. She was flushed with running. 'It's chloric ether and nitrate of potash, a highly diffusible stimulant. And there's a chance that sooner or later it may put him into a perspiration. But it will be worse than useless if the hot applications aren't kept up, the doctor said. You must raise his head and give it him in a spoon in very small doses. '

And then Meshach impassively submitted to the handling of his head and his mouth. He gurgled faintly in accepting the medicine, and soon his temples and the corners of his lips showed a very slight perspiration. But though the doses were repeated, and the fomentations assiduously maintained, no further result occurred, save that Meshach's eyes, according to the shifting of his head, perused new portions of the ceiling.

* * * * *

145

As the futile minutes passed, John grew more and more restless. He was obliged to admit to himself that Uncle Meshach was not dead, but he felt absolutely sure that he would never revive. Had not the doctor said as much? And he wanted desperately to hear that Aunt Hannah still lived, and to take every measure of precaution for her continuance in this world. The whole of his future might depend upon the hazard of the next hour.

'Look here, Nora, ' he said protestingly, while Rose was on one of her journeys to the kitchen. 'It's evidently not much use you stopping here, whereas there's no knowing what hasn't happened down at Church Street. '

'Do you mean you wish me to go down there? ' she asked coldly.

'Well, I leave it to your common sense, ' he retorted.

Rose appeared.

'Your father thinks I ought to go down to Church Street, ' said Leonora.

'What! And leave uncle? ' Rose added nothing to this question, but proceeded with her tasks.

'Certainly, ' John insisted.

Leonora was conscious of an acute resentment against her husband. The idea of her leaving Uncle Meshach at such a crisis seemed to her to be positively wicked. Had not John heard what Rose said to the doctor: 'Mother must stay here'? Had he not heard that? But of course he desired that Uncle Meshach should die. Yes, every word, every gesture of his in the sick-room was an involuntary expression of that desire.

'Why don't you go yourself, father? ' Rose demanded of him bluntly, after a pause.

'Simply because, if there *is* any illness, I shouldn't be any use. ' John glared at his daughter.

Then, quite suddenly, Leonora thought how vain, how pitiful, how unseemly, were these acrimonious conflicts of opinion in presence of the strange and awe-inspiring riddle in the blanket. An impulse seized her to give way, and she found a dozen reasons why she should desert Uncle Meshach for Aunt Hannah.

'Can you manage? ' she asked Rose doubtfully.

'Oh yes, mother, we can manage, ' answered Rose, with an exasperating manufactured sweetness of tone.

'Tell Carpenter to put the horse in, ' John suggested. 'I expect he's waiting about in the kitchen. '

'No, ' said Leonora, 'I'll pin my skirt up and walk. I shall be half way there before he's ready to start. '

When Leonora had departed, John redoubled his activity as a nurse. 'There's no object in changing the cloths as often as that, ' said Rose. But his suspense forbade him to keep still. Rose annoyed him excessively, and the nervous energy which should have helped towards self-control was expended in concealing that annoyance. He felt as though he should go mad unless something decisive happened very soon. To his surprise, just after the hall clock (which was always kept half-an-hour fast) had sounded three through the dark passages of the apprehensive house, Rose left the room. He was alone with what remained of Uncle Meshach. He moved the blanket, and touched the cloth which lay on Meshach's heart. 'Not too hot, that, ' he said aloud. Taking the cloth he walked to the fire, where was a large saucepan full of nearly boiling water. He picked up the lid of the saucepan, dropped it, crossed over to the washstand with a brusque movement, and plunged the cloth into the cold water of the ewer. Holding it there, he turned and gazed in a sort of abstract meditation at Uncle Meshach, who steadily ignored him. He was possessed by a genuine feeling of righteous indignation against his uncle.... He drew the cloth from the ewer, squeezed it a little, and approached the bed again. And as he stood over Meshach with the cloth in his hand, he saw his wife in the doorway. He knew in an instant that his own face had frightened her and prevented her from saying what she was about to say.

'How you startled me, Nora! ' he exclaimed, with his surpassing genius for escaping from an apparently fatal situation.

She ran up to the bed. 'Don't keep uncle uncovered like that, ' she said; 'put it on. ' And she took the cloth from his hand. 'Why, ' she cried, 'it's like ice! What on earth are you doing? Where's Rose? '

'I was just taking it off, ' he replied. 'What about aunt? '

'I met the girls down the road, ' she said. 'Your aunt is dead. '

* * * * *

A few minutes later Uncle Meshach's rigid frame suffered a convulsion; the whole surface of his skin sweated abundantly; his eyes wavered, closed, and opened again; his mouth made the motion of swallowing. He had come back from unconsciousness. He was no longer an enigma, wrapped in supercilious and inflexible calm; but a sick, shrivelled little man, so pitiably prostrate that his condition drew the sympathy out of Leonora with a sharp violent pain, as very cold metal burns the fingers. He could not even whisper; he could only look. Soon afterwards Dr. Hawley returned, explaining that the anxiety of a husband about to be a father had called him too soon by several hours. The doctor, who had been informed of Aunt Hannah's death as he entered the house, said at once, on seeing him, that Uncle Meshach had had a marvellous escape. Then, when he had succoured the patient further, he turned rather formidably to Leonora.

'I want to speak to you, ' he said, and he led her out of the room, leaving Rose, Ethel, and John in charge of Meshach.

'What is it, doctor? ' she asked him plaintively on the landing.

'Which is your bedroom? Show it me, ' he demanded. She opened a door, and they both went in. 'I'll light the gas, ' he said, doing so. 'And now, ' he proceeded, 'you'll kindly retire to bed, instantly. Mr. Myatt is out of danger. ' He smiled warmly, just as he had smiled when he predicted that Meshach would probably not recover.

'But, doctor, ' Leonora protested.

'Instantly, ' he said, forcing her gently on to the sofa at the foot of the two beds.

'But some one ought to go down to Church Street to look after things, ' she began.

'Church Street can wait. There's no hurry at Church Street now. '

'And uncle hasn't been told yet... I'm not at all over-tired, doctor. '

'Yes, mother dear, you are, and you must do as the doctor orders. ' It was Ethel who had come into the room; she touched Leonora's arm caressingly.

'And where are you girls to sleep? The spare room isn't— —'

'Oh, mother! — —Just listen to her, doctor! ' said Ethel, stroking her mother's hand, as though she and the doctor were two old and sage persons, and Leonora was a small child.

'They think I'm ill! They think I'm going to collapse! ' The idea struck her suddenly. 'But I'm not. I'm quite well, and my brain is perfectly clear. And anyhow, I'm sure I can't sleep. ' She said aloud: 'It wouldn't be any use; I shouldn't sleep. '

'Ah! I'll attend to that, I'll attend to that! ' the doctor laughed. 'Ethel, help your mother to bed. ' He departed.

'This is really most absurd, ' Leonora reflected. 'It's ridiculous. However, I'm only doing it to oblige them. '

Before she was entirely undressed, Rose entered with a powder in a white paper, and a glass of hot milk.

'You are to swallow *this*, mother, and then drink *this*. Here, Eth, hold the glass a second. '

And Leonora accepted the powder from Rose and the milk from Ethel, as they stood side by side in front of her. Great waves seemed to surge through her brain. In walking to the bed, she saw herself all white in the mirror of the wardrobe.

'My face looks as if it was covered with flour, ' she said to Ethel, with a short laugh. It did not occur to her that she was pale. 'Don't forget to— —' But she had forgotten what Ethel was not to forget. Her head reeled as it lay firmly on the pillow. The waves were waves of sound now, and they developed into a rhythm, a tune. She had barely time to discover that the tune was the Blue Danube Waltz, and that she was dancing, when the whole world came to an end.

* * * * *

She awoke to feel the radiant influence of the afternoon sun through the green blinds. Impregnated with a delicious languor, she slowly stretched out her arms, and, lifting her head, gazed first at the intricate tracery of the lace on her silk nightgown, and then into the silent dreamy spaces of the room. Everything was in perfect order; she guessed that Ethel must have trod softly to make it tidy before leaving her, hours ago. John's bed was turned down, and his pyjamas laid out, with all Bessie's accustomed precision. Presently she noticed on her night-table a sheet of note-paper, on which had been written in pencil, in large letters: 'Ring the bell before getting up. ' She could not be sure whether the hand was Ethel's or Rose's. 'Oh! ' she thought, 'how good my girls are! ' She was quite well, quite restored, and slightly hungry. And she was also calm, content, ready to commence existence anew.

'I suppose I had better humour them, ' she murmured, and she rang the bell.

Bessie entered. The treasure was irreproachably neat and prim in her black and white.

'What time is it, Bessie? ' Leonora inquired.

'It's a straight-up three, ma'am. '

'Then I must have slept for eleven hours! How is Mr. Myatt going on? '

Bessie dropped her hands, and smiled benevolently: 'Oh! He's much better, ma'am. And when the doctor told him about poor Miss Myatt, ma'am, he just said the funeral must be on Saturday because he didn't like Sunday funerals, and it wouldn't do to wait till Monday. He didn't say nothing else. And he keeps on telling us he shall be well enough to go to the funeral, and he's sent master down to Guest's in St. Luke's Square to order it, and the hearse is to have two horses, but not the coaches, ma'am. He's asleep just now, ma'am, and I'm watching him, but Miss Rose is resting on Miss

Milly's bed in case, so I can come in here for a minute or two. He told the doctor and master that Miss Myatt was took with one of them attacks at half-past eleven o'clock, and he went for Dr. Adams as lives at the top of Oldcastle Street. Dr. Adams wasn't in, and then he saw a cab—it must have been coming from the ball, ma'am, but Mr. Myatt didn't know as there was any ball—and he drove up to Hillport for Dr. Hawley, him being the family doctor. And then he said he felt bad-like, and he thought he'd come here and send master across the way for Dr. Hawley. And he got out of the cab and paid the cabman, and then he doesn't remember no more. Wasn't it dreadful, ma'am? I don't believe he rightly knew what he was doing, the poor old gentleman! '

Leonora listened. 'Where are Miss Ethel and Miss Milly? ' she asked.

'Master said they was to go to Oldcastle to order mourning, ma'am. They've but just gone. And master said he should be back himself about six. He never slept a wink, ma'am; nor even sat down. He just had his bath, and Miss Ethel crept in here for his clothes. '

'And have you been to bed, Bessie? '

'Me? No, ma'am. What should I go to bed for? I'm as well as well, ma'am. Miss Milly slept in Miss Rose's bedroom, for a bit, and Miss Ethel on the sofy in the drawing-room—not as you might call that sleeping. Miss Rose said you was to have some tea before you got up, ma'am. Shall I tell cook to get it now? '

'I really think I should prefer to have it downstairs, Bessie, thanks, ' said Leonora.

'Very well, ma'am. But Miss Rose said— —'

'Yes, but I will have it downstairs. In three-quarters of an hour, say. '

'Very well, ma'am. Now is there anything I can do for you, ma'am? '

While dressing, very placidly and deliberately, and while thinking upon all the multitudinous things that seemed to have happened in her world during her long slumber, Leonora dwelt too upon the extraordinary loving kindness of this hireling, who got twenty pounds a year, half-a-day a week, and a day a month. On the first of every month Leonora handed to Bessie one paltry sovereign, thirteen shillings, and the odd fourpence in coppers. She wondered fancifully if she would have the effrontery to requite the girl in coin on the next pay-day; and she was filled with a sense of the goodness of humanity. And then there crossed her mind the recollection that she had caught John in a wicked act on the previous night. Yes; he had not imposed on her for a moment; and she perceived clearly now that murder had been in his heart. She was not appalled nor desolated. She thought: 'So that is murder, that little thing, that thing over in a minute! ' It appeared to her that murder in the concrete was less dreadful than murder in the abstract, far less horrible than the strident sound of the word on the lips of a newsboy, or the look of it in the 'Signal. ' She felt dimly that she ought to be shocked, unnerved, terrified, at the prospect of living, eating, and sleeping with a man who had meant to kill. But she could not summon these sensations. She merely experienced a kind of pity for John. She put the episode away from her, as being closed, accidental, and unimportant. Uncle Meshach was alive.

A few minutes before four o'clock, she went quietly into the sick-room. Bessie, sitting upright between the beds, put her finger to her lips. Uncle Meshach was asleep on Ethel's bed, and on the other bed lay Rose, also asleep, stretched in a negligent attitude, but fully dressed and wearing an old black frock that was too tight for her. The fire burned brightly.

'Tea is ready in the drawing-room, ma'am, ' Bessie whispered, 'and Mr. Twemlow has just called. He's waiting to see you. '

* * * * *

'So you know what has happened to us? '

'Yes, ' he said, 'I met your husband on St. Luke's Square. But I heard something before that. At one o'clock, a man told me at Knype Station that Mr. Myatt had cut his throat on your doorstep. I didn't believe it. So I called up Twemlow & Stanway over the 'phone and got on to the facts. '

'What things people say! ' she exclaimed.

'I guess you've stood it very well, ' he remarked, gazing at her, as with quick, sure movements of her gracile hands she poured out the tea.

152

'Ah! ' she murmured, flushing, 'they sent me to bed. I have only just got up. '

'I know exactly when you went to bed, ' he smiled.

His tone filled her with satisfaction. She had hoped and expected that he would behave naturally, that he would not adopt the desolating attitude of gloom prescribed by convention for sympathisers with the bereaved; and she was not disappointed. He spoke with an easy and cheerful sincerity, and she was exquisitely conscious of the flattery implied in that simple, direct candour which seemed to say to her, 'You and I have no need of convention—we understand each other. ' Perhaps never in her life, not even in the wonderful felicities of girlhood, had Leonora been more peacefully content than during those moments of calm succeeding stress, as she met Arthur's eyes in the intimacy of a fraternal confidence. The large room was so tranquil, the curtains so white, and the sunlight so benignant in the caress of its amber horizontal rays. Rose lay asleep upstairs, Ethel and Millicent were at Oldcastle, John would not return for two hours; and she and Arthur were alone together in the middle of the long quiet chamber, talking quietly. She was happy. She had no fear, neither for herself nor for him. As innocent as Rose, and more innocent than Ethel, she now regarded the feverish experience of the dance as accidental, a thing to be forgotten, an episode of which the repetition was merely to be avoided; Death and the fear of Death had come suddenly and written over its record in the page of existence. Her present sanity and calmness and mild bliss and self-control—these were to last, these were the real symptoms of her condition, and of Arthur's condition. No! The memory of the ball did not trouble her; it had not troubled her since she awoke after the sedative. She had entered the drawing-room without a qualm, and the instant of their meeting, anticipated on the previous night as much in terror as in joy, had passed equably and serenely. Relying on his strength, and exulting in her own, she had given him her hand, and he had taken it, and that was all. She knew her native force. She knew that she had the precious and rare gift of common sense, and she was perfectly convinced that this common sense, which had never long deserted her in the past, could never permanently desert her in the future. She imagined that nothing was stronger than common sense; she had small suspicion that in their noblest hours men and women have invariably despised common sense, and trampled it underfoot as the most contemptible of human attributes. Therefore she was content and unalarmed. And she found pleasure even in trifles, as, for example, that the maid had set two cups-and-saucers and two only; the duality struck her as delicious. She looked close at Arthur's sagacious, shrewd, and kindly face, with the heavy, clipped moustache, and the bluish chin, and those grey hairs at the sides of the forehead. 'We belong to the same generation, he and I, ' she thought, eating bread and butter with relish, 'and we are not so very old, after all! ' Aunt Hannah was incomparably older, ripe for death. Who could be profoundly moved by that unimportant, that trivial, demise? She felt very sorry for Uncle Meshach, but no more than that. Such sentiments may have the appearance of callousness, but they were the authentic sentiments of Leonora, and Leonora was not callous. The financial aspect of Aunt Hannah's death, as it affected John and herself and the girls and their home, did not disturb her. She was removed far above finance, far above any preoccupation about the latter years, as she sat talking quietly and blissfully with Arthur in the drawing-room.

'Yes, ' she was telling him, 'it was just opposite the Clayton-Vernons' that I met them. '

'Where the elm-trees spread over the road? ' he questioned.

She nodded, pleased by his minute interest in her narrative and by his knowledge of the neighbourhood. 'I saw them both a long way off, walking quickly, under a gas-lamp. And it's very curious, but although I was so anxious to know what had happened, I couldn't go on to meet them—I was obliged to wait until they came up. And they didn't notice me at first, and then Ethel shrieked out: "Oh, it's mother! " And Milly said: "Aunt Hannah's dead, mother. Is Uncle Meshach dead? " You can't understand how queer I felt. I felt as if Milly would go on asking and asking: "Is father dead? Is Bessie dead? Is Bran dead? Are you dead? "'

'I know, ' he said reflectively.

She guessed that he envied her the strange nocturnal adventure. And her secret pride in the adventure, which hitherto she had endeavoured to suppress, suddenly became open and legitimate. She allowed her face to disclose the thought: 'You see that I too have lived through crises, and that I can appreciate how wonderful they are. ' And she proceeded to give him all the details of Aunt Hannah's death, as she had learnt them from Ethel and Milly during the walk

154

home through sleeping Hillport: how the servant had grown alarmed, and had called a neighbour by breaking a bedroom window with a broomstick, leaning from Aunt Hannah's window, and how the neighbour's eldest boy had run for Dr. Adams and had caught him in the street just as he was returning home, and how Aunt Hannah was gone before the boy came back with Dr. Adams, and how no one could guess what had happened to Uncle Meshach, and no one could suggest what to do, until Ethel and Milly knocked at the door.

'Isn't it all strange? Don't you think it's strange? ' Leonora demanded.

'No, ' he said. 'It seems strange, but it isn't really. Such things are always happening. '

'Are they? ' She spoke naïvely, with a girlish inflection and a girlish gesture.

'Well, of course! ' He smiled gravely, and yet humorously. And his eyes said: 'What a charming simple thing you are! ' And she liked to think of his superiority over her in experience, knowledge, imperturbability, breadth of view, and all those kindred qualities which women give to the men they admire.

They could not talk further on the subject.

'By the by, how's your foot? ' he inquired.

'My foot? '

'Yes. You hurt it last night, didn't you, after I'd gone? '

She had completely forgotten the trifling fiction, until it thus rather startlingly reappeared on his lips. She might easily have let it die naturally, had she chosen; but she could not choose. She had a whim to kill it violently, romantically.

'No, ' she said, 'I didn't hurt it. '

'It was your husband was telling me. '

She went on joyously and fearfully: 'Some one asked me to dance, after—after the Blue Danube. And I didn't want to; I couldn't. And so I said I had hurt my foot. It was just one of those things that one says, you know! '

He was embarrassed; he had no remark ready. But to preserve appearances he lowered the corners of his lips and glanced at the copper tea-kettle through half-closed eyes, feigning to suppress a private amusement. She was quite aware, however, that she had embarrassed him. And just as, a minute earlier, she had liked him for his lordly, masculine, philosophic superiority, so now she liked him for that youthful embarrassment. She felt that all men were equally child-like to women, and that the most adorable were the most child-like. 'How little you understand, after all! ' she thought. 'Poor boy, I unlatched the door, and you dared not push it open! You were afraid of committing an indiscretion. But I will guide and protect you, and protect us both. '

This was the woman who, half an hour ago, had been exulting in the adequacy of her common sense. Innocent and enchanting creature, with the rashness of innocence!

'I guess I couldn't dance again after the Blue Danube, either, ' he said at length, boldly.

She made no answer; perhaps she was a little intimidated; but she looked at him with eyes and lips full of latent vivacity.

'That was why I left, ' he finished firmly. There was in his tone a hint of that engaging and piquant antagonism which springs up between lovers and dies away; he had the air of telling her that since she had invited a confession she was welcome to it.

She retreated, still admiring, and said evenly that the ball had been a great success.

Soon afterwards Ethel and Milly unexpectedly entered the room. They had put on the formal aspect of dejection which they deemed proper for them, but on perceiving that their elders were talking quite naturally, they at once abandoned constraint and became natural too. From the sight of their unaffected pleasure in seeing Arthur Twemlow again, Leonora drew further sustenance for her mood of serene content.

'Just fancy, Mr. Twemlow, ' Millicent burst out. 'We walked all the way to Oldcastle, and we never thought, and no one reminded us. It's father's fault, really. '

'What is father's fault, really? '

'It's Thursday afternoon and the shops were all shut. We shall have to go to-morrow morning. '

'Ah! ' he said. 'The stores don't shut on Thursday afternoon in New York. '

'Mother will be able to come with us to-morrow morning, ' said Ethel, and approaching Leonora she asked: 'Are you all right, mother? '

This simple, familiar conversation, and the free movements of the girls, and the graver suavity of Arthur and herself, seemed to Leonora to constitute a picture, a scene, of mysterious and profound charm.

Arthur rose to depart. The girls wished him to stay, but Leonora did not support them. In a house where an aged relative lay ill, and that relative so pathetically bereaved, it was not meet that a visitor should remain too long. Immediately he had gone she began to anticipate their next meeting. The eagerness of that anticipation surprised her. And, moreover, the environment of her life closed quickly round her; she could not ignore it. She demanded of herself what was Arthur's excuse for calling, and how it was that she should be so happy in the midst of woe and death. Her joyous confidence was shaken. Feeling that on such a day she ought to have been something other than a delicate châtelaine idly dispensing tea in a drawing-room, she went upstairs, determined to find some useful activity.

The light was failing in the sick-room, and the fire shone brighter. Bessie had disappeared, and Rose sat in her place. Uncle Meshach still slept.

'Have you had a good rest, my dear? ' she whispered, kissing Rose fondly. 'You had better go downstairs. I've had some tea, and I'll take charge here now. '

Leonora

'Very well, ' the girl assented, yawning. 'Who's that just gone? '

'Mr. Twemlow. '

'Oh, mother! ' Rose exclaimed in angry disappointment. 'Why didn't some one tell me he was here? '

* * * * *

'The cortège will move at 2.15, ' said the mourning invitation cards, and on Saturday at two o'clock Uncle Meshach, dressed in deep black, sat on a cane-chair against the wall in the bedroom of his late sister. He had not been able to conceive Hannah's funeral without himself as chief mourner, and therefore he had accomplished his own recovery in the amazing period of fifty hours; and in addition to accomplishing his recovery he had given an uninterrupted series of the most minute commands concerning the arrangements for the obsequies. Protests had been utterly useless. 'It will kill him, ' said Leonora to the doctor as Meshach, risen straight out of bed, was getting into a cab at Hillport that morning to drive to Church Street. 'It may, ' old Hawley answered. 'But what can one do? ' Smiling, first at Meshach, and then at Leonora, the doctor had joined his aged patient in the cab and they had gone off together.

Next to the cane-chair was Hannah's mahogany bed, which had been stripped. On the bed lay a massive oaken coffin, and, accurately fitted into the coffin, lay the withered remains of Meshach's slave. The prim and spotless bedroom, with its chest of drawers, its small glass, its three-cornered wardrobe, its narrow washstand, its odd bonnet-boxes, its trunk, its skirts hung inside-out behind the door, its Bible with the spectacle-case on it, its texts, its miniature portraits, its samplers, framed in maple, and its engraving of the infant John Wesley being saved from the fire at Epworth Vicarage, framed in gold, was eloquent of the habits of the woman who had used it, without ambition, without repining, and without hope, save an everlasting hope, for more than fifty years.

Into this room, obedient to the rigid etiquette of an old-fashioned Five Towns funeral, every person asked to the burial was bound to come, in order to take a last look at the departed, and to offer a few words of sympathy to the chief mourner. As they entered—Stanway, David Dain, Fred Ryley, Dr. Hawley, Leonora, the servant, and lastly Arthur Twemlow—unwillingly desecrating the almost sæcular

158

modesty of the chamber, Meshach received them one by one with calmness, with detachment, with the air of the curator of the museum. 'Here she is, ' his mien indicated. 'That is to say, what's left. Gaze your fill. ' Beyond a monotonous 'Thank ye, thank ye, ' in response to expressions of sympathy for him, and of appreciation of Hannah's manifold excellences, he made no remarks to any one except Leonora and Arthur Twemlow.

'Has that ginger wine come? ' he asked Leonora anxiously. The feast after the sepulture was as important, and as strictly controlled by etiquette, as the lying-in-state. Leonora, who had charge of the meal, was able to give him an affirmative.

'I'm glad as you've come, ' he said to Twemlow. 'I had a fancy for you to see her again as soon as they told me you was back. Her makes a good corpse, eh? '

Twemlow agreed. 'To die suddenly, that's the best, ' he murmured awkwardly; he did not know what to say.

'Her was a good sister, a good sister! ' Meshach pronounced with an emotion which was doubtless genuine and profound, but which superficially resembled that of an examiner awarding pass-marks to a pupil. 'By the way, Twemlow, ' he added as Arthur was leaving the room, 'didst ever thrash that business out wi' our John? I've been thinking over a lot of things while I was fast abed up yon'. '

Arthur stared at him.

'Thou knowst what I mean? ' continued Meshach, putting his thin tremulous hand on the edge of the coffin in order to rise from the chair.

'Yes, ' Arthur replied, 'I know. I haven't settled it yet, I haven't had time. '

'I should ha' thought thou'dst had time enough, lad, ' said Meshach.

Then the undertaker's men adjusted the lid of the coffin, hiding Aunt Hannah's face, and screwed in the eight brass screws, and clumped down the dark stairs with their burden, and so across the pavement between two rows of sluttish sightseers, to the hearse. Uncle Meshach, with the aid only of his stick, entered the first coach; John

Stanway and Fred Ryley—the rules of precedence were thus inflexible! —occupied the second; and Arthur Twemlow, with the family lawyer and the family doctor, took the third. Leonora remained in the house with the servant to spread the feast.

The church was barely four hundred yards away, and in less than half an hour they were all in the house again; all save Aunt Hannah, who had already, in the vault of the Myatts, passed the first five minutes of the tedium of waiting for the Day of Judgment. And now, as they gathered round the fish, the fowl, the ham, the cake, the preserves, the tea, the wines and the spirits, etiquette demanded that they should be cheerful, should show a resignation to the will of heaven, and should eat heartily. And although the rapid-ticking clock on the mantelpiece in the parlour pointed only to a little better than three o'clock they were obliged to eat heartily, for fear of giving pain to Uncle Meshach; to drink much was not essential, but nothing could have excused abstention from the solid fare. The repast, actively conducted by the mourning host, was not finished until nearly half-past four. Then Twemlow and the doctor said that they must leave.

'Nay, nay, ' Meshach complained. 'There's the will to be read. It's right and proper as all the guests should hear the will, and it'll take nobbut a few minutes. '

The enfeebled old man talked more and more the dialect which his father and mother had talked over his cradle.

'Better without us, old friend! ' the doctor said jauntily. 'Besides, my patients! ' And by dint of blithe obstinacy he managed to get away, and also to cover the retreat of Twemlow.

'I shall call in a day or two, ' said Arthur to Uncle Meshach as they shook hands.

'Ay! call and see th' old ruin! ' Meshach replied, and dropping back into his chair, 'Now, Dain! ' he ordered.

David Dain drew a long white envelope from his breast pocket.

'"This is the last will and testament of me, Hannah Margaret Myatt, "' the lawyer began to read quickly in his thick voice, '"of Church Street, Bursley, in the county of Stafford, spinster. I commit my body to the grave and my soul to God in the sure hope of a blessed resurrection through my Redeemer the Lord Jesus Christ. I bequeath ten pounds each to my dear nephew John Stanway, and to his wife Leonora, to purchase mourning at my decease, and five pounds each for the same purpose to my dear great-nephew Frederick Wellington Ryley, and to my great-nieces Ethel, Rosalys, and Millicent Stanway, and to any other children of the said John and Leonora Stanway should they have such, and should such children survive me. " This will is dated twelve years ago, ' the lawyer stopped to explain. He continued: "'I further bequeath to my great-nephew Frederick Wellington Ryley the sum of two hundred and fifty pounds. "'

'Something for you there, Frederick Wellington Ryley! ' exclaimed Stanway in a frigid tone, biting his thumb and looking up at the ceiling.

Ryley blushed. He had scarcely spoken during the meal, and he did not break his silence now.

With much verbiage the will proceeded to state that the testatrix left the residue of her private savings to Meshach, 'to dispose of absolutely according to his own discretion, ' in case he should survive her; and that in case she should survive him she left her private savings and the whole of the estate of which she and Meshach were joint tenants to John Stanway.

'There is a short codicil, ' Dain added, 'which revokes the legacy of two hundred and fifty pounds to Mr. Ryley in case Mr. Myatt should survive the testatrix. It is dated some six months ago. '

'Kindly read it, ' said Stanway coldly.

'With pleasure, ' the lawyer agreed, and he read it.

'Then, as it turns out, ' Stanway remarked, looking defiantly at his uncle, 'Ryley gets nothing but five pounds under this will. '

'Under this will, nephew, ' the old man assented.

'And may one inquire, ' Stanway persisted, 'the nature of your intentions in regard to aunt's savings which she leaves you to dispose of according to your discretion? '

'What dost mean, nephew? '

Leonora saw with anxiety that her husband, while intending to be calm, pompous, and superior, was, in fact, losing control of himself.

'I mean, ' said John, 'are you going to distribute them? '

'No, nephew. They're well enough where they lie. I shall none touch 'em. '

Stanway gave the sigh of a martyr who has sufficient spirit to be disdainful. Throwing his serviette on the disordered table, he pushed back his chair and stood up. 'You'll excuse me now, uncle, ' he said, bitterly polite, 'I must be off to the works. Ryley, I shall want you. ' And without another word he left the room and the house.

* * * * *

Leonora was the last to go. Meshach would not allow her to stay after the tea-things were washed up. He declined firmly every offer of help or companionship, and since the middle-aged servant made no objection to being alone with her convalescent master, Leonora could only submit to his wishes.

When she was gone he lighted his pipe. At seven o'clock, the servant came into the parlour and found him dozing in the dark; his pipe hung loosely from his teeth.

'Eh, mester, ' she cried, lighting the gas. 'Hadn't ye better go to bed? Ye've had a worriting day. '

'Happen I'd better, ' he answered deliberately, taking hold of the pipe and adjusting his spectacles.

'Can ye undress yeself? ' she asked him.

'Ay, ' he said, 'I can do that, wench. My candle! '

And he went carefully up to bed.

CHAPTER X

IN THE GARDEN

'Father's in a horrid temper. Did anything go wrong? ' said Rose, when Leonora reached Hillport.

'No, ' Leonora replied. 'Where is he? '

'In the drawing-room. He says he won't have any tea. '

'You must remember, my dear, that your father has been through a great deal this last day or two. '

'So have all of us, as far as that goes, ' Rose stated ruthlessly. 'However— —' She turned away, shrugging her shoulders.

Leonora wondered by means of what sad experience Rose would ultimately discover that, whereas men have the right to cry out when they are hurt, it is the whole business of a woman's life to suffer in cheerful silence. She sat with the girls during tea, drinking a cup for the sake of form, and giving them disconnected items of information about the funeral, which at their own passionate request they had been excused from attending. The talk was carried on in low tones, so that the rattle of a spoon in a saucer sounded loud and distinct. And in the drawing-room John steadily perused the 'Signal, ' column by column, from the announcement of 'Pink Dominoes' at the Hanbridge Theatre Royal on the first page, to the bait of a sporting bookmaker in Holland at the end of the last. The evening was desolating, but Leonora endured it with philosophy, because she appreciated John's state of mind.

It was the disclosure of the legacy of two hundred and fifty pounds to Fred Ryley, and of the recent conditional revocation of that legacy, which had galled her husband's sensibilities by bringing home to him what he had lost through Aunt Hannah's sudden death and through the senile whim of Uncle Meshach to alter his will. He could well have tolerated Meshach's refusal to distribute Aunt Hannah's savings immediately (Leonora thought), had the old man's original testament remained uncancelled. Once upon a time, Ryley, the despised poor relation, the offspring of an outcast from the family, was to have been put off with two hundred and fifty pounds, and the bulk of the Myatt joint fortune was to have passed in any case to John. The withdrawal of the paltry legacy, as shown in the codicil, was the outward and irritating sign that Ryley had been lifted from his humble position to the level of John himself. John, of course, had known months ago that he and Ryley stood level in the hazard of gaining the inheritance, but the history of the legacy, revealed after the funeral, aroused his disgusted imagination, as it had not been roused before.

He was beaten; and, more important, he knew it now; he had the incensed, futile, malevolent, devil-may-care feeling of being beaten. He bitterly invited Fate not to stop at half-measures but to come on and do her worst. And Fate, with that mysterious responsiveness which often distinguishes her movements, came on. 'Of course! I might have expected it! ' John exclaimed savagely, two days later, when he received a circular to the effect that a small and desperate minority of shareholders were trying to put the famous brewery company into liquidation under the supervision of the Court. The shares fell another five in twenty-four hours. The Bursley Conservative Club knew positively the same night that John had 'got out' at a ruinous loss, and this episode seemed to give vigorous life to certain rumours, hitherto faint, that John and his uncle had violently quarrelled at his aunt's funeral, and that when Meshach died Fred Ryley would be found to be the heir. Other rumours, that Ethel Stanway and Fred Ryley were about to be secretly married, that Dain would have been the owner of Prince but for the difference between guineas and pounds, and that the real object of Arthur Twemlow's presence in the Five Towns was to buy up the concern of Twemlow & Stanway, were received with reserve, though not entirely discredited. The town, however, was more titillated than perturbed, for every one said that old Meshach, for the sake of the family's good name, would never under any circumstances permit a catastrophe to occur. The town saw little of Meshach now—he had almost ceased to figure in the streets; it knew, however, the Myatt pride in the Myatt respectability.

* * * * *

Leonora sympathised with John, but her sympathy, weakened by his surliness, was also limited by her ignorance of his real plight, and by the secret preoccupation of her own existence. From the evening of the funeral the desire to see Arthur again, to study his features, to hear his voice, definitely took the uppermost place in her mind. She thought of him always, and she ceased to pretend to herself that this was not so. She continually expected him to call, or to meet some one who had met him, or to receive a letter from him. She forced her memory to reconstitute in detail his last visit to Hillport, and all the exacerbating scene of the funeral feast, in order that she might dwell tenderly upon his gestures, his glances, his remarks, the inflections of his voice. The eyes of her soul were ever beholding his form. Even at breakfast, after the disappointment of the post, she would indulge in ridiculous hopes that he might be abroad very early and would look in, and not until bedtime did she cease to listen for his ring at the front door. No chance of a meeting was too remote for her wild fancy. But she dared not breathe his name, dared not even adumbrate an inquiry; and her husband and daughters appeared to have entered into a compact not to mention him. She did not take counsel with herself, examine herself, demand from herself what was the significance of these symptoms; she could not; she could only live from one moment to the next engrossed in an eternal expectancy which instead of slackening became hourly more intense and painful. Towards the close of the afternoon of the third day, in the drawing-room, she whispered that something decisive must happen soon, soon.... The bell rang; her ears caught the distant sound for which they had so long waited. Shuddering, she thanked heaven that she was alone. She could hear the opening and closing of the front door. In three seconds Bessie would appear. She heard the knob of the drawing-room door turn, and to hide her agitation she glanced aside at the clock. It was a quarter to six. 'He will stay the evening, ' she thought.

'Mr. Dain, ' Bessie proclaimed.

'Oh, how do you do, Mrs. Stanway? Stanway not come in yet, eh? ' said the stout lawyer, approaching her hurriedly with his fussy, awkward gait.

She could have laughed; but the visit was at any rate a distraction.

A few minutes later John arrived.

'Dain will stay for tea, Nora. Eh, Dain? ' he said.

'Well—thanks, ' was Dain's reply.

She asked herself, with sudden misgiving, what new thing was afoot.

After tea, the two men were left together at the table.

'Mother, ' Ethel inquired eagerly, coming into the drawing-room, 'why are father and Mr. Dain measuring the dining-room? '

'I don't know, ' said Leonora. 'Are they? '

'Yes, Mr. Dain has got ever such a long tape. '

Leonora went into the kitchen and talked to the cook.

The next morning an idea occurred to her. Since the funeral, the girls had been down to see Uncle Meshach each afternoon, and Leonora had called at Church Street in the forenoon, so that the solitude of the old man might be broken at least twice a day. When she had suggested the arrangement to her husband, John had answered stiffly, with an unimpeachable righteousness, that everything possible must be done for his uncle. On this fourth day, Leonora sent Ethel and Milly in the morning, with a message that she herself would come in the afternoon, by way of change. The phrase that sang in her head was Arthur's promise to Meshach: 'I shall call in a day or two. ' She knew that he had not yet called. 'Don't wait tea, if I should be late, dears, ' she said smilingly to the girls; 'I may stay with uncle a while. ' And she nearly ran out of the house.

* * * * *

When they had had tea, and when Leonora had performed the delicate feat of arranging Uncle Meshach's domestic affairs without affronting his servant, she sat down opposite to him before the fire in the parlour.

'You're for stopping a bit, eh? ' he said, as if surprised.

'Well, ' she laughed, 'wouldn't you like me to? '

'Oh, ay! ' he admitted readily, 'I'st like it well enough. I don't know but what you aren't all on ye very good—you and th' wenches, and Fred as calls in of nights. But it's all one to me, I reckon. I take no pleasure i' life. Nay, ' he went on, 'it isn't because of *her*. I've felt as I was done for for months past. I mun just drag on. '

'Don't talk like that, uncle. ' She tried conventionally to cheer him. 'You must rouse yourself. '

'What for? '

She sought a good answer to this conundrum. 'For all of us, ' she said lamely, at length.

'Leonora, my lass, ' he remarked drily, 'you're no better than the rest of 'em. '

And as she sat there in the age-worn parlour, and thought of the distant days of his energy, when with his own hands he had pulled down a wall and replaced it by a glass partition, and of the night when he lay like a corpse on Ethel's bed at the mercy of his nephew, and of Aunt Hannah resting in the cold tomb just at the end of the street, her heart was filled for a moment with an awful, ineffable, devastating sadness. It seemed to her that every grief, anxiety, apprehension was joy itself compared to this supreme tragedy of natural decay.

'Shall I light the gas? ' she suggested. The room was always obscure, and that evening happened to be a sombre one.

'Ay! '

'There! ' she said brightly, when the gas flared, 'that's better, isn't it? Aren't you going to smoke? '

'Ay! '

In reaching a second spill from the spill-jar on the mantelpiece she noticed the clock. It was only a quarter past five. 'He may call yet, ' she dreamed, and then a more piquant thought: 'He may be at home when I get back. '

There was a perfunctory knock at the house-door. She started.

'It's the "Signal" lad, ' Meshach explained. 'He keeps on bringing it, but I never look at it. '

She went into the lobby for the paper, and then read aloud to Uncle Meshach the items of local news. The clock showed a quarter to six. Suddenly it struck her that Arthur Twemlow might have called quite early in the afternoon and that Meshach might have forgotten to tell her. If he had perchance called, and perchance informed Meshach that he was going on to Hillport, and if he had walked up by the road while she came down by the fields! The idea was too dreadful.

'Has Mr. Twemlow been to see you yet? ' she demanded, after a long silence, pretending to be interested in the 'Signal. '

'No, ' said Meshach; 'why dost ask? '

'I remembered he said he should. '

'He'll come, he'll come, ' Meshach murmured confidently. 'Dain's been in, ' he added, 'wi' papers to sign, probate o' Hannah's will. Seemingly John's not satisfied, from what Dain hints. '

'Not satisfied with what? ' Flushing a little, she dropped the paper; but she was still busily employed in expecting Arthur to arrive.

'Eh, I canna' tell you, lass. ' Meshach gave a grim sigh. 'You know as I altered my will? '

'Jack mentioned it. '

'Me and her, we thought it over. It was her as first said that Fred was getting a nice young chap, and very respectable, and why should he be left out in the cold? And so I says to her, I says, "Well, you can make your will i' favour o' Fred, if you've a mind. " "Nay, Meshach, " her says, "never ask me to cut out our John's name. " "Well, " I says to her, "if you won't, I will. It'll give 'em both an even chance. Us'n die pretty near together, me and you, Hannah, it'll be a toss-up, " I says. Wasn't that fair? ' Leonora made no reply. 'Wasn't that fair? ' he repeated.

She could not be sure, even then, whether Uncle Meshach had devised in perfect seriousness this extraordinary arrangement for dealing justly between the surviving members of the Myatt family, or whether he had always had a private humorous appreciation of the fantastic element in it.

'I don't know, ' she said.

'Well, lass, ' he continued persuasively, sitting up in his chair, 'us ignored young Fred for more till twenty year. And it wasna' right. Hannah said it wasna' right as Fred should suffer for his mother and his grandfeyther. And then us give Fred and your John an equal chance, and John's lost, and now John isna' satisfied, by all accounts. ' She gazed at him with a gentle smile. 'Why dostna' speak, lass? '

'What am I to say, uncle? '

'Wouldst like me to make a new will, and halve it between John and Fred? It wouldna' be fair to Fred, not rightly fair, because he's run his risk for th' lot. But wouldst like it, lass? '

There was a trace of the old vitality in his shrivelled features, as he laid this offering on the altar of her feminine charm.

'Oh, do, uncle! ' she was about to say eagerly, but she thought in the same instant of John standing over Meshach's body, with the ice-cold cloth in his hand, and something, some dim instinct of a fundamental propriety, prevented her from uttering those words. 'I would like you to do whatever you think right, ' she answered with calmness.

Meshach was evidently disappointed.

'I shall see, ' he ejaculated. And after a pause, 'John's i' smooth water again, isn't he? I meant to ask Dain. '

'I think so, ' said Leonora.

She had become restive. Soon afterwards she bade him good-night and departed. And all the way up to Hillport she speculated upon the chances of finding Arthur in her drawing-room when she got home.

* * * * *

As she passed through the hall she knew at once that Arthur was not in the house and had not been there; and the agitation of her heart subsided suddenly into the melancholy stillness of defeated hope. She sadly admitted that she no longer knew herself, and that the

Leonora of old had been supplanted by a creature of incalculable moods, a feeble victim of strange crises of secret folly. Through the open door of the drawing-room she could see Rose reading, and Millicent searching among a pile of music on the piano. Bessie emerged from the dining-room with a white cloth and the crumb-tray.

'Master's in there, ' said Bessie; 'they didn't wait tea, ma'am. '

Leonora went into the dining-room, where John sat alone at the bare mahogany, smoking. With her deep knowledge of him, she detected instantly that he had been annoyed by her absence from tea. The condition of the sharp end of his cigar showed that he was perturbed, fretful, and perhaps in a state of suspense. 'Well, ' she thought with resignation, 'I may as well play the wife, ' and she sat down in a chair near him, put her purse on the table, and smiled generously. Then she raised her veil, loosed the buttons of her new black coat, and began to draw off her gloves.

'I've been waiting for you, ' he said, and to her surprise his tone was extremely pacific.

'Have you? ' she answered, intensifying all her alluring grace. 'I hurried home. '

'Yes, I wanted to ask you——' He stopped, ostensibly to put the cigar into his meerschaum holder.

She perceived that the desire to ingratiate fought within him against his vexation, and she wondered, with a touch of cynicism, what new scheme had got possession of him, and how her assistance was necessary to it.

'Would you like to go and live in the country, Nora? ' He looked at her audaciously for a moment and then his eyes shifted.

'For the summer, you mean? '

'Yes, ' he said, 'for the summer and the winter too. Somewhere out Sneyd way. '

'And leave here? '

'Exactly. '

'But what about the house, Jack? '

'Sell it, if you like, ' said John lightly.

'Oh, no! I shouldn't like that at all, ' she replied, nervously but amiably. She wished to believe that his suggestion about selling the house was merely an idle notion thrown out on the spur of the moment, but she could not.

'You wouldn't? '

She shook her head. 'What has made you think of going to live in the country? ' she asked him, using a tone of gentle, mild curiosity. 'How should you get to the works in the morning? '

'There's a very good train service from Sneyd to Knype, ' he said. 'But look here, Nora, why wouldn't you care to sell the house? '

It was perfectly clear to her that, having mortgaged her house, he had now made up his mind to sell it. He must therefore still be in financial difficulties, and she had unwittingly misled Uncle Meshach.

'I don't know, ' she answered coldly. 'I can't explain to you why. But I shouldn't. ' And she privately resolved that nothing should induce her to assent to this monstrous proposal. Her heart hardened to steel. She felt prepared to suffer any unpleasantness, any indignity, rather than give way.

'It isn't as if Hillport wasn't changing, ' he went on, politely argumentative. 'It is changing. In another ten years all the decent estates will have been broken up, and we shall be left alone in the middle of streets of villas rented at nineteen guineas to escape the house duty. You know the sort of thing.... And I've had a very fair offer for the place. '

'Whom from? '

'Well, Dain. I know he's wanted the house a long time. Of course, he's a hard nut to crack, is Dain. But he went up to two thousand,

and yesterday I got him to make it guineas. That's a good price, Nora. '

'Is it? ' she exclaimed absently.

'I should just imagine it was! ' said John.

So it was expected of her that she should surrender her home, her domain, her kingdom, the beautiful and mellow creation of her intelligence; and that she should surrender it to David Dain, and to the impossible Mrs. Dain, and to their impossible niece. She remembered one of Milly's wicked tales about Mrs. Dain and the niece. Milly had met Mrs. Dain in the street, and in response to an inquiry about the health of the hypochondriacal niece, Mrs. Dain, gorgeously attired, had replied: 'Her had but just rallied up off th' squab as I come out. ' These were the people who wanted to evict her from her house. And they would cover its walls with new papers, and its floors with new carpets, in their own appalling taste; and they would crowd the rooms with furniture as fat, clumsy, and disgusting as themselves. And Mrs. Dain would hold sewing meetings in the drawing-room, and would stand chattering with tradesmen at the front door, and would drive out to Sneyd to pay a call on Leonora and tell her how *pleased* they all were with the place!

'Do you absolutely need the money, John? ' She came to the point with a frank, blunt directness which angered him.

'I don't absolutely need anything, ' he retorted, controlling himself. 'But Dain made the offer— —'

'Because if you do, ' she proceeded, 'I dare say Uncle Meshach— —'

'Look here, my girl, ' he interrupted in turn, 'I've had exactly as much of Uncle Meshach as I can stand. I know all about Uncle Meshach, what I wanted to know was whether you cared to sell the house. ' And then he added, after hesitating, and with a false graciousness, 'To oblige me. '

There was a marked pause.

'I really shouldn't like to sell the house, John, ' she answered quietly. 'It was aunt's, and— —'

'Enough said! enough said! ' he cried. 'That finishes it. I suppose you don't mind my having asked you! '

He walked out of the room in a rage.

Tears came into her eyes, the tears of a wounded and proud heart. Was it conceivable that he expected her to be willing to sell her house?... He must indeed be in serious straits. She would consult Uncle Meshach.

The front door banged. And then Rose entered the room.

Leonora drove back the tears.

'Your father has been suggesting that we sell this house, and go and live at Sneyd, ' she said to the girl in a trembling voice. 'Aren't you surprised? ' She seldom talked about John to her daughters, but at that moment a desire for sympathy overwhelmed her.

'I should never be surprised at anything where father was concerned, ' said Rose coldly, with a slight hint of aloofness and of mental superiority. 'Not at anything. '

Leonora got up, and, leaving the room, went into the garden through the side door opposite the stable. She could hear Millicent practising the Jewel Song from Gounod's *Faust*. As she passed down the sombre garden the sound of the piano and of Milly's voice in the brilliant ecstatic phrases of the song grew fainter. She shook violently, like a child who is recovering from a fit of sobs, and without thinking she fastened her coat. 'What a shame it is that he should want to sell my house! What a shame! ' she murmured, full of an aggrieved resentment. At the same time she was surprised to find herself so suddenly and so deeply disturbed.

* * * * *

At the foot of the long garden was a low fence separating it from the meadow, and in the fence a wicket from which ran a faint track to the main field-path. She leaned against the fence, a few yards away from the wicket, at a spot where a clump of bushes screened the house. No one could possibly have seen her from the house, even had the bushes not been there; but she wished to isolate herself completely, and to find tranquillity in the isolation. The calm spring night, chill but not too cold, cloudy but not too dark, favoured her intention. She gazed about her at the obscure nocturnal forms of things, at the silent trees, and the mysterious clouds gently rounded in their vast shape, and the sharp slant of the meadow. Far below could be seen the red signal of the railway, and, mapped in points of light on the opposite slope, the streets of Bursley. To the right the eternal conflagration of the Cauldon Bar furnaces illumined the sky with wavering amber. And on the keen air came to her from the distance noises, soft but impressive, of immense industrial activities.

She thought she could decipher a figure moving from the field-path across the gloom of the meadow, and as she strained her eyes the figure became an indubitable fact. Presently she knew that it was Arthur. 'At last! ' her heart passionately exclaimed, and she was swept and drenched with happiness as a ship by the ocean. She forgot everything in the tremendous shock of joy. She felt as though she could have waited no more, and that now she might expire in a bliss intense and fatal, in a sigh of supreme content. She could not stir nor speak, and he was striding towards the wicket unconscious of her nearness! She coughed, a delicate feminine cough, and then he turned aside from the direction of the wicket and approached the fence, peering.

'Is that you? ' he asked.

'Yes. '

Across the fence they clasped hands. And in spite of her great wish not to do so she clutched his hand tightly in her long fingers, and held it for a moment. And as she felt the returning pressure of his large, powerful, protective grasp, she covered—but in imagination only—she covered his face, which she could shadowily see, with brave and abandoned kisses; and she whispered to him, but unheard: 'Admit that I am made for love. ' She feared, in those beautiful and shameless instants, neither John, nor Ethel and Milly, nor even Rose. She knew suddenly why men and women leave all— honour, duty, and affection—and follow love. Then her arm dropped, and there was silence.

'What are you doing here? ' She was unable to speak in an ordinary tone, but she spoke. Her voice exquisitely trembled, and its vibrations said everything that the words did not say.

'Why, ' he answered, and his voice too bore strange messages, 'I called at Church Street and Mr. Myatt said you had only been gone a few minutes, and so I came right away. I guessed I should overtake you. I don't know what he would think. ' Arthur laughed nervously.

She smiled at him, satisfied. And how well she knew that her smiling face, caught by him dimly in the obscurity of the night, troubled him like an enchanting and enigmatic vision!

After they had looked at each other, speechless, for a while, the strong influence of convention forced them again into unnecessary, irrelevant talk.

'What's this about you selling this place? ' he inquired in a low, mild tone.

'Have you heard? '

'Yes, ' he said, 'I did hear something. '

'Ah! ' she murmured, wrinkling her forehead in a pretty make-believe of woe—the question of the sale had ceased to be acute: 'I just came out here to think about it. '

'But you aren't really going to——'

'No, of course not. '

She had no desire to discuss the tedious affair, because she was infallibly certain of his entire sympathy. Explanations on her side, and assurances on his, were equally superfluous.

'But won't you come into the house? ' She invited him as a sort of afterthought.

'Why? ' he demanded bluntly.

She hesitated before replying: 'It will look so queer, us staying here like this. ' As soon as she had uttered the words she suspected that she had said something decisive and irretrievable.

He put his hands into the pockets of his overcoat and walked several times to and fro a few paces. Then he stopped in front of her.

175

'I guess we are bound to look queer, you and I, some day. So it may as well be now, ' he said.

It was in this exchange of sentences that their mutual passion became at length articulate. A single discreet word spoken quickly, and she might even yet perhaps have withdrawn from the situation. But she did not speak; she could not speak; and soon she knew that her own silence had bound her. She yielded herself with poignant and magnificent joy to the profound drama which had been magically created by this apparently commonplace dialogue. The climax had been achieved, and she was conscious of being lifted into a sublime exultation, and of being cut off from all else in the world save him. She looked at him intently with a sadness that was the cloak of celestial rapture. 'How courageous you are! ' her soft eyes said. 'I should never have dared. What a *man*! ' It seemed to her that her heart would break under the strain of that ecstasy. She had not imagined the possibility of such bliss.

'Listen! ' he proceeded. 'I ought to be in New York—I oughtn't to be here. I must tell you. Scarcely a fortnight ago, one afternoon while I was working in my office in Fourteenth Street, I had a feeling I would be bound to come over. I said to myself the idea was preposterous. But the next thing I knew I was arranging to come. I couldn't believe I was coming. Not even when I had booked my berth and boarded the steamer, not even when the steamer was actually passing Sandy Hook, could I believe that I was really coming. I said to myself I was mad. I said to myself that no man in his senses could behave as I was behaving. And when I got to Southampton I said I would go right back. And yet I couldn't help getting into the special for London. And when I got to London I said I would act sensible and go back. But I met young Burgess, and the next thing I knew I was at Euston. And here I am pretending that it's my new London branch that brings me over, and doing business I don't want to do in Knype and Cauldon and Bursley. And I'm killing myself—yes, I am; I tell you I couldn't stand much more—and I wouldn't be sure I wasn't killing you. Some folks would say the whole thing was perfectly dreadful, but I don't care so long as you— so long as you don't. I'm not conceited really, but it looks like conceit—me talking like this and assuming that you're ready to stand and listen. I assure you it isn't conceit. I only know—that's all. It's difficult for you to say anything—I can feel that—but I'd like you just to tell me you're glad I came and glad I've spoken. I'd just like to hear that. '

176

She gazed fondly at him, at the male creature in whom she could find only perfection, and she was filled with glorious pride that her image should have drawn this strong, shrewd self-possessed man across the Atlantic. It was incredible, but it was true. 'And, ' said the secret feminine in her, 'why not? '

He waited for her answer, facing her.

'Oh, yes! ' she breathed. 'Oh, yes!... I'm glad—I'm so glad. '

'I wish, ' he broke out, 'I wish I could explain to you what I think of you, what I feel about you. You're so quiet and simple and direct and yet—you don't know it, but you are. You're absolutely the most—Oh! it's no use. '

She saw that he was growing very excited, and this, too, gave her deep pleasure.

'We're in a hell of a fix! ' he sighed.

Like many women, she took a fearful, almost thrilling joy in hearing a man swear earnestly and religiously.

'That's it, ' she said, 'there's nothing to be done? '

'Nothing to be done? ' he demanded, imperiously. 'Nothing to be done? '

She examined his face, which was close to hers, with a meditative, expectant smile. She loved to see him out of repose, eager, masterful, and daring. 'What is there to be done? ' she asked.

'I don't know yet, ' he said firmly, 'I must think. ' Then, in a delicious surrender, she felt towards him as though they were on the brink of a rushing river, and he was about to pick her up in his arms, like a trifle, and carry her safely through the flood; and she had the illusion of pressing her face, which she knew he adored, against his shoulder.

'Oh, you innocent angel! ' he cried, seizing her hand (she let it lie inert), 'do you suppose I'm the sort of man to sit down and cross my legs and say that fate, or whatever you call it, hasn't done me right? Do you suppose that two sensible persons like you and me are going to be beaten by a mere set of circumstances? We aren't children, and we aren't fools. '

'But— —'

'You're not afraid, are you? ' He drank in her charm.

'What of? '

'Anything. '

'It's when you aren't there, ' she murmured tenderly. She really thought, then, that by some marvellous plan he would perform the impossible feat of reconciling the duty of fulfilling love with all the other duties.

'I shall reckon it up, ' he said. 'Ah! '

Silence fell. And with the feel of the grass under her feet, and the soft clouds overhead, and the patient trees, and the glare in the southern smoke, and the lamps of Bursley, and the solitary red signal in the valley, she breathed out her spirit like an aerial essence, and merged into unity with him. And the strange far-off noises of nocturnal industry wandered faintly across the void and seemed fraught with a mysterious significance. Everything, in that unique hour, had the same mysterious significance.

'Mother! ' Millicent's distant voice, fresh and strong and pure in the night, chanted the word startlingly to the first notes of a phrase from the Jewel Song. 'Mother! Aren't you coming in? ' The girl finished the phrase with inviting gaiety, holding the final syllable. And the sound faded, went out, like the flare of a rocket in the sky, and the dark stillness was emphasised.

They did not move; they did not speak; but Leonora pressed his hand. The passing thought of the orderly, multifarious existence of the house behind her, of the warmed and lighted rooms, of the preoccupied lives, only increased the felicity of her halcyon dream. And in the dreamy and brooding silence all things retreated and gradually lapsed away, and the pair were left sole amid the ineffable spaces of the universe to listen to the irregular beatings of their own hearts. Time itself had paused.

'Mother! ' Millicent sang again, nearer, more strongly and purely in the night. 'We are waiting for you to come in! ' She varied a little the phrase from the Jewel Song. 'To come in! ' The long sustained notes seemed to become a beautiful warning, and then the sound expired.

Leonora withdrew her hand.

'I shall think it out, and write you to-morrow, ' Arthur whispered, and was gone.

* * * * *

The next day, after a futile morning of hesitations, Leonora decided in the afternoon that she would go out for a walk and return in some definite state of mind. She loosed Bran, and the dog, when he had finished his elephantine gambades, followed her close at heel, with all stateliness, to the wide marsh on the brow of the hill. Here she began actively and seriously to cogitate.

John was sulking; and it was seldom that he sulked. He had not spoken to her again, neither on the previous evening nor at breakfast; he had said nothing whatever to any one, except to tell Bessie that he should not be at home for dinner; on committee-meeting days, when he was engaged at the Town Hall, John sometimes dined at the Tiger. His attitude produced small effect on Leonora. She was far too completely absorbed in herself to be perturbed by the offensive symptoms of her husband's wrath. She had neglected even to call on Uncle Meshach; and as she strolled about the marsh she thought vaguely and perfunctorily that she must see Uncle Meshach soon and acquaint him with John's difficulties.

Pride as much as joy and alarm filled her heart. She was proud of her perilous love; she would have liked proudly to confide it to some friend, some mature and brilliant woman who knew the world and understood things, and who would talk rationally; it seemed to her that this secret idyll, at once tender and sincere and rather dashing, was worthy of pride. She knew that many women, languishing in the greyness of an impeccable and frigid domesticity, would be capable of envying her; she remembered that, in reading the newspapers, she had sometimes timidly envied the heroines of the matrimonial court who had bought romance at the price of esteem and of peace. Then suddenly the whole matter slipped into unreality, and she could not credit it. Was it possible that she, a respectable matron, a known figure, the mother of adult daughters, had fallen in love with a man not her husband, had had a secret interview with her lover, and was anticipating, not a retreat, but an advance? And she thought, as every honest woman has thought in like case: 'This may happen to others; one hears of it, one reads about it; but surely it cannot have happened to *me*! ' And when she had admitted that it had in fact happened to her, and had perceived with a kind of shock that the heroines of the matrimonial court were real persons, everyday creatures of flesh-and-blood, she thought, again like the rest: 'Ah! But my affair is different from all the others. There is something in it, something indefinable and precious, which makes it different. '

She said: 'Can one help falling in love? Can one be blamed for that? '

For John she had little compassion, and the gay and feverish existence of New York spread out invitingly before her in a vision full of piquant contrasts with the death-in-life of the Five Towns! But her beloved girls! They were an insuperable barrier. She could not leave them; she could not forfeit the right to look them in the eyes without embarrassment... And then the next moment—somehow, she did not know how—the difficulty of the girls was arranged. And she had departed. She had left the Five Towns for ever. And she was in the train, in the hotel, on the steamer; she saw every detail of the escape. Oh! The rapture! The tremors! The long sigh! The surrender! The intense living! Surely no price could be too great....

No! Common sense, the acquirement of forty years, supervened, and informed her wild heart, with all the cold arrogance of sagacity, that these imaginings were vain. She felt that she must write a brief and firm letter to Arthur and tell him to desist. She saw with extraordinary clearness that this course was inevitable. And lest her resolution might slacken, she turned instantly towards home and began to hurry. The dog glanced up questioningly, and hurried too.

'Why! ' she reflected. 'People would say: "And her husband's aunt scarcely cold in her grave! "' She laughed scornfully.

A carriage overtook her. It was Mrs. Dain's, coming from the direction of Oldcastle.

'Good afternoon to you, ' Mrs. Dain shouted, without stopping, and then, when she caught sight of Bran: 'Bless us! The dog hasn't brukken his leg after all! '

'Broken his leg! ' Leonora repeated, astonished. The carriage was now in front of her.

'Our Polly come in this morning and sat hersen down on a chair and told us as your dog had brukken his leg. What tales one hears! ' Mrs. Dain had to twist her stout neck dangerously in order to finish the sentence.

'I should think so! ' was Leonora's private comment, her gaze fixed on the scarlet of Mrs. Dain's nodding bonnet.

In the little room off the dining-room Leonora dipped pen in ink to write to Arthur. She wrote the date, and she wrote the word 'Dear. ' And she could not proceed. She knew that she could not compose a letter which would be effective. She went to the window and looked out, biting the pen. 'What am I to do? ' she whispered, in terror. 'What am I to do? ' Then she saw Ethel running hard down the drive to the front door.

'Oh, mother! ' The pale girl burst into the room. 'Father's done something to himself. Fred's come up. They're bringing him. '

* * * * *

John Stanway had called at the chemist's in the Market Place and had given a circumstantial description of an accident to Bran. It appeared that while Carpenter was washing the waggonette, Bran being loose in the stable-yard, the groom had suddenly slipped the lever of the carriage-jack and the off hind wheel had caught Bran's hind leg and snapped it like a piece of wood. The chemist had suggested prussic acid, and John had laughingly answered that perhaps the chemist would be good enough to come up and show them how to administer prussic acid to a dog of Bran's size in great pain. John explained that the animal was now fast by the collar, and he had demanded a large dose of morphia, together with a hypodermic instrument. Having obtained these, and precise instructions for their use, John had hurried away. It was not till three hours had elapsed that a startling suspicion had disturbed the chemist's easy mind. By that time, his preparations completed, John had dropped unconscious from the arm-chair in his office at the works, and Bursley was provided with one of those morbid sensations which more than joy or triumph electrify the stagnant pulses of a provincial town. Scores of persons followed the cab which conveyed Stanway from the works to his house; and on the route most of the inhabitants seemed to know in advance, by some strange intuition, that the vehicle was coming, and at their windows or at their gates (according to social status) they stood ready to watch it pass. And even after John had entered his home and had been carried upstairs, and the cab and the policeman had gone, and the doctor had gone, and Fred Ryley and Mr. Mayer, the works manager, had gone, a crowd still remained on the footpath, staring at the gravelled drive and at the front door, silent, patient, implacable.

The doctor had tried hot coffee, artificial respiration, and other remedies, but without the least success, and he had reluctantly departed, solemn for once, leaving four women to understand that there was nothing to do save to wait for the final sigh. The inactivity was dreadful for them. They could only look at each other and think, and move to and fro aimlessly in the large bedroom, and light the gas at dusk, and examine from moment to moment those contracted pupils and that damp white brow, and listen for the faint occasional breaths. They did not think the thoughts which, could they have foreseen the situation, they might have expected to think. It did not occur to them to search for the causes of the disaster, nor to speculate upon its results in regard to themselves: they surrendered to the supreme fact. They were all incapable of logical and ordered reflections, and in the hushed torpor of their secret hearts there wandered, loosely, little disconnected ideas and sensations; as that the Stanway family was at length getting its full share of vicissitude and misfortune, that John was after all more important and more truly dominant and more intimately a part of their lives than they had imagined, that this affair was a thousand miles removed from that of Uncle Meshach, that they were fully supplied with mourning, and that suicide was mysteriously different from their previous notion of it. The impressive thoughts, the obvious thoughts—that if their creeds were sound, a soul was about to enter into eternal torment, and that their lives would be violently changed, and that they would be branded before the world as the wife and the daughters of a defaulter and a self-murderer—did not by any means absorb their minds in those first hours.

Leonora

In the attitude of the girls towards Leonora there was a sort of religious deference, as of priestesses to one soon to be sacrificed. 'She is the central figure of the tragedy, ' they had the air of saying to each other. 'We feel the affliction, but it cannot be demanded from us that we should feel it as she feels it. We are only beginning to live; we have the future; but she—she will have nothing. She will be the widow. ' And the significance of that terrible word—all that it implied of social diminishment, of feeding on memory, and of mere waiting for death—seemed to cling about Leonora as she stood restlessly observant by the bed. And when Rose urged her to drink some tea, she could not help drinking the tea humbly, from a sense of the duty of doing what she was told. It was not Rose's fault that Rose was superior, and that only twenty-four hours ago she had coldly informed her mother that no act of her father's would surprise her. Leonora resigned herself to humility.

'Mamma, ' said Millicent, creeping into the room after an absence, 'Uncle Meshach is here with Mr. Twemlow, and he says he's coming in. Must he? '

'Of course, darling, ' Leonora answered, without turning her head.

Uncle Meshach appeared, leaning on his stick and on Arthur's arm. He wore his overcoat and even his hat, and a white knitted muffler encircled his shrivelled neck in loose folds. No one spoke as the old and feeble man, with short uncertain steps, drew Arthur towards the bed and gazed at his dying nephew. Meshach looked long, and sighed. Suddenly he demanded of Leonora in a whisper:

'Is he unconscious? '

Leonora nodded.

Drawing a little nearer to the bed, Meshach signed to Millicent to approach, and gave her his stick. Then he unbuttoned his overcoat, and his coat, and the flap-pocket of his trousers, and after much searching found a box of matches. He shook out a match clumsily, and struck it, and came still nearer to the bed. All wondered apprehensively what the old man was going to do, but none dared interfere or protest because he was so old, and so precariously attached to life, and because he was the head of the family. With his thin, veined, trembling hand, he passed the lighted match close across John's eyeballs; not a muscle twitched. Then he extinguished the match, put it in the box, returned the box to his pocket, and buttoned the pocket and his coats.

'Ay! ' he breathed. 'The lad's unconscious right enough. Let's be going. '

Taking his stick from Milly, he clutched Arthur's arm again, and very slowly left the room.

After a moment's hesitation Leonora followed and overtook them at the bottom of the stairs; it was the first time she had forsaken the bedside. She was surprised to see Fred Ryley in the hall, self-conscious but apparently determined to be quite at home. She remembered that he said he should come up again as soon as he had arranged matters at the works.

'Just take Mr. Myatt to the cab, will you? ' said Twemlow quietly to Fred. 'I'll follow. '

'Certainly, ' Fred agreed, pulling his moustache nervously. 'Now, Mr. Myatt, let me help you. '

'Ay! ' said Meshach. 'Thou shalt help me if thou'n a mind. ' As he was feeling for the step with his stick he stopped and looked round at Leonora. 'Lass! ' he exclaimed, 'thou toldst me John was i' smooth water. ' Then he departed and they could hear his shuffling steps on the gravel.

Twemlow glanced inquiringly at Leonora.

'Come in here, ' she said briefly, pointing to the drawing-room. They entered; it was dark.

'Your uncle made me drive up with him, ' Arthur explained, as if in apology.

She ignored the remark. 'You must go back to New York—at once, ' she told him, in a dry, curt voice.

'Yes, ' he assented, 'I suppose I'd better. '

'And don't write to me—until after I have written. '

184

'Oh, but— —' he began.

She thought wildly: 'This man, with his reason and his judgment, has not the slightest notion how I feel, not the slightest! '

'I must write, ' he said in a persuasive tone.

'No! ' she cried passionately and vehemently. 'You aren't to write, and you aren't to see me. You must promise, absolutely. '

'For how long? ' he asked.

She shook her head. 'I don't know, I can't tell. '

'But isn't that rather— —'

'Will you promise? ' she cried once more, quite loudly and almost fiercely. And her accents were so full of entreaty, of command, and of despair, that Arthur feared a nervous crisis for her.

'If you wish it, ' he said, forced to yield.

And even then she could not be content.

'You give me your word to do nothing at all until you hear from me?'

He paused, but he saw no alternative to submission. 'Yes. '

She thanked him, and without shaking hands or saying good-night she went upstairs and resumed her place by the bedside. She could hear Uncle Meshach's cab drive away.

'How came Mr. Twemlow to be here, mother? ' Rose demanded quietly.

'I don't know, ' Leonora replied. 'He must have been at uncle's. '

When the doctor had been again and gone, and various neighbours and the 'Signal' reporter had called to inquire for news, and the hour was growing late, Ethel said to her mother, 'Fred thinks he had better stay all night. '

Leonora

'But why? ' Leonora asked.

'Well, mother, ' said Milly, 'it's just as well to have a man in the house. '

'He can rest on the Chesterfield in the drawing-room, ' Ethel added. 'Then if he's wanted — —'

'Yes, yes, ' Leonora agreed. 'And tell him he's very kind. '

At midnight, Fred was reading in the drawing-room, the man in the house, the ultimate fount of security for seven women. Bessie, having refused positively to go to bed, slept in a chair in the kitchen, her heels touching the scrap of hearthrug which lay like a little island on the red tiles in front of the range. Rose and Millicent had retired to bed till three o'clock. Ethel, as the eldest, stayed with her mother. When the hall-clock sounded one, meaning half past twelve, Leonora glanced at her daughter, who reclined on the sofa at the foot of the beds; the girl had fallen into a doze.

John's condition was unchanged; the doctor had said that he might possibly survive for many hours. He lay on his back, with open eyes, and damp face and hair; his arms rested inert on the sheet; and underneath that thin covering his chest rose and fell from time to time, with a scarcely perceptible movement. It seemed to Leonora that she could realise now what had happened and what was to happen. In the nocturnal solemnity of the house filled with sleeping and quiescent youth, she who was so mature and so satiate had the sensation of being alone with her mate. Images of Arthur Twemlow did not distract her. With the full strength of her mind she had shut an iron door on the episode in the garden; it was as though it had never existed. And she gazed at John with calm and sad compassion. 'I would not sell my home, ' she reflected, 'and here is the consequence of refusal. ' She wished she had yielded — and she could perceive how unimportant, comparatively, bricks-and-mortar might be — but she did not blame herself for not having yielded. She merely regretted her sensitive obstinacy as a misfortune for both of them. She had a vision of humanity in a hurried procession, driven along by some force unseen and ruthless, a procession in which the grotesque and the pitiable were always occurring. She thought of John standing over Meshach with the cold towel, and of Meshach passing the flame across John's dying eyes, and these juxtapositions appeared to her intolerably mournful in their ridiculous grimness.

Impelled by a physical curiosity, she lifted the sheet and scrutinised John's breast, so pallid against the dark red of his neck, and bent down to catch the last tired efforts of the heart within. And the idea of her extraordinary intimacy with this man, of the incessant familiarity of more than twenty years, struck her and overwhelmed her. She saw that nothing is so subtly influential as constant uninterrupted familiarity, nothing so binding, and perhaps nothing so sacred. It was a trifle that they had not loved. They had lived. Ah! she knew him so profoundly that words could not describe her knowledge. He kept his own secrets, hundreds of them; and he had, in a way, astounded and shocked her by his suicide. Yet, in another way, this miserable termination did not at all surprise her; and his secrets were petty, factual things of no essential import, which left her mystic omniscience of him unimpaired.

She looked at his eyes, and thought pitifully: 'These eyes cannot see that I uncover him. ' Then she looked again at his breast, which heaved in shallow respirations. And at the moment he exhaled a sigh, so softly delicate and gentle that it might have been the sigh of an infant sinking to sleep. She put her ear quickly to the still breast, as to a sea-shell, and listened intently, and caught no rumour of life there. Startled, she glanced at the jaw, which had dropped, and then at Ethel dozing on the sofa.

The room was filled for her with the majestic sound of trumpets, loud, sustained, and thrilling, but heard only by the soul; a noble and triumphant fanfare announcing the awful advent of those forces which are beyond the earthly sense. John's body lay suddenly deserted and residual; that deceitful brain, and that lying tongue, and that murderous hand had already begun to decay; and the informing fragment of eternal and universal energy was gone to its next manifestation and its next task, unconscious, irresponsible, and unchanged. The ineptitude of human judgments had been once more emphasised, and the great excellence of charity.

'Ethel, ' said Leonora timorously, waking with a touch the young and beautiful girl whose flushed cheek was pressed against the cushion of the sofa. 'He's gone.... Call Fred. '

CHAPTER XI

THE REFUSAL

Fifteen months after John's death, and the inquest on his body, and the clandestine funeral, Leonora sat alone one evening in the garden of the house at Hillport. She wore a black dress trimmed with jet; a narrow band of white muslin clasped her neck, and from her shoulders hung a long thin antique gold chain, once the ornament of Aunt Hannah. Her head was uncovered, and the mild breeze which stirred the new leaves of the poplars moved also the stray locks of her hair. Her calm and mature beauty was unchanged; it was a common remark in the town that during the past year she had looked handsomer than ever, more content, radiant, and serene. 'And it's not surprising, either! ' people added. The homestead appeared to be as of old. Carpenter was feeding Prince in the stable; Bran lay huge and benign at the feet of his mistress; the borders of the lawn were vivid with bloom; and within the house Bessie still ruled the kitchen. No luxury was abated, and no custom altered. Time apparently had nothing to show there, save an engagement ring on Bessie's finger. Many things, however, had occurred; but they had seemed to occur so placidly, and the days had been so even, that the term of her widowhood was to Leonora more like three months than fifteen, and she often reminded herself: 'It was last spring, not this, that he died. '

'The business is right enough! ' Fred Ryley had said positively, with an emphasis on the word 'business, ' when he met Leonora and Uncle Meshach in family council, during the first week of the disaster; and Meshach had replied: 'Thou shalt prove it, lad! ' The next morning Mr. Mayer, the manager, and everybody on the bank, learned that Fred, with old Myatt at his back, was in sole control of the works at Shawport; creditors breathed with relief; and the whole of Bursley remembered that it had always prophesied that Fred's sterling qualities were bound to succeed. Meshach lent several thousands of pounds to Fred at five per cent., and Fred was to pay half the net profits of the business to Leonora as long as she lived. The youth did not change his lodgings, nor his tailor, nor his modest manners; but he became nevertheless suddenly important, and none appreciated this fact better than Mr. Mayer, whose sandy hair was getting grey, and who, having six children but no rich great-uncle, could never hope to earn more than three pounds a week. Fred was now an official member of the Myatt clan, and, in the town, men of position, pompous individuals who used to ignore him, greeted the sole principal of Twemlow & Stanway's with a certain cordiality. After an interval his engagement to Ethel was announced. Every evening he came up to Hillport. The couple were ardently and openly in love; they expected always to have the dining-room at their private disposal, and they had it. Ethel simply adored him, and he was immeasurably proud of her. Even in presence of the family they would sit hand in hand, making no attempt to conceal their bliss. For the rest Fred's attitude to Leonora was very affectionate and deferential; it touched her, though she knew he worshipped her ignorantly. Rose and Millicent wondered 'what Ethel could see in him'; he was neither amusing nor smart nor clever, nor even vivacious; he had little acquaintance with games, music, novels, or the feminist movement; he was indeed rather dull; but they liked him because he was fundamentally and invariably 'nice. ' At the close of the year of Stanway's death, Fred had paid to Leonora four hundred and fifty pounds as her share of the profits of the firm for nine months. But long before that Leonora was rich. Uncle Meshach had died and left her the Myatt fortune for life, with remainder to the three girls absolutely in equal shares. Fred was the executor and trustee, and Fred's own share of the bounty was a total remission of Meshach's loan to him. Thus it is that providence watches over the wealthy, the luxurious, and the well-connected, and over the lilies of the field who toil not.

Aroused from lethargy by the dramatic circumstances of her father's death, Rose had resumed her reading with a vigour that amounted almost to fury. In the following January she miraculously passed the Matriculation examination of London University in the first division, and on returning home she informed Leonora that she had decided to go back to London and study medicine at a hospital for women.

But of the three girls, it was Millicent who had made the most history. Millicent was rapidly developing the natural gift, so precious to the theatrical artist, of existing picturesquely in the eye of the public. When the rehearsals of *Princess Ida* began for the annual performance of the Operatic Society Milly confidently expected to receive the principal part, despite the fact that Lucy Turner, who had the prescriptive right to it, was once more in a position to sing; and Milly was not disappointed. As a heroine of comic opera she now accounted herself an extremely serious person, and it soon became apparent that the conductor and his prima donna would have to decide between them who was to control the rehearsals while Milly was on the stage. One evening a difference of opinion as to the *tempo* of a song and chorus reached the condition of being acute. Exasperated by the pretty and wayward child, the conductor laid down his stick and lighted a cigarette, and those who knew him knew that the rehearsal would not proceed until the duel had been fought to a finish. Milly thought hard and said: 'Mr. Corfe says the Hanbridge people would jump at me! ' 'My good girl, ' the conductor replied, 'Mr. Corfe's views on the acrobatic propensities of the Hanbridge people are just a shade off the point. ' Every one laughed, except Milly. She possessed little appreciation of wit, and she had scarcely understood the remark; but she had an objection to the laughter, and a very strong objection to being the conductor's good girl. The instant result was that she vowed never again to sing or act under his baton, and took the entire Society to witness; her place was filled by Lucy Turner. The Hanbridge Society happened to be doing *Patience* that year, and they justified Mr. Corfe's prediction. Moreover, they hired the Hanbridge Theatre Royal for six nights. On the first night Milly was enthusiastically applauded by two thousand people, and in addition to half a column of praise in the 'Signal, ' she had the happiness of being mentioned in the district news of the 'Manchester Guardian' and the 'Birmingham Daily Post. ' She deemed it magnificent for her; Leonora tried to think so too. But on the fourth day the Hanbridge conductor was in bed with influenza; and the Bursley conductor, upon a flattering request, undertook his work for the remaining nights. Milly broke her vow; her practical common sense was really wonderful. On the last and most glorious night of the six, after responding to several frenzied calls, Milly was inspired to seize the conductor in the wings and drag him with her before the curtain. The effect was tremendous. The conductor had won, but he very willingly admitted that, in losing, the adorable chit had triumphed over him. The episode was gossip for many days.

And this was by no means the end of the matter. The agent-in-advance of one of the touring musical-comedy companies of Lionel Belmont, the famous Anglo-American manager, was in Hanbridge during that week, and after seeing Milly in the piece he telegraphed to Liverpool, where his company was, and the next day the manager visited Hanbridge incognito. Then Harry Burgess began to play a part in Millicent's history. Harry had abandoned his stool at the Bank, expressing his intention to undertake some large commercial enterprise; he had persuaded his mother to find the capital. The leisurely search for a large commercial enterprise precisely suited to

Harry's tastes necessitated frequent sojourns in London. Harry became a man-about-town and a member of the renowned New Fantastics Club. The New Fantastics were powerful supporters of the dramatic art, and the roll of the club included numerous theatrical stars of magnitudes varying from the first to the tenth. It was during one of the club's official excursions—in pantechnicon vans—to a suburban theatre where a good French actress was performing, that Harry made the acquaintance of that important man, Louis Lewis, Belmont's head representative in Europe. Louis Lewis, over champagne, asked Harry if he knew a Millicent Stanway of Bursley. The effect of the conversation was that Harry came home and astounded Milly by telling her what Louis Lewis had authorised him to say. There were conferences between Leonora and Milly and Mr. Cecil Corfe, a journey to Manchester, hesitations, excitations, thrills, and in the end an arrangement. Millicent was to go to London to be finally appraised, and probably to sign a contract for a sixteen-weeks provincial tour at three pounds a week.

* * * * *

Leonora's prevailing mood was the serenity of high resolve and of resignation. She had renounced the chance of ecstasy. She was sad, but she was not unhappy. The melancholy which filled the secret places of her soul was sweet and radiant, and she had proved the ancient truth that he who gives up all, finds all. Still in rich possession of beauty and health, she nevertheless looked forward to nothing but old age—an old age of solitude and sufferance. Hannah and Meshach were gone; John was gone; and she alone seemed to be left of the elder generations. In four days Ethel was to be married. Already for more than three months Rose had been in London, and in a fortnight Leonora was to take Millicent there. And when Ethel was married and perhaps a mother, and Rose versed and absorbed in the art and craft of obstetrics, and the name of Millicent familiar in the mouths of clubmen, what was Leonora to do then? She could not control her daughters; she could scarcely guide them. Ethel knew only one law, Fred's wish; and Rose had too much intellect, and Millicent too little heart, to submit to her. Since John's death the house had been the abode of peace and amiability, but it had also been Liberty Hall. If sometimes Leonora regretted that she could not more dominantly impress herself upon her children, she never doubted that on the whole the new republic was preferable to the old tyranny. What then had she to do? She had to watch over her girls, and especially over Rose and Milly. And as she sat in the garden with Bran at her feet, in the solitude which foreshadowed the more poignant solitude to come, she said to herself with passionate maternity: 'I shall watch over them. If anything occurs I shall always be ready. ' And this blissful and transforming thought, this vehement purpose, allayed somewhat the misgivings which she had long had about Millicent, and which her recent glimpses into the factitious and erratic world of the theatre had only served to increase.

It was Milly's affair which had at length brought Leonora to the point of communicating with Arthur Twemlow. In the first weeks of widowhood, the most terrible of her life, she could not dream of writing to him. Then the sacrifice had dimly shaped itself in her mind, and while actually engaged in fighting against it she hesitated to send any message whatever. And when she realised that the sacrifice was inevitable for her, when she inwardly knew that Arthur and the splendid rushing life of New York must be renounced in obedience to the double instinct of maternity and of repentance, she could not write. She felt timorous; she was unable to frame the sentences. And she procrastinated, ruled by her characteristic quality of supineness. Once she heard that he had been over to London and gone back; she drew a deep breath as though a peril had been escaped, and procrastinated further. Then came the overtures from Lionel Belmont, or at least from his agents, to Milly. Belmont was a New Yorker, and the notion suddenly struck her of writing to Arthur for information about Belmont. It was a capricious notion, but it provided an extrinsic excuse for a letter which might be followed by another of more definite import. In the end she was obliged to yield to it. She wrote, as she had performed every act of her relationship with Arthur, unwillingly, in spite of her reason, governed by a strange and arbitrary impulse. No sooner was the letter in the pillar-box than she began to wonder what Arthur would say in his response, and how she should answer that response. She grew impatient and restless, and called at the chief Post Office in Bursley for information about the American mails. On this evening, as Leonora sat in the garden, Milly was reciting at a concert at Knype, and Ethel and Fred had accompanied her. Leonora, resisting some pressure, had declined to go with them. Assuming that Arthur wrote on the day he received her missive, his reply, she had ascertained, ought to be delivered in Hillport the next morning, but there was just a chance that it might be delivered that night. Hence she had stayed at home, expectant, and—with all her serenity—a little nervous and excited.

Carpenter emerged from the region of the stable and began to water some flower-beds in the vicinity of her seat.

'Terrible dry month we've had, ma'am, ' he murmured in his quiet pastoral voice, waving the can to and fro.

She agreed perfunctorily. Her mind was divided between suspense concerning the postman, contemplation of the placid vista of the remainder of her career, and pleasure in the languorous charm of the May evening.

Bran moved his head, and rising ponderously walked round the seat towards the house. Then Carpenter, following the dog with his eyes, smiled and touched his cap. Leonora turned sharply. Arthur Twemlow himself stood on the step of the drawing-room window, and Bessie's white apron was just disappearing within.

In the first glance Leonora noticed that Arthur was considerably thinner. She was overcome by a violent emotion that contained both fear and joy. And as he approached her, agitated and unsmiling, the joy said: 'How heavenly it is to see him again! ' But the fear asked: 'Why is he so worn? What have you been doing to him all these months, Leonora? ' She met him in the middle of the lawn, and they shook hands timidly, clumsily, embarrassed. Carpenter, with that inborn delicacy of tact which is the mark of a simple soul, walked away out of sight, and Bran, receiving no attention, followed him.

'Were you surprised to see me? ' Arthur lamely questioned.

In their hearts a thousand sensations struggled, some for expression, others for concealment; and speech, pathetically unequal to the swift crisis, was disconcerted by it almost to the verge of impotence.

'Yes, ' she said. 'Very. '

'You ought not to have been, ' he replied.

His tone alarmed her. 'Why? ' she said. 'When did you get my letter?'

'Just after one o'clock to-day. '

'To-day? '

'I was in London. It was sent on to me from New York. '

She was relieved. When she saw him first at the window, she had a lightning vision of him tearing open her letter in New York, jumping instantly into a cab, and boarding the English steamer. This had frightened her. It was, if not exactly reassuring, at any rate less terrifying, to learn that he had flown to her only from London.

'Well, ' he exclaimed, 'how's everybody? And where are the girls? '

She gave the news, and then they walked together to the seat and sat down, in silence.

'You don't look too well, ' she ventured. 'You've been working too hard. '

He passed his hand across his forehead and moved on the seat so as to meet her eyes directly.

'Quite the reverse, ' he said. 'I haven't been working half hard enough. '

'Not half hard enough? ' she repeated mechanically.

As his eyes caught hers and held them she was conscious of an exquisite but mortal tremor; her spine seemed to give way. The old desire for youth and love, for that brilliant and tender existence in which were united virtue and the flavour of sin, dalliance and high endeavour, eternal appetite and eternal satisfaction, rushed wondrously over her. The life which she had mapped out for herself suddenly appeared miserable, inadequate, even contemptible. Was she, with her rich blood, her perfect health, her proud carriage, her indestructible beauty, and her passionate soul, to wither solitary in the cold shadow? She felt intensely, as every human heart feels sometimes, that the satisfactions of duty were chimerical, and that the only authentic bliss was to be found in a wild and utter abandonment to instinct. No matter what the cost of rapture, in self-respect or in remorse, it was worth the cost. Why did not mankind rise up and put an end to this endless crucifixion of instinct which saddened the whole earth, and say gloriously, 'Let us live'? And in a moment dalliance without endeavour, and the flavour of sin without virtue, were beautiful ideals for her. She could have put her arms round Arthur's neck and drawn him to her, and blotted out all the past and sullied all the future with one kiss. She wondered what recondite force dissuaded her from doing so. 'I have but to lift my arms and smile, ' she thought.

'You've been very cruel, ' said Arthur. 'I wouldn't have believed you could have been so cruel. I guess you didn't know how cruel you were. Why didn't you write before? '

'I couldn't, ' she answered submissively. 'Didn't you understand? ' The question was not quite ingenuous, but she meant it well.

'I understood at first, ' he said. 'I knew you would want to wait. I knew how upset you'd be—I—I think I knew all you'd feel.... But it will soon be eighteen months ago. ' His voice was full of emotion. Then he smiled, gravely and charmingly. ' However, it's finished now, and I'm here. '

His indictment was very kind, very mild; but she could see how he had suffered, and that his wrath against her had been none the less genuine because it was the wrath of love. She grew more and more humble before his gaze so adoring and so reproachful. She knew that she had been selfish, and that she had ransomed her conscience as much at his expense as at her own. She perceived the vital inferiority of women to men—that quality of callousness which allows them to commit all cruelties in the name of self-sacrifice, and that lack of imagination by which they are blinded to the wounds they deal. Women have brief moods in which they judge themselves as men judge them, in which they escape from their sex and know the truth. Such a mood came then to Leonora. And she wished ardently to compensate Arthur for the martyrdom which she had inflicted on him. They were close to one another. The atmosphere between them was electric. And the darkness of a calm and delicious night was falling. Could she not obey her instinct, and in one bright word, one word laden with the invitation and acquiescence of femininity, atone for her sin against him? Could she not shatter the images of Rose and Milly, who loved her after their hard fashion, but who would never thank her for her watchful affection—would even resent it? Vain hope!

'Oh! ' she exclaimed grievously, trying uselessly to keep the dream of joyous indulgence from fading away. 'I must tell you—I cannot leave them! '

'Leave whom? '

'The girls—Rose and Milly. I daren't. You don't know what I went through after John's death—and I can't desert them. I should have told you in my next letter. '

Her tones moved not only him but herself. He was obliged at once to receive what she said with the utmost seriousness, as something fully weighed and considered.

'Do you mean, ' he demanded, 'that you won't marry me and come to New York? '

'I can't, I can't, ' she replied.

He got up and walked along the garden towards the meadow, so far that in the twilight her eyes could scarcely distinguish his figure against the bushes. Then he returned.

'Just let me hear all about the girls. ' He stood in front of her.

'You see, ' she said entreatingly, when she had hurried through her recital, 'I couldn't leave them, could I? '

But instead of answering, he questioned her further about Milly's projects, and made suggestions, and they seemed to have been discussing the complex subject for an hour before she found a chance to reassert, plaintively: 'I couldn't leave them. '

'You're entirely wrong, ' he said firmly and authoritatively. 'You've just got an idea fixed in your head, and it's all wrong, all wrong. '

'It isn't as if they were going to be married, ' she obstinately pursued the sequence of her argument. 'Ethel now — —'

'Married! ' he cried, roused. 'Are we to wait patiently, you and I, until Rose and Milly choose to get married? ' He was bitterly scornful. 'Is that our rôle? I fancy I know something about Rose and Milly, and allow me to tell you they never will get married, neither of them. They aren't the marrying sort. Not but what that's beside the point!... Yes, ' he continued, 'and if there ever were two girls in this world able to look after themselves without parental assistance Rose and Milly are those two. '

196

'You don't understand women; you don't know, you don't understand, ' she murmured. She was shocked and hurt by this candid and hostile expression of opinion concerning Rose and Milly, whom hitherto he had always appeared to like.

'No, ' he retorted with solemn resentment. 'And no other man either!... Before, when they needed your protection perhaps, when your husband was alive, you would have left Rose and Milly then, wouldn't you?... Wouldn't you? '

'Oh! ' the exclamation escaped her unawares. She burst into a sob. She had not meant to cry, but she was crying.

He sat down close to her, and put his hand on her shoulder, and leaned over her. 'My dearest girl, ' he whispered in a new voice of infinite softness, 'you've forgotten that you have a duty to yourself, and to me, as well as to Rose and Milly. Our lives want looking after, too. We're human creatures, you know, you and I. This row that we're having now has occurred thousands of times before, but this time it's going to be settled with common sense, isn't it? ' And he kissed her with a kiss as soft as his voice.

She sighed. Still perplexed and unconvinced, she was nevertheless in those minutes acutely happy. The mysterious and profound affinity of the flesh had made a truce between the warring principles of the male and of the female; a truce only. To the left of the house, over the Marsh, the last silver relics of day hung in the distant sky. She looked at the dying light, so provocative of melancholy in its reluctance to depart, and at the timidly-appearing stars and the sombre trees, and her thought was: 'World, how beautiful and sad you are! '

Bran emerged forlorn from the gloom, and rested his great chin confidingly on her knees.

'Bran! ' she condoled with him through her tears, stroking the dog's head tenderly, 'Ah! Bran! '

Arthur stood up, resolute, victorious, but prudent and magnanimous too. He put one foot on the seat beside her, and leaned forward on the raised knee, tapping his stick. 'I've hired a flat over there, ' he said low in her ear, 'such as can't be gotten outside of New York. And in my thoughts I've made a space for you in New York, where it's life and no mistake, and where I'm known, and where my interests are. And if you didn't come I don't know what I should do. I tell you fair I don't know what I should do. And wouldn't your life be spoilt? Wouldn't it? But it isn't the flat I've got, and it isn't the space I've sort of cleared, and it isn't the ruin and smash for you and me—it isn't so much these things that make me feel wicked when I think of the mere possibility of you refusing to come, as the fundamental injustice of the thing to both of us. My dear girl, no one ever understood you as I do. I can see it all as well as if I'd been here all the time. You took fright after—after his death. Women are always more frightened after the danger's over than at the time, especially when they're brave. And you thought, "I must do something very good because it was on the cards I might have been very wicked. " And so it's Rose and Milly that mustn't be left... I'm not much of an intellect, outside crocks, you know, but there's one thing I can do, I *can* see clear?... Can't I see clear? '

Their hands met in the dog's fur. She was still crying, but she smiled up at him admiringly and appreciatively.

'If Rose and Milly want a change any time, ' he continued, 'let 'em come over. And we can come to Europe just as often as you feel that way... Eh? '

'Why, ' she meditated, 'cannot this last for ever? ' She felt so feminine and illogical, and the masculine, masterful rationality of his appeal touched her so intimately, that she had discovered in the woe and the indecision of her situation a kind of happiness. And she wished to keep what she had got. At length a certain courage and resolution visited her, and summoning all her sweetness she said to him: 'Don't press me, please, please! In a fortnight I shall be in London with Milly.... Will you wait a fortnight? Will you wait that long? I know that what you say is—You will wait that long, won't you? You'll be in London then to meet us? '

'God! ' he exclaimed, deeply moved by the fainting, beseeching poignancy of her voice, 'I will wait forty fortnights. And I guess I shall be in London. '

She sank back on the reprieve as on a pillow.

'Of course I'll wait, ' he repeated lightly, and his tone said: 'I understand. Life isn't all logic, and allowances must be made.

Women are women—that's what makes them so adorable—and I'm not in a hurry. '

They did not speak further.

A moving patch of white on the path indicated Bessie.

'If you please, ma'am, shall I set supper for five? ' she asked vivaciously in the summer darkness.

There was a silence.

'I'm not staying, Bessie, ' said Twemlow.

'Thank you, sir. Come along, Bran, come kennel. '

The great beast slouched off, and left them together.

* * * * *

'Guess who's been! ' Leonora demanded of her girls and Fred, with feverish gaiety, when they returned from the concert. The dining-room was very cheerful, and brightly lit; outside lay the dark garden and Bran reflective in his kennel. No one could guess Arthur, and so Leonora had to tell. They were surprised; and they were interested, but not for long. Millicent was preoccupied with her successful performance at the concert; and Ethel and Fred had had a brilliant idea. This couple were to commence married life modestly in Uncle Meshach's house; but the place was being repaired and redecorated, and there seemed to be an annoying probability that it would not be finished for immediate occupation after the short honeymoon—Fred could only spare 'two week-ends' from the works. Why should they not return on the very day when Leonora and Milly were to go to London and keep house at Hillport during Leonora's absence? Such was the brilliant idea, one of those domestic ideas whose manifold excellences call for interminable explanation and discussion. The name of Arthur Twemlow was not again mentioned.

CHAPTER XII

IN LONDON

The last day of the dramatic portion of Leonora's life was that on which she went to London with Milly. They were up early, in order to catch the morning express, and, before leaving, Leonora arranged with the excited Bessie all details for the reception of Ethel and Fred, who were to arrive in the afternoon from their honeymoon. 'I will drive, ' she said to Carpenter when the cart was brought round, and Carpenter had to sit behind among the trunks. Bessie in her morning print and her engagement ring stood at the front door, and sped them beneficently away while clinging hard to Bran.

As the train rushed smoothly across the vast and rich plain of Middle England, Leonora's thoughts dwelt on the house at Hillport, on her skilled and sympathetic servants, on Prince and Bran, and on the calm and the orderliness and the high decency of everything. And she pictured the homecoming of Ethel and Fred from Wales— Fred stiff and nervous, and Ethel flushed, beautiful, and utterly bewitching in the self-consciousness of the bride. 'May I call her Mrs. Fred, ma'am? ' Bessie had asked, recoiling from the formality of 'Mrs. Ryley, ' and aware that 'Miss Ethel' was no longer possible. Leonora saw them in the dining-room consuming the tea which Bessie had determined should be the final word of teas; and she saw Bessie, in that perfect black of hers and that miraculous muslin, waiting at table with a superlative and cold primness that covered a desire to take Ethel in her arms and kiss her. And she saw the pair afterwards, dallying on the lawn with Bran at dusk, simple, unambitious, unassuming, content; and, still later, Fred meticulously locking up the great house, so much too large and complicated for one timid couple, and Ethel standing at the top of the stairs as he extinguished the hall-gas. These visions of them made her feel sad— sad because Ethel could never again be that which she had been, and because she was so young, inexperienced, confiding, and beautiful, and would gradually grow old and lose the ineffable grace of her years and situation; and because they were both so innocent of the meaning of life. Leonora yearned for some magic to stay the destructive hand of time and keep them ever thus, young, naïve, trustful, and unspoilt. And knowing that this could not be, she wanted intensely to shield, and teach, and advise them. She whispered, thinking of Ethel: 'Ah! I must always be near, within reach, within call, lest she should need me. '

'Mother, shall you go with me to see Mr. Louis Lewis to-morrow? ' Milly demanded suddenly when the train halted at Rugby.

'Yes, of course, dear. Don't you wish me to? '

'Oh! I don't mind, ' said Milly grandly.

Two well-dressed, middle-aged men entered the compartment, which, till then, Leonora and Milly had had to themselves; and while duly admiring Leonora, they could not refrain from looking continually at Millicent; they talked to one another gravely, and they made a pretence of reading newspapers, but their eyes always returned furtively to Milly's corner. The girl was not by any means confused by the involuntary homage, which merely heightened her restless vitality. She chattered to her mother; she was pert; she looked out of the window; she tapped the floor with her brown shoes. In the unconscious process of displaying her individuality for admiration, she was never still. The fair, pretty face under the straw hat responded to each appreciative glance, and beneath her fine blue coat and skirt the muscles of the immature body and limbs played perpetually in graceful and free movement. She was adorable; she knew it, Leonora knew it, the two middle-aged men knew it. Nothing—no pertness, no audacity, no silliness, no affectation—could impair the extraordinary charm. Leonora was exceedingly proud of her daughter. And yet she reflected impartially that Millicent was a little fool. She trembled for Millicent; she feared to let her out of sight; the idea of Millicent loose in the world, with no guide but her own rashness and no protection but her vanity, made Leonora feel sick. Nevertheless, Millicent would soon be loose in the world, and at the best Leonora could only stand in the background, ready for emergency.

At Euston they were not surprised to see Harry. The young man was more dandiacal and correct than ever, and he could cut a figure on the platform; but Leonora observed the pallor of his thin cheeks and the watery redness of his eyes. He had come to meet them, and he insisted on escorting them to their hotel in South Kensington.

'Look here, ' he said in the cab, 'I've one dying request to make before the luggage drops through the roof. I want you both to come and dine with me at the Majestic to-night, and then we'll go to the Regency. Lewis has given me a box. By the way, I told him he might rely on me to take you up to see him to-morrow. '

'Shall we, mother? ' Milly asked carelessly; but it was obvious that she wished to dine at the Majestic.

'I don't know, ' said Leonora. 'There's Rose. We're going to fetch Rose from the hospital this afternoon, Harry, and she will spend the evening with us. '

'Well, Rose must come too, of course, ' Harry replied quickly, after a slight hesitation. 'It will do her good. '

'We will see, ' said Leonora. She had known Harry from his infancy, and when she encountered him in these latter days she was always subject to the illusion that he could not really be a man, but was rather playing at manhood. Moreover, she had warned Arthur Twemlow of their arrival and expected to find a letter from him at the hotel, and she could make no arrangements until she had seen the letter.

They drove into the courtyard of the select and austere establishment where John Stanway had brought his wife on her wedding journey. Leonora found that it had scarcely changed; the dark entrance lounge presented the same appearance now as it had done more than twenty years ago; it had the same air of receiving visitors with condescension; the whole street was the same. She grew thoughtful; and Harry's witticisms, as he ceremoniously superintended their induction into the place, served only to deepen the shadow in her heart.

'Any letters for me? ' she asked the hall porter, loitering behind while Millicent and Harry went into the *salle à manger*.

'What name, madam? No, madam. '

But during luncheon, to which Harry stayed, a flunkey approached bearing a telegram on silver. 'In a moment, ' she thought, 'I shall know when we are to meet. ' And she trembled with apprehension. The flunkey, however, gave the telegram to Millicent, who accepted it as though she had been accepting telegrams at the hands of flunkeys all her life.

'*Miss* Stanway, ' she smiled superiorly with her chin forward, perceiving the look on Leonora's face. She tore the envelope. 'Lewis says I am to go to-day at four, instead of to-morrow. Hooray! the sooner it's over, the sooner to sleep, though the harbour bar be mo—oaning. Ma, that's the very time you have to meet Rose at the hospital. Harry, you shall take me. '

Leonora would have preferred that Harry and Millicent should not go alone together to see Mr. Louis Lewis. But she could not bring herself to break the appointment with Rose, who was extremely sensitive; nor could she well inform Harry, at this stage of his close intimacy with the family, that she no longer cared to entrust Milly to his charge.

She left the hotel before the other two, because she had further to drive. The hansom had scarcely got into the street when she instructed the driver to return.

'Of course you will settle nothing definitely with Mr. Lewis, ' she said to Milly. 'Tell him I wish to see him first. '

'Oh, mother! ' the girl cried, pouting.

* * * * *

At the New Female and Maternity Hospital in Lamb's Conduit Street Leonora was shown to a bench in the central hall and requested to sit down. The clock over the first landing of the double staircase indicated three minutes to four. During the drive she had begun by expecting to meet Arthur on his way to the hotel, and even in Piccadilly, where delays of traffic had forced upon her attention the glittering opulence and afternoon splendour of the London season, she had still thought of him and of the interview which was to pass between them. But here she was obsessed by her immediate environment. The approach to the hospital, through sombre squalid streets, past narrow courts in which innumerable children tumbled and yelled, disturbed and desolated her. It appeared that she had entered the secret breeding-quarter of the immense city, the obscene district where misery teemed and generated, and where the revolting fecundity of nature was proved amid surroundings of horror and despair. And the hospital itself was the very centre, the innermost temple of all this ceaseless parturition. In a corner of the hall, near a door, waited a small crowd of embossed women, young and middle-aged, sad, weary, unkempt, lightly dressed in shabby shapeless clothes, and sweltering in the summer heat; a few had babies in their arms. In the doorway two neatly attired youngish women, either doctors or students, held an animated and interminable conversation, staring absent-mindedly at the attendant crowd. A pale nurse came hurrying from the back of the hall and vanished through the doorway, squeezing herself between the doctors or students, who soon afterwards followed her, still talking; and then one by one the embossed women began to vanish through the doorway also. The clock gently struck four, and Leonora, sighing, watched the hand creep to five minutes and to ten beyond the hour. She gazed up the well of the staircases, and in imagination saw ward after ward, floor above floor of beds, on which lay repulsive and piteous creatures in fear, in pain, in exhaustion. And she thought with dismay how many more poor immortal souls went out of that building than ever went into it. 'Rose is somewhere up there, ' she reflected. At a quarter past four a stout white-haired lady briskly descended the stairs, and, after being accosted twice by officials, spoke to Leonora.

'You are Mrs. Stanway? My name is Smithson. I dare say your daughter has mentioned it in her letters. ' The famous dean of the hospital smiled, and paused while Leonora responded. 'Just at the moment, ' Miss Smithson continued, 'dear Rosalys is engaged, but I hope she will be down directly. We are very, very busy. Are you making a long stay in London, Mrs. Stanway? The season is now in full swing, is it not? '

Leonora could find little to say to this experienced spinster, whom she unwillingly admired but with whom she was not in accord. Miss Smithson uttered amiable banalities with an evident intention to do nothing more; her demeanour was preoccupied, and she made no further reference to Rose. Soon a nurse respectfully called her; she hastened away full of apologies, leaving Leonora to meditate upon her own shortcomings as a serious person, and upon the futility of her existence of forty-one years.

Another quarter of an hour elapsed, and then Rose ran impetuously down the stone steps.

'Mother, I'm so glad to see you! Where's Milly? ' she exclaimed eagerly, and they kissed twice.

As she answered the greeting Leonora noticed the lines of fatigue in Rose's face, the brilliancy of her eyes, the emaciation of the body beneath her grey alpaca dress, and that air of false serenity masking hysteric excitement which she seemed to have noticed too in all the other officials—the doctors or students, the nurses, and even the dean.

'Are you ready now, dear? ' she asked.

'Oh, I can't possibly come to-day, mother. Didn't Miss Smithson tell you? I'm awfully sorry I can't. But there's a very important case on. I can only stay a minute. '

'But, my child, we have arranged to take you to the theatre, ' Leonora was on the point of expostulating. She checked herself, and placidly replied: 'I'm sorry, too. When shall you be free? '

'Might be able to get off to-morrow. I'll slip out in the morning and send you a telegram. '

'I should like you to try and be free to-morrow, my dear. You seem as if you needed a rest. Do you take any exercise? '

'As much as I can. '

'But you know, Rose——'

'That's all right, mater, ' Rose interrupted confidently, patting her mother's arm. 'We can look after ourselves here, don't you worry. Have you seen Mr. Twemlow yet? '

'Not yet. Why? '

'Nothing. But he called to see me yesterday. We're great friends. I must run back now. '

Leonora departed with the girl's hasty kiss on her lips, realising that she had fallen to the level of a mere episodic interest in Rose's life. The impassioned student of obstetrics had disappeared up the staircase before Leonora could reach the double-doors of the entrance. The mother was dashed, stricken, a little humiliated. But as she arranged the folds of her beautiful dress in the hansom which was carrying her away from Lamb's Conduit Street towards South

Kensington, she said to herself firmly, 'I am not a ninny, after all, and I know that Rose will be ill soon. And there are things in that hospital that I could manage better. '

'Mr. Twemlow came to see you just after you left, ' said Harry when he restored Milly to her mother at half-past five. 'I asked him to join us at dinner, but he said he couldn't. However, he's coming to the theatre, to our box. '

'You must excuse us from dining with you to-night, Harry, ' was Leonora's reply. 'We'll meet you at the theatre. '

'Yes, Harry, ' said Millicent coldly. 'We really can't come to-day. '

'The hand of the Lord is heavy upon me, ' Harry murmured. And he repeated the phrase on leaving the hotel.

Neither he nor Millicent had shown much interest in Rose's defection. The dandy seemed to be relieved, and Millicent said, 'How stupid of her! ' Milly had returned from the visit to Mr. Louis Lewis in a state of high self-satisfaction. Leonora was told that Mr. Lewis was simply the most delightful and polite man that Milly had ever met; he would be charmed to see Mrs. Stanway, and would make an appointment. Meanwhile Milly gave her mother to understand that the affair was practically settled. She knew the date when the tour of *Princess Puck* started, and the various towns which it would include; and Mr. Lewis had provided her with a box for the next afternoon at the Queen's Theatre, where the piece had been most successfully produced a month ago; the music she would receive by post; and the first rehearsal of the No. I. Company would occur within a week or so. Millicent walked in flowery paths. She saw herself covered with jewels and compliments, flattered, adored, worshipped, and leading always a life of superb luxury. And this prophetic dream was not the conception of a credulous fancy, but the product of the hard and calculating shrewdness which she possessed. She was aware of the importance of Mr. Louis Lewis, who, on behalf of Lionel Belmont, absolutely controlled three West End theatres; and she was also aware of the effect which she had had upon him. She knew that in her personality there was a mysterious something which intoxicated, not all the men with whom she came in contact, but most of them, and men of utterly different sorts. She did not trouble to attempt any analysis of that quality; she accepted it as a natural phenomenon; and she meant to use it ruthlessly, for she was almost incapable of pity or gratitude. It was, for instance, her intention to drop Harry; she had no further use for him now. She was learning to forget her childish awe of Leonora: a very little time, and she would implacably force her mother to recognise that even the semblance of parental control must cease.

'And I am to have my photograph taken, mamma! ' she exclaimed triumphantly. 'Mr. Lewis says that Antonios in Regent Street will be only too glad to take it for nothing. He's going to send them a line. '

Leonora was silent. Deep in her heart she made a gesture of appeal to each of her daughters—to Ethel who was immersed in love, to Rose who was absorbed by a vocation, and to this seductive minx whose venal lips would only smile to gain an end—and each seemed to throw her a glance indifferent or preoccupied, and to say, 'Presently, presently. When I can spare a moment. ' And she thought bitterly how Rose had been content to receive her mother in the public hall of the hospital.

* * * * *

They were late in arriving at the theatre because the cab could not get through Piccadilly, and Harry was impatiently expecting them in the foyer. His brow smoothed at once when he caught sight of them, and he admired their dresses, and escorted them up the celebrated marble stairs with youthful pride.

'I thought no one was going to supervene, ' he smiled. 'I was afraid you'd all been murdered in patent asphyxiating hansoms. I don't know what's happened to Twemlow. I must leave word with the people here which box he's to come to. '

'Perhaps he won't come, ' thought Leonora. 'Perhaps I shall not see him till to-morrow. '

Harry's box was exactly in the middle of the semi-circle of boxes which surround the balcony of the Regency Theatre. They were ushered into it with the precautions of silence, for the three hundred and fifty-fifth performance of *The Dolmenico Doll*, the unique musical comedy from New York, had already commenced. Leonora and Milly sat in front, and Harry drew up a chair so that he might whisper in their ears; he was very talkative. Leonora could see nothing clearly at first. Then gradually the crowded auditorium arranged itself in her mind. She perceived the semi-circle of boxes, each exactly like their own, and each filled with women quite as elegantly gowned as she and Millicent, and men as dandiacal and correct as Harry; and in the balcony and in the stalls were serried regular rows of elaborate coiffures and shining bald heads; and all the seats seemed to be pervaded by the glitter of gems, the wing-like beating of fans, and the restless curving of arms. She had not visited London for many years, and this multitudinous and wholesale opulence startled her. Under other circumstances she would have enjoyed it intensely, and basked in it as a flower in the sunshine; to-night, however, she could not dismiss the image of Rose in the gaunt hospital in Lamb's Conduit Street. She knew the comparison was crude; she assured herself that there must always be rich and poor, idle and industrious, gay and sorrowful, elegant and shabby, arrogant and meek; but her discomfort none the less persisted, and she had the uneasy feeling that the whole of civilisation was wrong, and that Rose and the earnest ones were justified in their scorn of such as her. And concurrently she dwelt upon Ethel and Fred at that hour, and listened with anxiety for the opening of the box-door and the entry of Arthur Twemlow.

She imagined that owing to their late arrival she must have missed the one essential clue to the plot of *The Dolmenico Doll*, and as the gorgeously decorated action was developed on the dazzling stage she tried in vain to grasp its significance. The fall of the curtain came as a surprise to her. The end of the first act had left her with nothing but a confused notion of the interior of a confectioner's shop, and young men therein getting tipsy and stealing kisses, and marvellously pretty girls submitting to the robbery with a nonchalance born of three hundred and fifty four similar experiences; and old men grotesque in a dissolute senility; and sudden bursts of orchestral music, and simpering ballads, and comic refrains and crashing choruses; and lights, *lingerie*, picture-hats and short skirts; and over all, dominating all, the set, eternal, mechanical, bored smile of the pretty girls.

'Awfully good, isn't it? ' said Harry, when the generous applause had ceased.

'It's simply lovely, ' Milly agreed, fidgeting on her chair in juvenile rapture.

'Yes, ' Leonora admitted. And she indeed thought that parts of it were amusing and agreeable.

'Of course, ' Harry remarked hastily to Leonora, '*Princess Puck* isn't at all like this. It's an idyll sort of thing, you know. By the way, hadn't I better go out and offer a reward for the recovery of Twemlow? '

He returned just as the curtain went up, bringing a faint odour of whisky, but without Twemlow.

A few moments later, while the principal pretty girl was warbling an invitation to her lover amid the diversions of Narragansett Pier, the latch of the door clicked and Arthur noiselessly entered the box. He nodded cheerfully, murmuring 'Sorry I'm so late, ' and then shook hands with Leonora. She could not find her voice. In the hazard of rearranging the seats, an operation which Harry from diffidence conducted with a certain clumsiness, Arthur was placed behind Milly while Leonora had Harry by her side.

'You've missed all the first act, and everyone says it's the best, ' Milly remarked, leaning towards Arthur with an air of intimacy. And Harry expressed agreement.

'But you must remember I saw it in New York two years ago, ' Leonora heard him whisper in reply.

She liked his avuncular, slightly quizzical attitude to them. He reinforced the elder generation in the box, reducing by his mere presence the two young and callow creatures to their proper position in the scheme of things.

And now the question of her future relations with Arthur, which hitherto she had in a manner shunned, at once became peremptory for Leonora. She was conscious of a passionate tenderness for him; he seemed to her to have qualities, indefinable and exquisite touches of character, which she had never observed in any other human being. But she was in control of her heart. She had chosen, and she knew that she could abide by her choice. She was uplifted by the force of one of those tremendous and invincible resolutions which women alone, with their instinctive bent towards martyrdom, are capable of making. And the resolution was not the fruit of the day, the result of all that she had recently seen and thought. It was a resolution independent of particular circumstances, a simple admission of the naked fact that she could not desert her daughters. If Ethel had been shrewd and worldly, and Rose temperate in her altruism, and Milly modest and sage, the resolution would not have been modified. She dared not abandon her daughters: the blood in her veins, the stern traits inherited from her irreproachable ancestors, forbade it. She might be convinced in argument—and she vividly remembered everything that Arthur had said—she might admit that she was wrong, that her sacrifice would be futile, and that she was about to be guilty of a terrible injustice to Arthur and to herself. No matter! She would not leave the girls. And if in thus obstinately remaining at their service she committed a sin, she could only ask pardon for that sin. She could only beg Arthur to forgive her, and assure him that he would forget, and submit to his reproaches in silence and humility. Now and then she gazed at him, but his eyes were always fixed on the stage, and the corners of his mouth turned down into a slightly ironic smile. She wondered if he expected to be able to persuade her, and whether an opportunity to convince him and so end the crisis would occur that evening, or whether she would be compelled to wait through another night.

At last the adventures of the Dolmenico Doll were concluded, the naughty kisses regularised, the old men finally befooled, the glory extinguished, the music hushed. The audience stood up and began to chatter, and the women curved their long arms backward to receive white cloaks from the men. Arthur led the way out with Milly, and as the party slowly proceeded through the crush into the foyer, Leonora could hear the impetuous and excited child delivering to him her professional views on the acting and the singing.

'Well, Burgess, ' Arthur said, in the portico, 'I guess we'll see these ladies home, eh? ' And he called to a commissionaire: 'Say, two hansoms. '

In a minute Leonora and Arthur were driving together along the scintillating nocturnal thoroughfare; he had put Harry and Millicent into the other hansom like school children. And in the sudden privacy of the vehicle Leonora thought: 'Now! ' She looked up at him furtively from beneath her eyelashes. He caught the glance and shook his head sadly.

'Why do you shake your head? ' she timidly began.

His kind shrewd eyes caressed her. 'You mustn't look at me so, ' he said.

'Why? '

'I can't stand it, ' he replied. 'It's too much for me. You don't know—you don't know. You think I'm calm enough, but I tell you the top of my head has nearly come off to-day. '

'But I——'

'Listen here, ' he ran on. 'Let me finish up. What I said a fortnight ago was quite right. It was absolutely unanswerable. But there was something about your letter that upset me. I can't tell you what it was—only it made my heart beat. And then yesterday I happened to go and worry out Rose at that awful hospital. And then Milly to-night! I know how you feel. I've got it to the eighth of an inch. And I've thought: "Suppose I do get her to New York, and she isn't happy? " Well, it's right here: I've settled to sell my business over there, and fix up in London. What do I care for New York, anyway? I don't care for anything so long as we can be happy. I've been a bachelor too long. And if I can be alone with you in this London, lost in it, just you and me! Oh, well! I want a woman to think about—one woman all mine. I'm simply mad for it. And we can only live once. We shan't be short of money. Now don't look at me any more like you did. Say yes, and let's begin right away and be happy. '

'Do you really mean——? ' She was obliged thus, in weak unfinished phrases, to gain time in order to recover from the shock.

'I'm going to cable to-morrow morning, ' he said, joyously. 'Not that there's so much hurry as all that, but I shall feel better after I've cabled. I'm silly, and I want to be silly.... I wouldn't live in New York for a million now. And don't you think we can keep an eye on Rose and Millicent, between us? '

'Oh, Arthur! '

She breathed a long, deep sigh, shutting her eyes for an instant; and then the beautiful creature, with all her elegance and her appearance of impassive and fastidious calm, permitted herself to move infinitesimally, but perceptibly, closer to him in the hansom; and her spirit performed the supreme feminine act of acquiescence and surrender. She thought passionately: 'He has yielded to me—I will be his slave. '

'I shall call you Leo, ' he murmured fondly. 'It occurred to me last night. '

She smiled, as if to say: 'How charmingly boyish you are! '

'And I must tell you—but see here, we shall be at your hotel too soon. ' He pushed at the trap-door. 'Say, driver, go up Park Lane and along Oxford Street a bit. '

Then he explained to her how he had refused Harry's invitation to dinner, and had arrived late at the theatre, solely that he might not have to talk to her until they could talk in solitude.

As, later, the cab rolled swiftly southwards through the mysterious dark avenues of Hyde Park, Leonora had the sensation of being really alone with him in the very heart of that luxurious, voluptuous, and decadent civilisation for which she had always yearned, and in which she was now to participate. The feeling of the beauty of the world, and of its catholicity and many-sidedness, returned to her. She gave play to her instincts. And, revelling in the self-confidence and the masterful ascendency which underlay Arthur's usual reticent demeanour, she resumed with exquisite relief her natural supineness. She began to depend on him. And she foresaw how he would reason diplomatically with Rose, and watch between Milly and Mr. Louis Lewis, and perhaps assist Fred Ryley, and do in the best way everything that ought to be done; and how she would reward him with the consolations of her grace and charm, her feminine arts, and her sweet acquiescence.

'So you've come, ' exclaimed Milly, rather desolate in the drawing-room of the hotel.

'Yes, Miss Muffet, ' said Arthur, 'we've come. Where is the youth? '

'Harry? I made him go home. '

Leonora smiled indulgently at Millicent with her pretty pouting face and her adorable artificiality, lounging on one of the sofas in the vast garish chamber. And her thoughts flew to Ethel, and existence in Bursley. The Myatt family had risen, flourished, and declined. Some of its members were dead, in honour or in dishonour; others were scattered now. Only Ethel and Fred remained; and these two, in the house at Hillport (which Leonora meant to give them), were beginning again the eternal effort, and renewing the simple and austere traditions of the Five Towns, where luxury was suspect and decadence unknown.

Lightning Source UK Ltd.
Milton Keynes UK
18 March 2010

151570UK00002B/91/A